Everywhere that Mary Went

Lisa Scottoline

CORONET BOOKS
Hodder and Stoughton

First published in the USA in 1993
by HarperPaperbacks

First published in paperback in 1995
by Hodder and Stoughton
A division of Hodder Headline PLC

A Coronet paperback

10 9 8 7 6 5 4 3 2 1

ISBN 0 340 62903 7

Printed and bound in Great Britain by
Cox & Wyman Ltd, Reading, Berkshire

Hodder and Stoughton
A division of Hodder Headline PLC
338 Euston Road
London NW1 3BH

For Franca, and for Kiki

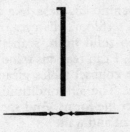

"All rise! All persons having business before this Honorable Judge of the United States District Court are admonished to draw near and be heard!" trumpets the courtroom deputy.

Instantly, sports pages vanish into briefcases and legal briefs are tossed atop the stock quotes. Three rows of pricey lawyers leap to their wingtips and come to attention before a vacant mahogany dais. Never before has a piece of furniture commanded such respect.

"The District Court for the Eastern District of Pennsylvania is now in session! God save the United States and this honorable court!" The deputy casts an eye in the direction of the dais and pauses significantly. "The Honorable William A. Bitterman, presiding."

Judge Bitterman sweeps onto the dais on cue and stands behind his desk like a stout regent surveying his serfdom. His eyes, mere slits sunk deep into too-solid flesh, scan the courtroom from on high. I can read his mind: Everything is in order. The counsel tables gleam. The marble floor sparkles. The air-conditioning freezes the blood of lesser life forms. And speaking of same, the lawyers wait and wait.

"You won't mind the delay, counsel," the judge says indifferently, sinking into a soft leather throne. "After all, waiting is billable too."

An uncertain chuckle circulates among the crowd in the back of the courtroom. None of us defense lawyers likes to admit it, but we will bill the time—we have to bill it to someone and it might as well be you. The plaintiffs' bar doesn't sweat it. A contingency fee has more cushion than an air bag.

"Well, well, well," the judge mutters, without explanation, as he skims the motion papers on his desk. Judge Bitterman might have been handsome in a former life, but his enormous weight has pushed his features to the upper third of his face, leaving beneath a chin as bulbous as a bullfrog's. Rumor has it he gained the weight when his wife left him years ago, but there's no excuse for his temperament, which is congenitally lousy. Because of it my best friend, Judy Carrier, calls him Bitter Man.

"Good morning, Your Honor," I say, taking my seat at counsel table. I try to sound perky and bright, and not at all how I feel, which is nervous and fearful. I'm wearing my navy-blue Man Suit; it's perfect for that special occasion when a girl wants to look like a man, like in court or at the auto mechanic's. The reason I'm nervous is that this oral argument is only my second—the partners in my law firm hog the arguments for themselves. They expect associates to learn how to argue by watching them do it. Which is like saying you can learn to ride a bike by watching other people ride them.

"Good morning, Your Honor," says opposing counsel, Bernie Starankovic. Starankovic blinks a lot and wears a bad suit. I feel a twinge of guilt for what I'm about to say about him in open court—that he's too incompetent to represent our client's employees in a class action for age discrimination. If I win this motion, the class action will evaporate, our client's liability will plunge from megabucks to chump change, and its aged ex-employees will end up living on Social Security and 9-Lives. Defense lawyers consider this a victory.

"Good morning, class," replies Judge Bitterman.

I force a fraudulent chuckle. The boys in the back do likewise.

"Ha-ha-ha!" Starankovic laughs loudly. "Ha-ha-ha!" The bogus sound caroms harshly off the walls of the cavernous courtroom, ricocheting like a subatomic particle long after everyone has fallen silent.

"Duly noted, Mr. Starankovic," says Bitter Man dryly, and Starankovic wilts into his chair.

The judge's eyes shift in my direction. "Miz DiNunzio!"

"Yes, Your Honor!" I pop up and grin, like an overeducated jack-in-the-box. Popping up and grinning isn't something they taught me in law school, but they should have, since it's a damn sight more useful than Property. I learned it on the job, and it's become a conditioned response to more stimuli than you can count. I'm up for partnership in two months.

"You've done your homework for this morning, haven't you, Miz DiNunzio? I expect no less from a former student of mine."

Bitter Man's chubby lips part in a smile, but it's not a friendly one. I recognize the smile from when I did time as his research assistant, during my second year at Penn. I spent three afternoons a week finding cases for his soporific article on federal court jurisdiction. No matter how good the cases, they were never good enough for him. He always smiled that smile right before he tore into me, in the true Socratic tradition, asking me question after question until he had proven, as a matter of logic, that I was taking up too much space in the universe.

"Miz DiNunzio? Are you with us?" the judge asks.

I nod, in a caffeinated way. My nervousness intensifies. Red, angry blotches burst into bloom, one by one, beneath my starchy blouse. In two minutes, my chest will look like a thatch of crimson roses on a snow-covered field. Very attractive.

Bitter Man turns to Starankovic. "Mr. Starankovic, we've never met, but I trust you've done your homework too. After all, you're fighting for your life today, aren't you? Or at least the next best thing—a very large contingency fee."

Starankovic springs to his feet, blinking rhythmically. "The fee is of no moment to me, Your Honor, I can assure you. My only concern is for my clients, a veritable generation of golden-agers who have been ruthlessly victimized by defendant corporation, at a time in their lives when they should be able to relax, relying on the fact that their hard-earned pensions—"

"Very good, Mr. Starankovic. You get an A for enthusiasm," Bitter Man snaps, which shuts Starankovic down in mid-homily. Then the judge studies the motion papers before him, ignoring us both.

I'm not sure whether to remain standing, so I steal a glance at Starankovic. He's swaying stiffly, like a sunflower before a thunderstorm. I take a chance and sit down.

"Miz DiNunzio!" says Bitter Man.

"Yes, Your Honor!" I pop up and grin.

"Approach the podium!"

I hear Starankovic snicker, which proves he doesn't deserve my sympathy. I walk to the lectern with apparent confidence and adjust the microphone to girl height. "May it please the Court, my name is Mary DiNunzio—"

"Miz DiNunzio," Bitter Man says. "I have your name, remember?"

"Yes, Your Honor. Sorry, Your Honor." I clear my throat to the sound of muffled laughter. "As you may know, Your Honor, I'm presenting this Motion to Strike Class Action Allegations on behalf of Harbison's The Hardware People. Harbison's is a national chain of hardware stores. It employs over—"

"I don't need the prospectus, Miz DiNunzio. I've heard of the company."

"Yes, Your Honor."

"I'd have to be deaf, dumb, and blind not to have heard of the company, after that inane jingle of theirs. You know their jingle."

"Their jingle?"

"Yes, their jingle. Their anthem. Their team song. I hear it everywhere—on my television, on my car radio—every fifteen minutes. You said you represent them, Miz DiNunzio, so I'm sure you know it. Do you?"

I nod uncertainly.

"Then sing it."

"*Sing it,* Your Honor?"

"You heard me," he says evenly.

A hush settles over the back of the courtroom. Each one of them is thanking God he's not in my pumps. I look down at the podium. My heart is pounding, my ears tingling. I curse Bitter Man, for humiliating me, and Richard Nixon, for appointing him to the federal bench.

"Pretty please? With a cherry on top?" The judge's voice is thick with sarcasm.

Not a soul in the gallery laughs. The court-room deputy avoids my eye, busily examining the buttons of the tape recorder. Christ. It'll be on tape. "Your Honor—"

"Miz DiNunzio!" Bitter Man is suddenly furi-ous; he looks like a volcano about to blow. "Sing!"

The courtroom is as quiet and stone-cold as death.

I close my eyes. I want to be somewhere else, anywhere else but here. I'm back in my girlhood, back in midnight mass on Christmas Eve, lost in the airy heights of "Ave Maria." I open my mouth and the notes fly out, unexpectedly clear and strong. They soar high over the congregation like the hymn, lovely and resonant in the wintry air. "Harbison's The Hardware People. We take the haaaaard out of hardware!"

When I open my eyes, Bitter Man's anger has evaporated. "That was quite . . . beautiful," he says.

I can't tell if he's being sarcastic, and I don't care. "May I begin my argument, Your Honor?"

"You may."

So I do, and the argument sounds punchy and right, fueled by my fury at the judge. I rattle off the local court rules that Starankovic has broken, then segue into my cases, transforming each into the parable of the Careless Lawyer Who Undermined Our System of Justice. Bitterman begins to bare his canines in an encouraging way, which means he's either happy or hungry. I finish my argument and return to counsel table.

"Your Honor, if I may respond," Starankovic says. He pushes down the shiny pants that are static-clinging to his socks and walks to the podium like a Christian into the Roman Colosseum. "May it please the Court, I'm Bernard—"

"Save it, Mr. Starankovic. We both know that defense counsel is right on the law. Your conduct as class counsel has been a disgrace—even my law clerks could do better. How could you miss the deadline on your motion for class certification? It's the one thing you have to do and you couldn't even do that right."

"But Your Honor . . ."

Bitter Man holds up a hand that looks like a mound of Play-Doh. "Stifle, Mr. Starankovic, as Archie Bunker used to say." He glances around the room to see if anyone appreciates his joke. The gallery is too terrified to laugh, but the courtroom deputy smiles broadly. Your tax dollars at work.

"Yes, Your Honor." Starankovic bows slightly.

"Now, Mr. Starankovic, even though Miz DiNunzio thinks she has you, you and I know that I have total discretion in deciding whether to grant her motion. I may grant it or I may deny it purely as a matter of my own inherent powers. Am I right?"

Starankovic nods.

"Of course I am. So your work is cut out for you. Your job is to give me your best argument. Give me one good reason why I shouldn't grant Miz DiNunzio's motion."

Starankovic blinks rapidly. "Your Honor, if I may, the class is composed—"

Bitter Man holds up a finger. "I said, one good reason."

"I was about to, Your Honor. The class is composed of some five hundred employees, and counting—"

"No. No. You're not listening, Mr. Starankovic. Repeat after me. 'The one good reason . . .'"

Starankovic licks his dry lips. "The one good reason . . ."

"'You shouldn't grant the motion . . .'"

"You shouldn't grant the motion . . ."

"'Is . . .'" Bitter Man finishes with a flourish, waving his hand in the air like a conductor.

"Is . . ."

"No, you idiot! I'm not going to finish the sentence for you. *You* finish the sentence."

"I knew that, Your Honor. I'm sorry." The man is sweating bullets. "It's hard to explain. I—"

"One good reason!" the judge bellows.

Starankovic jumps.

The courtroom deputy looks down. The gallery holds its breath. I wonder why judges like Bitter Man get appointments for life. The answer is: because of presidents like Nixon. Someday the electorate will make this connection, I know it.

"I made some mistakes, Your Honor, I admit it," Starankovic blurts out. "I was having a rough time, my mother had just passed, and I missed a lot of deadlines. Not just on this case—on others too. But it won't happen again, Your Honor, you have my word on that."

Bitter Man's face is a mask of exaggerated disbelief. He grabs the sides of the dais and leans way over. "*This* is your best argument? *This* is the one good reason?"

Starankovic swallows hard.

I feel awful. I almost wish I'd never brought the motion in the first place.

"*This* is the best you can come up with? The one good reason I shouldn't grant the motion is that you were making a lot of mistakes at the time—*and this was just one of them?*"

"Your Honor, it's not like—"

"Mr. Starankovic, you said your only concern was for your clients. Isn't that right?"

"Yes, Your Honor."

"Do you care enough to give them the best lawyer possible?"

"Yes, Your Honor."

"Would the best lawyer possible fail to file his motion for class certification on time?"

"No . . . Your Honor."

"But you failed to do so, didn't you?"

Starankovic blinks madly.

"Didn't you?"

Starankovic opens his mouth, but nothing comes out.

"Didn't you fail to do so, Mr. Starankovic? Yes or no will do."

"Yes," he says quietly.

"Then you are not the best lawyer possible, are you?"

There is silence as Starankovic looks down. He can't bring himself to say it. He shakes his head once, then again.

Socrates would have stopped there, but Bitter Man is just warming up. He drags Starankovic through every deadline he blew and every phone call he failed to return. I can barely witness the spectacle; the back rows are shocked into silence. Poor Starankovic torques this way and that, eyelids aflutter, but Bitterman's canines are sunk deep in his neck, pinning him to the floor. There's nowhere to run, nowhere to hide. There's only pain and suffering.

When it's over, Bitter Man issues his decision from the bench. With a puffy smile, he says, "Motion granted."

"Thank you, Your Honor," I say, dry-mouthed.

"Thank you, Your Honor," says Starankovic, hemorrhaging freely. He shoots me a look that could kill.

"Next!" says Bitter Man.

I stuff my papers in my briefcase and turn to go, as another corporate shill takes my place at counsel table. The pews are jam-packed with us, padded shoulder to padded shoulder, because the argument schedule is so late. I hurry by the freshly shaved suits in rep ties and collar pins. I feel like I'm fleeing the scene of a murder. I avoid the eyes of the men in the gallery, some amused, others curious. I don't want to think about who sat among them at this time last year.

I promised myself.

I'm almost past the back row when someone grabs my elbow. It's the only other woman in this horde of pinstriped testosterone, and her red-lacquered nails dig into my arm.

"This has gone far enough!" the woman says.

"What do you mean?" My chest still feels tight, blotchy. I have a promise to keep and I'm failing fast. I try to avoid looking at the pew where she sits, but I can't help it. It's where my husband sat with his first-grade class and watched me argue my first motion. The rich mahogany of the pew has been burnished to a high luster, like a casket.

"He hates us! He hates women lawyers!" she

says. She punches the bridge of her glasses with a finger. "I think it's high time we did something about it."

I only half hear her. All I can think about is Mike. He sat right in this row and had to quiet the class as they fidgeted, whispered, and giggled through the entire argument. He sat at the end of the pew, his arm rested right here. I touch the knobby arm rest with my fingertips. It feels just like his shoulder used to feel: strong, solid. As if it would never give way. I don't want to move my hand.

"We have to file a complaint of judicial misconduct. It's the only thing that will stop him. I know the procedure. You file the complaint with the Clerk of the Third Circuit, then it goes to the Chief Judge and . . ."

Her words grow faint. My fingertips on the shoulder of wood put me in touch with Mike, and in touch with that day. It was a morning like this one. My first argument in court. I remember my own nervous excitement, presenting the motion almost automatically, in a blur. Bitter Man ruled for me in the end, which caused the first-graders to burst into giddy applause. Mike's face was lit up by a proud smile that didn't fade even when Bitter Man went ballistic, pounding his gavel. . . .

Crack! Crack! Crack!

Reality.

I pull my hand from the cold, glossy wood of the pew. Mike isn't here, Mike is gone. I feel my chest flush violently. "I have to go."

"Wait? How will I find you? I need you to sign

the complaint," the woman says, grasping at my arm. "I have at least two other incidents. If we don't do something about this, no one else will!"

"Let me go, I have to go." I yank my arm from her grasp and bang through the courtroom doors.

My promise is broken; my head is flooded with a memory. Mike and I celebrated the night I won the motion. We made love, so sweetly, and then ate pizza, a reverse of our usual order. Afterward he told me he felt sorry for the employees whose discrimination case I had gotten dismissed.

"You're a softie," I said.

"But you love me for it," he said.

Which was true. Two months later, Mike was dead.

And I began to notice a softer-hearted voice than usual creeping into my own consciousness. I don't know for sure whose voice it is, but I think the voice is Mike, talking to me still. It says the things he would say, it's picked up where he left off. Lately it's been whispering to me that my on-the-job sins are piling up. That each hash mark for the corporate defense is a black mark for my soul.

Judgment day will come, it says. *It's just a matter of time.*

2

t's exactly 11:47 when I get back to my office at Stalling & Webb, one of Philadelphia's holy trinity of corporate megafirms. I can't help but know the time exactly, given the view from my office. It's a regulation associate cubicle except for the fact that the window behind my desk is entirely consumed by the immense yellow clock face on top of Philadelphia's City Hall, which is directly across the street. If you have to have a clock looming over your shoulder as you work, it's one of the nicest: an old-timey clock, round as the moon and almost as large. Ornate hands, curlicued with Victorian ironwork, move precisely on time, silently pointing to Roman numerals of

somber black. Nobody senior to me wanted this
office because of the clock, but I didn't mind it. I
always know what time it is, which is good for a
lawyer. As Socrates said, time is money.

I swivel around in my chair and look at the
clock. 11:48. 11:49. I don't like it so much anymore, though I'm not sure why. 11:50. *It's only
a matter of time.*

"Snap out of it, Mare," says a distinctive voice
from the doorway. My secretary, Brent Polk,
comes in with a stack of yellow message slips and
coffee on a tray. Brent's a slim, good-looking
man with hazel eyes and a thatch of jet-black
hair. He's also gay, but only Judy and I are privy
to that bit of job-threatening information. Judy
nicknamed him Bent in honor of his sexual
preference; he loves it, but we can't call him that
around the other secretaries. They think he has a
girlfriend in Massachusetts and can't decide
whether to get married. The perfect camouflage—
a man who won't commit. He blends right in.

"Coffee, what a great idea. Brent, you're a
man among men."

"Don't I wish." He sets the coffee and the
messages down on my desk. "Look, I even have
the tray today. Aren't you proud of me?" Brent's
ticked off because one of Stalling's commandments is THOU SHALT NOT CARRY COFFEE WITH-
OUT A TRAY because it will stain the carpets, and
he got reprimanded last week for not using one.

I pick up the YOU WANT IT WHEN? mug gratefully. All the coffee mugs talk back at Stalling,
because the employees can't.

"Now listen, Mare, you got another call from

Mystery Man. This is ridiculous. We should change your phone numbers. It's been going on for a year."

"Don't exaggerate. It hasn't been a year."

"Yes it has, off and on. It seems like it's more often now, too—this guy must have nothing better to do. Are you getting more calls at home?"

"When did he call?" Lately I've noticed the calls have fallen into a pattern, occurring when I get back to the office or home from work. I get the feeling that someone knows when I'm coming and going, which is not a good feeling to have. If Brent knew the whole story, he'd call out the National Guard. But I'm not sure the whole thing isn't coincidental.

"What difference does it make when he called? He called."

"Let's hold off. I've had the same phone number since I started here. All the clients know it. I hate to change for no good reason. People hate that."

"Arrrrgh," he growls in frustration, and reaches for my throat.

"Back, back. I'm telling you: You don't screw up your clients without good cause. Then they go away, and you're broke."

"But, Mary, it's sceevy. Did you ever think about what this guy's doing when you answer the phone?" He wrinkles his nose in disgust. "I had an Uncle Morty who—"

"Brent, please."

"Well it's the truth."

"All right. Let it sit for a while. If it keeps on happening, we'll change the numbers, okay?"

"Yes, bwana," he says with a sigh.

"Good."

His dark eyes light up wickedly. "Wait'll the big kahuna hears you won that motion. He and Delia are gonna celebrate tonight at the Four Seasons." Brent's connected like nobody's business at Stalling. The latest dirt is that the senior partner on the *Harbison's* case, Sam Berkowitz, is having an affair with his secretary. "I figure she'll leave at five and he'll leave ten minutes later. This time I'm gonna win. I can feel it."

"What do you mean, you're going to win?"

"You want in? It's only a buck." Brent pulls a wrinkled piece of steno paper out of his pants pocket and reads from it. "I bet he could wait ten minutes, but Janet says only five. Maggie bet he'll tough it out for half an hour. Lucinda says they'll leave together, but she's crazy. He's got his position to think of. Not *that* position, *this* position." He laughs.

"You mean you have a pool going?"

"Yeah." He slips the paper back into his pocket.

"You're shameless. You don't know they're having an affair."

"What, are you kidding? Everybody knows it."

"But he's married."

Brent rolls his eyes. "So was I."

"You were young. It's different."

"Please. I can't believe you've lived this long, you're so naive. Take a look at Delia next time you're up there. She's edible."

"She's okay-looking, but—"

"Okay-looking? She's a knockout. I'm gay,

dear, not blind, and neither is Berkowitz. He's got the hots. Everybody's talking about it. Where there's smoke, there's fire."

I make a finger crucifix and ward him off with it. "Blasphemer! The man is chairman of the department!"

"Oh, excuse me, I forgot. Your idol, Berkowitz, King of Kings. You know what I heard about him?"

"What?"

"You have to promise not to freak when I tell you, or I'm not going to tell you anything else. Ever again." He wags a finger at me through a too-long shirtsleeve. Black, of course, the only color he wears. "Especially about this partnership crap."

"What did you hear?"

"Promise, Mary."

"Tell me! We're talking my job here."

He leans over my desk. I can smell the Obsession on his neck. "I heard that no matter what they say, Berkowitz is authorizing only two partners from litigation. Two, not three. Two, and that's it."

"Not three? They said three!"

"Yeah? Well that was then and this is now. They don't want to divide up that pie any more than they have to."

"So they're just going to fire one of us? I can't believe it."

"Here we go. I knew I shouldn't have told you."

"How are they going to choose between the three of us? We all have the same evaluations, and we all bill over two thousand hours a year. We've indentured ourselves to this fucking firm, now they're gonna lop one of us off?" I rub my forehead on the front, where it's beginning to pound. I'm convinced that this is the partnership lobe. It's right next to the bar exam lobe and the SAT lobe.

"It won't be you, Mare. You just won a big motion."

"What about Judy?"

"Judy's got it made. They need her to crank out those briefs."

"And Ned Waters, what about him? I don't want to see any of us fired, for Christ's sake. It'll be impossible to get another job. It's not like the eighties, when you could pick and choose."

"Listen to me, you're working my last nerve. Are you having lunch with Judy today?"

"Of course."

"Good. Go early. Talk it over with her. She'll straighten you out."

And she tries to, as we sit at a wobbly table by the wall in the Bellyfiller, a dingy restaurant in the basement of our office building. Judy drags me here all the time because the sandwiches are huge and the pickles are free. She doesn't mind that the atmosphere is dark and cruddy, the big-screen TV attracts all the wrong people, and the sawdust on the floor sometimes crawls.

"You're letting this make you nuts, Mary!" She throws up her long arms, with their Boeing-sized wingspan. Judy Carrier is six feet tall, and from northern California, where the women grow like sequoias.

"I can't help it."

"Why? You just won a motion, you dufus. You're undefeated. We should be celebrating."

"How can you be so relaxed about this?"

"How can you be so worried about it?"

I laugh. "Don't you ever worry, Judy?"

She thinks a minute. "Sure. When my father is belaying. Then I worry. His attention wanders, and he—"

"What's belaying?"

"You know, when you climb, you designate one person to—"

"I'm not talking about rock climbing. I mean about work, about partnership. Don't you ever worry about whether we'll make it?"

"Making partner is nothing compared with rock climbing," she says earnestly. "You make a mistake rock climbing and you're fucked."

"I'm sure."

"You should come sometime. I'll take you." She turns around and looks for our waitress for the third time in five minutes.

"Right. When pigs fly."

She turns back. "What did you say?"

"Nothing. So you really don't worry about making partner?"

"Nope."

"Why?"

"Because we're both good lawyers. You do the discrimination defense and I'm the entire appellate brief department. We'll make it." Judy grins easily, showing the many gaps between her teeth, which are somehow not unattractive on her. In fact, men look her over all the time, but she disregards them cheerfully. She loves Kurt, the sculptor she lives with, who has most recently hacked Judy's buttercup-yellow hair into a chunky Dutch-boy cut. She calls it a work in progress.

"You think it's that easy?"

"I know it is. Do the work, the rest will come. You'll see—"

"Here it is, ladies," interrupts our waitress, who hates us. Not that we're special; the waitresses here hate all the customers. She slides the plates off her arm and they clatter onto the center of the table. Then she stalks off, leaving Judy and me to sort the orders. We move the heavy plates around like bumper cars.

"Girl food coming at you," Judy says, pushing the garden salad and diet Coke to me. "Yuck."

"Gimme a break. If I were ten feet tall I could eat like a lumberjack too." I slide her the hoagie with double meat, a side order of potato salad, and a vanilla milkshake.

"But you're not. You're a little Italian shortie. Where I come from, we use you people for doorstops." Judy bites eagerly into her hoagie. She starts at the end, like the sword-swallower in the circus. "Actually, there *is* one thing I'm worried about," she says, chomping away.

"What?"

"You. I'm worried about you."

"Me?" I can't tell if she's kidding.

"Yes."

"The phony phone calls?" I take a gulp of soda. It tastes like aspartame.

"No, they'll go away. I'm talking real danger," she says, wiggling her eyebrows comically. "Ned Waters is after you."

"Oh, jeez. Don't start, Jude."

"He wants it, Mare. Better buy some new undies." Judy likes sex and talks about it frankly and naturally. Since I was raised a Catholic, I know her attitude is perverted and evil. Faxed from Satan himself.

"Judith, keep it clean."

She leans over confidentially. "Be prepared to deal with the man, because it's true. I heard it from Delia the Stone Fox."

"Delia? Berkowitz's secretary? How does she know?"

"She heard it from Annie Zirilli From South Philly."

I laugh. Judy loves to make up nicknames. Half the time, I don't know who she's talking about. "You mean Barton's secretary?"

"Right. Annie saw him mooning around his office yesterday and started up a conversation with him. He told her he's interested in someone but won't say who. He said the girl—that's what he said, too, the *girl*—doesn't even know herself, because he's too scared to tell her. Too *scared*, can you believe this guy? What a horse's ass!" She stabs at her milkshake with a straw.

"He's shy."

"In a kid, it's shyness. In a man, it's dysfunction. And I bet money you're the lucky victim, because he always tries to sit next to you at department meetings. Plus I've seen the way he looks at you." She makes googly eyes.

"Bull. If he were interested, he would have followed up in law school. After our big date."

"But you met Mike."

"Ned didn't know that. He didn't even call back."

Judy shakes her head. "Sounds just like Waters. A torrid love affair of the mind. This guy has intimacy issues out the wazoo, I'm telling you. He's too cool. Cool Waters, that's him. Run for cover." She plows into her potato salad with a soupspoon, like a bulldozer clearing heavy snow.

I watch her eat, thinking about Ned Waters. I still say he's shy, but it doesn't square with how handsome he is. Strong, masculine features, a smattering of large freckles, and unusual eyes of light green. "He has nice eyes."

"If you like Rosemary's baby."

"Come on. He was a hunk in law school."

"It's tough to be a hunk in law school, Mare. If your pupils respond to light, you can screw half the class."

I smile, remembering back to school when I had dinner with Ned. I was surprised when he asked me out, but not when he didn't call back, because he was so quiet on the date. He barely said a word; I yammered away to fill the silences. Of course, I didn't sleep with him or anything; that would have required 12,736 more dates, and even then I wouldn't have enjoyed it. Enjoying it didn't happen until Mike.

After lunch, Judy and I take a walk around the block, since it's a warm day in spring and Philadelphia's infamous humidity has yet to set in. We window-shop, checking out the displays at

Laura Ashley, Banana Republic, and Borders, a chic bookstore on Walnut Street. I like Borders, because it's made reading fashionable, and I like to read. Judy likes Borders because it has an espresso bar with big cookies. Big as flapjacks, she likes to say. I treat her to a big cookie, and we walk back to the office, with me feeling like the stumpy mommy to a child on growth hormones.

3

A black-mirrored elevator whisks us to the top of a black-mirrored monolith that is home to a major oil company, an investment banking house, and Stalling & Webb. Stalling has the building's top seven floors, which always remind me of the seven deadly sins I learned in parochial school. Sloth is the bottom floor, where Judy gets off, and the next stops are Anger, Gluttony, Envy, Lust, and Avarice. Pride is the penthouse. I get off on Envy, which is where Martin H. Chatham IV, the junior partner on *Harbison's*, has his office. I'll tell him about the big victory after I freshen up.

Stalling's ladies' rooms are like heaven. They're clean, palatial, all done in cumulus white. The Corian countertop boasts eight generous basins, each lined with fake gold. At the end of the countertop is a white cabinet stocked with all-you-can-eat toiletries—free Tampax, Band-Aids, mouthwash, and dental floss. There's even Neutrogena, which I use liberally.

I wash my face as the secretaries joke around with me. They started to be nicer to me after Mike died, killed by a hit-and-run driver as he rode his bike along the Schuylkill River. I became a Young Widow, a character many of them recognized from their romance paperbacks. The lawyers, who have no time to read anything, barely remarked Mike's passing, which was fine with me. It's private.

I blot my face with a pebbled paper towel and take off.

Martin's on the telephone but waves me in. I sit down in one of the Shaker chairs facing his Shaker desk. Everything in Martin's office is tasteful, in a Thomas Moser kind of way, except for the owls. Needlepointed owls stare from the pillows, ceramic owls glare from the bookshelves. I used to think the owls were a high-prep fetish, like whales, but there's a better explanation. Martin is boredom personified and must know it, so he's seized on an interest to make himself interesting. The owls fill the vacuum where his personality should be. Now everyone knows him as Martin, the Guy Who Likes Owls. See what I mean?

"I'm listening, Stuart," Martin says into the telephone.

Listening is Martin's forte. He listened when I told him my idea for this motion, even as he winced with distaste. Martin's of the gentleman's school of litigation, which considers it bad form to put your client's interests ahead of your squash partner's. It was Berkowitz who green-lighted the motion, because Berkowitz is a real lawyer and doesn't know from squash.

"Good enough, Stuart. Take care, big guy." Martin hangs up the telephone and immediately puts a finger to his lips, a tacit *whoooo!* He makes a note in his red day journal to bill his time and another in his blue telephone log to bill the call. Later, Martin will bill for the time it takes him to write a file memo about the call, and he'll bill for the cost of duplicating the memo. Martin makes $265 every hour and 15 cents every page. In the name of the Father, of the Son, and of the Holy Ghost.

"So, Mary, how did it go?" he asks blandly.

"Very well."

"Good news?" His washed-out blue eyes flicker with interest.

"We won, Martin."

"We won? We *won?*"

"He ruled from the bench. The class action is no more."

"Good God, Mary!" Martin pumps me for every detail of the argument. I edit out the "Ave Maria" and give him the colorized version, in which I star as Partnership Material, No Question. When I'm finished, Martin calls to see if Berkowitz is in. Then he grabs his suit jacket, because THOU SHALT NOT WALK AROUND

THE HALLS WITHOUT A JACKET, and dashes out.

I walk back to my office. I've done my job, which is to make Martin look good. That's why he goes alone to Berkowitz's office, to take credit for the win. Likewise, since Martin's raison d'être is to make Berkowitz look good, he'll let Berkowitz take the credit when he telephones Harbison's General Counsel. Because Berkowitz has made the GC look good to his CEO, the GC will send him more cases. ASAP. And partners who bring in the most business make the most money. You get the picture: The knee bone's connected to the thigh bone, the thigh bone's connected to the hip bone, and so on.

I should feel happy, but I don't. The victory lights up my Partnership Tote Board big-time, but it comes at a price. If Brent's information is right, my partnership could cost the firing of either of two fine lawyers, one of whom is my best friend.

And don't forget about the Harbison employees, says the little Mike-voice, come back again. *They were fired just when their pensions were about to vest, and the only mistake they made was choosing a lousy lawyer. Now they don't even have him anymore. Is that what you went to law school for?*

I try to shake off the voice when I hit my office. 2:25. I run out the day's string, listlessly dealing with the mail. I ask Brent to divide it into Good and Evil, with Good on the right and Evil on the left. The Good mail is advance sheets, which are paperback books summarizing recent court decisions. I'm supposed to read the Good mail, but if I did, cobwebs as heavy as suspension cables would grow from my butt to the chair. Instead, I put them in my out box so the messengers will shovel them onto someone else's desk. That's why they're Good.

The Evil Mail is everything else. It's Evil because your opponent's trying to fuck you. There's only one lawyerly response: Fuck back. For example, last week, in a case for Noone Pharmaceuticals, opposing counsel tried to fuck us into a settlement by threatening to publish company memoranda in the newspaper. So I'm writing a motion asking the Court to restrict the use of company documents to the lawsuit and to award Noone my fees in preparing the motion. This is primo fucking back, and you have to fuck back. If you don't fuck back, you'll get fucked.

Believe it or not, I usually enjoy this aspect of my profession, the head-banging and the back-fucking, but not today. Anxiety gnaws at the edges of my brain and I can't focus on the Evil mail. I turn to the unfinished brief for Noone. I read it over and over but the argument sounds like a verbal Mobius strip: Judge, you should restrict the documents to the lawsuit because documents should be restricted to lawsuits. I can't tell if it's a failure of concentration or of writing. I pack the draft in my briefcase and leave the office at dusk.

The remainder of the day's sunlight is blocked prematurely by Philadelphia's new and improved skyline. Developers went crazy after City Council permitted buildings to be taller than William Penn's hat, with the result that the city streets get dark too soon and there's a lot of empty office buildings sprouting like mushrooms in the gloom.

The air cools down rapidly as I reach Rittenhouse Square. I'm shivering like all the other superannuated yuppies, except that I refuse to wear Reeboks. If my shoes were too uncomfortable to walk in, I wouldn't buy them.

The square looks just like it does every evening this time of year. The old people huddle together on the benches, clucking worriedly about the young people, with their orange-striped hair and nose rings, as well as the homeless, with their shopping carts and superb tans. Runners circle the square for the umpteenth time. Walkers stride by in fast-forward, plugged into Walkmans. A pale young man on a bench looks me up and down, and then I remember.

Is someone watching me?

I look backward over my shoulder at the pale man on the bench, but he's joined by a girlfriend in a black beret. I look at the other people as I pass through the square, but they all look normal enough. Is one of them the some-one? Does one of them call me and do God-knows-what when I answer? My step quickens involuntarily.

I hurry inside when I reach my building. It's quiet in the entrance hall, the kind of absolute silence that settles in when a big old house is empty. I'm the only tenant here. My landlords are an elderly couple who live on the first two floors of the house. They're nice people, hand-holders after fifty years of marriage, off on another Love Boat cruise. I pick up my bills and catalogs from the floor and make sure the front door's locked.

I climb the stairs, wondering if the telephone will ring after I get in. I unlock the door and switch on the living room light. I glance at the telephone, but it's sitting there like a properly inanimate object. I breathe a sigh of relief and drop my briefcase with a thud.

"Honey, I'm home."

The tabby cat doesn't even look up from the windowsill. She's not deaf, she's indifferent. She wouldn't care if Godzilla drove a Corvette through the door, she's waiting for Mike to come home. In winter, the windowpane is dotted with her nose prints. In summer, her gray hairs cling to the screen.

"He's not coming back," I tell her. It's a reminder to both of us since the episode this morning in court.

I kick off my shoes and join her at the window, looking out at the apartments across the street. Most have plants on their windowsills, starved for light in the northern exposure. One has a turquoise Bianchi bike hanging in the window, like an advertisement to break in, and another has an antique rake. Most of my neighbors are home, cooking dinner or listening to music. The window directly across from mine has the shade drawn; it looks dark inside. I wonder if the person who lives there is the one who's been calling me. It's hard to imagine, since Mike knew all our neighbors. He was the friendly one.

"Come on, Alice. Let's close up." I nudge the cat and she jumps to the living room rug, her hindquarters twitching.

I yank on the string of the knife-edged blinds, which tumble to the windowsill with a *zzziiip*. I pad over to the other window, flat-footed without my heels, and am about to pull down the blinds when I hear the ignition of a car outside the window.

Strange. I didn't see a driver walk to the car, and it's not a car I recognize.

I let down the blinds but peek between them at the car. It's too dark out for me to see the driver.

The car's headlights blaze to life as it pulls out of its parking space and glides down the street. I don't know the make of the car; I'm not good at that. It's big, though, like the boats my father used to drive. An Oldsmobile, maybe. Before they tried to convince us that they're not the boats our fathers used to drive.

I watch the car disappear, as the telephone rings loudly.

I flinch at the sound. Is it the someone?

I pick up the receiver cautiously. "Hello?"

But the only response is static—a static I hear on many of the calls. It's him. My heart begins to pound as I put two and two together for the first time.

"Is this a car phone, you bastard? Are you watching my house, you sick—"

The tirade is severed by the dial tone.
"Fuck you!" I shout into the dead receiver.
Alice blinks up at me, in disapproval.

"Taste, *cara*," says my mother, holding out a wooden spoon with tomato sauce.

"Mmmm. *Perfetto*." I'm at my parents' row house in South Philly the next day, playing hooky because my twin sister's on parole from the convent. She only gets out once a year under the rules of her cloistered order, and isn't permitted phone calls or mail. I hate the convent for taking my twin from me. I can't believe that God, even if he does exist, would want to divide us.

"You all right, Maria?" My mother frowns behind her thick glasses, which make her brown eyes look supernaturally large. She's half blind from sewing lampshades in the basement of this very house, her childhood home. The kitchen is the only thing that's changed since then; the furniture and fixtures remain the same, stop-time. We still use the tinny black switchplate like a bulletin board, leaving notes among the dog-eared mass cards, a photo of JFK, and a frond of dried-out palm.

"I'm fine, Ma. I'm fine." I wouldn't dream of telling her I think I'm being watched. She's like a supersensitive instrument, the kind that calibrates air pressure—or lies. She has a jumpy needle, and the news would send it into the red zone.

"Maria? They're not treating you good at that office?" She scrutinizes me, the wooden spoon resting against her stretch pants like Excalibur in its scabbard.

"I've just been busy. It's almost time for them to decide who makes partner."

"*Dio mio!* They're lucky to have you! Lucky! The nuns said you were a genius! A genius!" A scowl contorts her delicate features. Even at seventy-three, she makes up in the morning and gets her hair done every Saturday at the corner, where they tease it to hide her bald spot.

"Catholic school standards, Ma."

"I should go up there to that fancy office! I should tell them how lucky they are to have my daughter be their lawyer!" She unsheaths the spoon and waves it recklessly in the air.

"No, Ma. Please." I touch her forearm to calm her. Her skin feels papery.

"They should burn in hell!" She trembles with agitation. I wrap my arms around her, surprised at her frailty.

"It's all right. Don't worry."

"Whaddaya two doing, the fox-trot?" jokes my father, puffing his cigar as he walks into the kitchen. He looks roly-poly in a thin short-sleeved shirt. It's almost transparent, made from some obscure synthetic fiber, and he's got the dago T-shirt on underneath. My father has dressed this way for as long as I can remember. When he's dressed up, that is.

"Out! Out of the kitchen with that cigar!" my mother shouts—of necessity, because my father never wears his hearing aid.

"Don't shoot!" He puts up both hands, then returns to the baseball game blaring in the living room.

My mother's magnified eyes are an inch from my nose. "When is he going to stop with those cigars? When?"

"He's been smoking cigars for sixty years, Ma. You think he'll quit soon?"

Suddenly, there's a commotion at the front door and I hear Angie shouting a greeting to my father. My mother and I hurry into the living room, where Angie is taking off her sweater.

"Hello, beautiful," she says, with a laugh. She always calls me that. It's her joke, since we're identical twins.

"Angie!" I lock her in a bear hug.

"Hey, that's too tight, let me go."

"No."

"Mare . . ."

"Not until you tell me you miss me."

"Ma, get her off of me, please."

"Let your sister alone. You're too old for that.

Too old." My mother swats me in the arm with the spoon.

"Too old to hug my own twin? Since when?"

She hits me again.

"Ouch! What is this, *Mommy Dearest?*" I let Angie go.

"Yeah, grow up," she says, with a short laugh. Her eyes look large and luminous under a short haircut—our childhood pixie resurrected. She's dressed in jeans and a Penn sweatshirt just like mine, having left her Halloween costume back at the convent. We're twins again, but for the hair and the fact that Angie looks rested and serene, with a solid spiritual core.

"Look at her, Ma, she looks so good!" I say. "Angie, you look great!"

"Stop, you." Angie can't take a compliment, never could.

"Turn around. Let me see."

She does a obligatory swish-turn in her jeans.

"You wearing underwear?"

She laughs gaily. For a split second, it's a snapshot of the twin I grew up with. I catch glimpses of the old Angie only now and then. The rest of the time, she's a twin I hardly know.

"*Basta*, Maria! *Basta!*" chides my mother happily.

"So you're out of uniform. I can't believe it."

"I changed at a Hojo's after I left." She sets her purse on the floor.

"Why?"

"No special reason. Tired of you making all those habit jokes, I guess."

"Me?"

"You."

"Well I love the sweatshirt. You look like your-self again."

"Like I didn't know you'd say that," Angie says.

"Look at this hair!" My mother runs an arthritic hand through Angie's hair. "So soft. Just like a baby's."

Angie smiles, and I wonder why she's so accepting of my mother's touch and not my own.

"Look at this hair, Matty!" my mother shouts delightedly. "Just like a baby's!"

My father smiles. "You got your baby back, Mama."

Angie positively glows in my mother's arms. "I can't get over how good you look, Ange. I think I'm in love," I say.

"Will you stop already?" She wiggles away from my mother, still smiling.

"Plus I'm not used to you looking so much better than me. You look like the *after* picture and I look like the *before*."

"That's because you work too hard."

"Tell me about it."

"Did you make a partner yet?"

"No, they decide in two months. I'm going crazy. I hate life." I wish I could tell her about the partnership rumors and the strange car, but we won't have any time alone unless I waylay her.

"And it's a hit! Out to right field! Might be deep enough . . . It is!" screams the Phillies announcer, Richie Ashburn, but my father's too excited at seeing Angie again to look at the television. My parents miss Angie, even though they're proud of her decision. They're proud of both their twins, the one who serves God, and the other who serves Mammon.

We troop into the kitchen to talk and drink percolated coffee from chipped cups. That's all we'll do today, as Richie Ashburn calls a high-decibel double-header to an empty living room. I start the ball rolling over the first cup, whining about my caseload, but my father quickly takes over the conversation. He can't hear when others talk, so his only choice is to filibuster. None of us minds this much, least of all my mother, who footnotes his narrative of their courtship.

My father takes a breather after lunch and my mother holds forth about the new butcher, who doesn't trim off enough fat. She tells a few stories of her own, mostly about our childhood, and I realize how badly she needs to talk to someone who can hear her. Angie must know this too, for she doesn't look bored, and, truth to tell, I'm not either. But we both draw the line after dinner, when she launches into the story of a maiden aunt's gallbladder operation. Angie seizes the opportunity to head for the bathroom and I follow her upstairs, hoping to get her alone. I reach the bathroom door just as she's about to close it.

"Ange, wait. It's me." I stick my foot in the door.

"What are you doing?" Angie looks at me through the crack.

"I want to talk to you."

"Move your foot. I'll be right out."

"What am I, the Boston Strangler? Let me in."

"I have to go to the bathroom."

"Number one or number two?"

"Mary, we're not kids anymore."

"Right. Number one or number two?"

She shakes her head. "Number one."

"Okay. So number one, you can let me in."

"It can't wait two minutes?"

"I don't want Mom to hear. Will you open the goddamn door?"

So she does, and I take a precarious seat on the curved edge of the tub, an old claw-and-ball-foot. Angie stands above me with her hands on her hips. "What is it?" she says.

"You can pee if you have to."

"I can wait. Why don't you tell me what you have to say."

A little ember of anger starts to glow inside my chest. "What's the big deal, Angie? We took baths together until we were ten years old. Now you won't let me in the bathroom?"

She closes the lid on the toilet seat and sits down on it with a quiet sigh. The old Angie would have snapped back, would have given as good as she got, but that Angie went into the convent and never came out. "Is something the matter?" she asks patiently.

By now my teeth are on edge. "No."

"Look, Mary, let's not fight. What's the matter?"

I look down at the tiny white octagons that make up the tile floor. The grout between them is pure as sugar. My father, a tile setter until he popped a disc in his back, regrouts the bathroom every year. The porcelain gleams like something you'd find at Trump Tower. My father does beautiful work.

"It's beautiful, isn't it?" Angie says.

I smile. We used to be able to read each other's minds; I guess Angie can still read mine. "What was it Pop always said?"

"'It's not a job, it's a *craft*.'"

"Right." I look up, and her face has softened. I take a deep breath. "I don't know where to start, Ange. So much is going on. At work. At home. I feel tense all the time."

"What's happening?"

"It's the last couple of weeks until they decide who's partner. I heard they're only picking two of us. Everything I do is under the microscope. Plus I've been getting these phony phone calls. And last night I could swear a car was watching me from across the street."

She frowns. "Are you sure?"

"Yeah."

"But why would anybody be watching you? You're not involved in any trouble, are you? I mean, in the work you do?"

"I don't do any criminal cases, if that's what you mean. Stalling would never touch anything like that."

From downstairs, my mother calls, "Angela! Maria! Dessert!"

Angie gets up. "Maybe it's your imagination. You always had a vivid imagination, you know."

"I did not."

"Oh, really? What about the time you hung garlic in our room, after that vampire movie we saw? It was on our bulletin board for a whole year. A foot-long ring of garlic."

"So?"

"So my sweaters smelled like pesto."

"But we never got any vampires."

She laughs. "You look stressed, Mary. You need to relax. So what if they don't make you partner? You're a great lawyer. You can get another job."

"Oh, yeah? Being passed over isn't much of a recommendation, and the market in Philly is tight. Even the big firms are laying people off."

"You need to stay calm. I'm sure everything will turn out all right. I would tell you that it's in God's hands, but I know what you'd say."

"Girls, your coffee's getting cold!" calls my mother.

"She's waiting for us," Angie says. "And I still have to go to the bathroom."

I get up, reluctantly. "I wish we could get time to talk, Ange. We never talk. I don't even know how you're doing. Are you okay?"

"I'm fine," she says, with a pat smile, the same smile you'd give to a bank teller.

"Really?"

"Really. Now go. I have to pee." She ushers me out the door. "I'll pray for you," she calls from inside.

"Terrific," I mumble, walking down the stairs to a darkened living room. The double-header is over, and my father is standing in front of the television watching the Phillies leave the field. Red, blue, and green lights flicker across his face in the dark. Despite the carnival on his features, I can see he's dejected. "They lose again, Pop?"

He doesn't hear me.

"They lose, Pop?" I shout.

He nods and turns off the ancient television with a sigh. It makes a small electrical crackle; then the room falls oddly silent. I hadn't realized how loud the volume was. He yanks the chattery pull chain on the floor lamp and the room lights up instantly, very bright. They must have a zillion-watt bulb in the lamp; the parchment shade is brown around the middle. I'm about to say something when I remember it might be because of my mother's eyesight.

"You want some cannoli, honey?" my father asks tenderly. He throws an arm around my shoulder.

"You got the chocolate chip, don't you? 'Cause if you don't, I'm leaving. I've had it with the service at this place."

"What kinda father would I be that I don't have the chocolate chip? Huh?" He gives me a squeeze and we walk into the kitchen together.

My mother clucks about the cold coffee as we sit down, and Angie joins us at the table. My father's soft shoulders slump over his coffee. We carry on the conversation around him, and my mother chatters anxiously through dessert. Something's wrong, but I can't figure out what it is. Angie senses it too, because after my father declines a cannoli for the second time, she gives me a discreet nudge.

"Pop," I say, "Have a cannoli. I'm eating alone here."

He doesn't even look up. I don't know if he doesn't hear me or what. Angie and I exchange glances.

"Pop!" Angie shouts. "You okay?"

My mother touches my hand. "Let him be. He's just tired."

My father looks up, and his milky brown eyes are wet. He squeezes them with two calloused fingers.

My mother deftly passes him a napkin. "Isn't that right, Matty? You're tired?"

"Ah, yeah. I'm tired." He nods.

"You're leading the witness, Ma," I say.

She waves me off like an annoying fly. "Your father and I were talking about Frank Rizzo last night. Remember, it was this time of year, Rizzo had the heart attack. It's a sin. He coulda been mayor again."

My father seems lost in thought. He says, half to himself, "So sudden. So young. We couldn't prepare."

"It's a sin," repeats my mother, rubbing his back. With her lipstick all gone, her lips look bloodless.

"Pop, Rizzo was almost eighty," I say, but Angie's look silences me. Her eyes tell me who they're grieving for. The one who loved percolated coffee, the Phillies, and even an occasional cigar—Mike. I feel a stab of pain inside; I wonder when this will stop happening. I rise stiffly. "I better get going. It's a school night."

My parents huddle together at the table, looking frozen and small.

Angie clears her throat. "Me too. I have to change back."

I walk to the screen door with its silly scroll-work *D*, looking out into the cool, foggy night. I remember nights like this from when I was little. The neighbors would sit out in beach chairs, the women gossiping in Italian and the men playing *mora*. Angie and I would sit on the marble stoop in our matching pajamas like twin mascots. It was a long time ago.

I wish I could feel that air again.

I open the screen door and walk down the front steps onto the sidewalk. The air is chilled from the fog, which hangs as low as the thick silver stanchions put in to thwart parking on the sidewalk. A dumb idea—all it does is force people to double-park on the main streets. Like my father says, in South Philly the cars are bigger than the houses.

Suddenly a powerful car barrels by, driving much too fast for this narrow street. It comes so near the curb in front of me that I feel a cold chill in its wake.

"Hey, buddy!" I shout after him, then do a double-take. It looks just like the car from last night.

I run into the middle of the street, squinting in the darkness. I catch sight of the car's flame-red taillights as it turns right at the top of the street and disappears into the dark. My father comes out of the house, followed by my mother.

"Pop! Did you see that car? What kind of car was that? Was that an Oldsmobile?"

"What?" He cups a hand behind his ear, making a lumpy silhouette in front of the screen door.

"Ma! Did you see that car?"

"What car?" she hollers, from behind her bullet-proof glasses.

Behind them both, at a distance, is Angie.

"I would say this is Evil mail, wouldn't you?" Brent asks grimly. He holds up a piece of white paper that reads:

CONGRATULATIONS ON YOUR
PARTNERSHIP, MARY

The letters are typed in capitals. It looks computer-generated, like the laser printers we use at Stalling. State-of-the-art. The paper is smooth. The note is unsigned.

I read it again. "Weird."

"Very."

"It's not a nice note, is it?"

"No." Brent's face looks tight.

"Who do you think it's from?"

"I have no idea. There's no return address, either."

"Let me see." I take the envelope, a plain white business envelope, and flip it over. On the front is my name and Stalling's address in capital letters. Also laser-printed. The stamp is a tiny American flag. "I don't understand."

"I do."

"What?"

"I think somebody's jealous of you, that's what I think. The news about your motion is all over the department. Everybody knows you won before Bitterman. It was a big deal for an associate. I even heard it in the secretaries' lunchroom, so you know the lawyers are talking about it."

"Really?"

"Sure. You're a star, kid. Your enemies will be comin' out of the woodwork now. It just proves my theory."

"What theory?"

"I never told you my theory?"

"You told me your cancellation theory, about how assholes marry each other. You never told me your theory about hate mail."

"Well. My theory is that you find out who your true friends are when something good happens to you, not when something bad happens to you. Everybody loves you when something bad happens to you. Then you're easy to love."

"That's sick, Brent."

"But true. And this is a good example. There

must be somebody who you think is your friend, but who isn't really. Not a true friend. They're jealous as shit of you, secretly competing with you. Whoever it is, they smile in your face."

His words make me uneasy. "Who?"

"Think about it. Who's competing with you right now to make partner? Judy and Ned. We know it can't be Judy, so that leaves Ned. I never liked that guy." He looks bitter.

My thoughts race ahead. Is the note connected to the car? To the phone calls? Is it one person or more than one? Holy Christ. I hand Brent the envelope. I don't even want it in my hand.

It's getting worse, says the Mike-voice. *First the calls. Then the car. Now a note.*

"Mary? You okay?"

I plop down into my chair. "I think this has something to do with the phone calls."

"Mystery Man?"

"Brent, something's the matter."

"What?"

"Close the door, okay?"

"Mare, what's going on?" He shuts the door and sinks into one of the chairs opposite my desk.

"I think somebody might be watching me. Following me."

"What?" His eyes widen.

I tell Brent about the car on my street and then at my parents' house. He barely lets me finish before he has a conniption. "You have to call the cops! Right this instant!" He points to the telephone on my desk. "What are you waiting for?"

"I can't do that. I'm not even sure about the car. Maybe I'm imagining—"

"Mary, you're not imagining *this!*" He waves the note in the air like a warning flag.

"I can't just call the cops. Can you imagine? Cops asking everyone in the department—even partners—about me? That would be terrific right now, right before the election."

"Mare, what's the matter with you? Someone is stalking you and you're worried about making partner?"

"They're not *stalking* me, you don't have to make it sound like that."

At that moment, my telephone rings and we exchange uneasy looks. Brent takes charge. "Let Lucinda get it. And they *are* stalking you. What do you think it's called when someone follows you around?"

The phone rings again, and Brent looks at it angrily. "Fuck! Can't she get off her ass for once? I pick up for *her!*"

The phone rings a third time.

I reach for it, but Brent heads me off. "No, let me. If it's that asshole, I'm gonna scream my fucking head off." He snatches up the receiver. "Ms. DiNunzio's office," he says, in a crisp telephone tenor. Then his face blanches. "Okay. Right now." He nods, hanging up.

"What?"

"Berkowitz wants to see you."

"Why? Is something the matter? Was that him?"

"It was Delia. She said he wants to see you right away."

"Great. This is all I need." I dig in my purse for my compact and check my reflection in its round mirror. A circle of dirty-blond hair, shoulder length. A circle of dark brown eye, an extended-wear contact lens afloat on its cornea. A circle of whitish teeth, straightened into Chiclets by orthodonture paid for in installments. Mike used to say I was pretty, but I don't feel pretty today.

"What are you doing? Get going! You're worse than Jack with that mirror," Brent says. Jack is his lover of five years, a bartender at Mr. Bill's, a gay bar on Locust Street. Judy calls him Jack Off, but Brent claims he thought of it first. "Go, girl, you'll be late!"

Berkowitz's corner office is on Pride, and Delia's desk blocks its entrance like a walnut barricade. She types as she listens to the teaching of Chairman Berkowitz through dictating earphones. Even the ugly headset doesn't mar her good looks. Lustrous red hair, a perfect nose, the sexiest pout in legal history. Brent is right. Delia *is* a stone fox.

"Hi, Delia."

"I'm busy." She doesn't look up but continues to hit the keys of her word processor with spiky acrylic nails. *Click-click-click-click.* It sounds like a hail on a rooftop. Too bad it will look like *jciy-wegwebcniquywgxnmai.* I know, I've seen her work.

"Oh. Sorry."

"He's in there." *Click-click-click. Oreuhbalkejeopn?*

"I'll just go in, then."

"Suit yourself."

This is even more attitude than I'm used to

from Delia; I wonder what's bothering her. I walk to the open doorway of Berkowitz's office, but his brawny back is to the door. A tailored English suit strains at its shoulder seams as Berkowitz hunches over. The only time Burberrys has dressed a major appliance.

"Go in already!" snaps Delia.

The command startles me into the sanctum sanctorum. Berkowitz is on the telephone and doesn't turn around. I walk the three city blocks to his desk and sit down in a massive leather wing chair. The decor here screams Street Kid Who Made God—I mean, Good. The desk is a baroque French antique with a surface that was polished by a Zamboni. The high-backed desk chair could have belonged to the Sun King. Photographs of Berkowitz's first, second, and third sets of children adorn curly-legged mahogany end tables. I feel like a scullery maid at Versailles.

"I don't care, Lloyd! I don't give *one flying fuck!*" Berkowitz bellows into the telephone, as he swivels around in his chair. "You tell that little bastard if he thinks he's going to fuck me, he has another thing coming! We can take his fucking little *pisher* of a firm, and we will!" Berkowitz is so engrossed in making what constitutes Terroristic Threats under the Pennsylvania Crimes Code that he's oblivious to me altogether. This is why Judy calls him Jerkowitz, but I think she's being unfair. Berkowitz grew up in tough West Philly and made it to the peaky-peak on sheer brainpower and force of will. If your Fortune 500 Company is in deep shit, he's one of the few lawyers in the country who can save your sorry ass. Guaranteed. But not in writing.

"Where the fuck does he get off? I told him what the agenda was, and he tries to make a fool out of me! He'll be offa this committee so goddamn fast it'll make his head spin!" Berkowitz is yelling at one of his apostles on the Rules Committee, which he chairs. It's a twelve-man panel of federal judges and prominent litigators that meets at our offices to propose changes in federal court rules. If something didn't go well at a recent meeting, heads will roll, and balls too. Everything rolling, off down the hall.

"Don't tell me to calm down! I *am* calm! . . . No! No! No! *You* deal with him then!"

Berkowitz slams down the telephone receiver. The glaze in his eyes tells me he's back on Girard Avenue, decades ago, fighting off the punks who want a peek at his foreskin. Or lack thereof.

Berkowitz shakes his head, his face still florid. "Can you believe this fucking guy? Can you fucking believe this guy?"

I gather the question is rhetorical and say nothing.

He rubs his eyes irritably and leans back in his chair. His look says, Heavy is the head that wears the crown. "You want my job, Mary, Mary, Quite Contrary?"

"What?"

"I'm asking you. You want it?" He isn't smiling.

"I don't understand."

"Do you want to be here someday? Run the department, head the committees? When I was your age, I wanted to be me so bad I was on fire." He gazes out of a massive window at the best view in the city. From his vantage point, you can see all the way to the Delaware River and the snaky black border it makes between Pennsylvania and New Jersey. An occasional tourist ferry travels in slow motion under the Ben Franklin Bridge. We ain't the port of call we used to be.

"I would have killed to be me," Berkowitz says absently. Suddenly he snatches a pack of Marlboros from his desk and lights one up, belching out a puff of smoke so thick it looks like the Industrial Revolution took place in his office. I pretend the smoke doesn't bother me, which it does, mightily. I try not to breathe.

"But you're not interested in this shit and neither am I. You're wondering why I called you up here." He takes a slow drag on the cigarette and squints at me through the smoke.

I nod, yes.

"Two reasons. One: That was a helluva result you got on the motion before Bitterman. I saw him at the Rules Committee meeting"—at this he winces—"and he told me you had great potential."

"Uh . . . thank you."

"He's an ugly bastard, isn't he?"

I laugh.

"Two: Harbison's GC is sending me a new case. You know how they like to spread their business around, get all the firms competing with each other. They sent the case to Masterson originally, but the GC thinks we can do a better job. We can, right?"

"Right." So we stole a case from Masterson, Moss & Dunbar, the firm at the apex of the holy trinity. We must have snaked them with our win before Bitter Man and some pillow talk by Berkowitz. He doesn't say these things, but I don't need a crib sheet to translate Latin One.

"It's another age discrimination case. They demoted a CFO, so it's very high-profile. And they won't settle. They want to crush the bastard." Berkowitz blows an enormous cloud of smoke upward, which is something he does at meetings when he thinks he's being considerate. "I'm assigning the case to you, Mary Mary. You make all the calls, just be sure you blind-copy me on the correspondence. I don't want to look like a smacked ass if the GC calls. There's a pretrial conference scheduled for today at three-thirty. It's your baby. Any questions?" He sucks on the cigarette throttled between his thick knuckles. Its red tip flashes on like a stoplight.

"And . . . Martin?"

"Forget Martin!" he says, breathing smoke. "You don't need Martin, do you?"

"No, I just . . . I thought he handled your matters."

"Well, he doesn't. I told him the other day. He's fine with it. You want this case or don't you?"

"I do. I do."

"Good. Then we're married." He erupts into laughter.

I laugh too, with relief and wonder.

"Now get out of my office. Can't you see I'm a busy man?"

I laugh again, but the meeting is over. I get up to leave.

"By the way, Ned Waters was in here bitching today. He heard that only two of you will be making partner in June. You hear anything like that, Mary, Queen of Scots?"

"No," I lie.

"Fine," he replies, knowing I'm lying. "It's not true."

"Good," I reply, knowing he's lying.

As I leave his office, I see that Delia's headset is off, resting at the base of her neck like a cheap choker. As I walk by, she's sipping tea in a genteel way from a white china cup. An affectation she's picked up from Berkowitz, who likes to stub out his Marlboro in the saucer.

"See you later, Delia."

"Ready to play with the big boys, Mary?" She looks daggers at me over the delicate cup.

Her expression bewilders me. "Guess so."

"You'd better be." Her lovely eyes glitter with hostility as she sets the cup down. It makes an unhappy sound when it crashes into the saucer.

"Are you mad at me for something, Delia?"

"You, Mary? Never. You're little Miss Perfect. Hail Mary, full of grace. He forgot that one, didn't he? But that's not one he'd know."

Before I can react, Berkowitz's hulking frame appears in the doorway. His cigarette is burnt all the way down to the V between his index and middle fingers, but he seems heedless of it. "Delia, I need you in here," he says gruffly.

"But I'm having a nice conversation with

Mary, Mr. Berkowitz." Her full lips curve upward in a sly smile.

"Now!" It sounds like a gunshot.

I jump, but Delia doesn't. Still smiling, she stands up and unfolds slowly, from her perky breasts on down. She and Berkowitz lock eyes, with him looking the stern principal to her naughty schoolgirl. As I turn to go, I hear the door of Berkowitz's office close behind them.

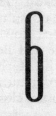

"Oh-ho!" Brent whoops behind the closed door of my office. "She's jealous of you, Mare. Sammie's giving you your big chance, and it's killing her. This ain't a law firm, it's a miniseries!"

"You think she's jealous?"

"That girl needs a spanking, and I bet I know who's gonna—"

"Jealous enough to send me that note?"

His face falls. "My God, Mary. I didn't think of that."

"Is she capable of it?"

"I only know what I hear about her. Sure, she's the type to send a hate note—she'd do it in a minute. But follow you around in a car? That's

— 58 —

a bit much. I'd sooner believe that of Waters. And he has more of a reason. It's his partnership you'd take." Brent bites at a thumbnail.

"I don't think it's Ned."

"Why?"

"Something tells me it's not him. I don't know; if anything, he seems kind of vulnerable. And why not Delia? Look, I don't know if she's having an affair with Berkowitz, and it doesn't matter. What if she has a crush on him and he's favoring me? Maybe that's enough to piss her off."

"They're having an affair, Mare. He left five minutes after her Monday night. Janet won four bucks."

I flash on the way Berkowitz looked at Delia before they closed the door. "Okay. So maybe they're having an affair. That would make her even more jealous, wouldn't it?"

He shakes his head, examining the ragged nail. "It's not her," he says with certainty.

"How do you know?"

"No typos."

So he's seen her work, too.

A while later, Judy drags me to the Bellyfiller for lunch, which is fine, because I'm not hungry. The place is packed with middle managers. They sit behind combination meat sandwiches, pretending not to be interested in the soap opera on the big-screen TV. I tell Judy about the car that drove by my parents' house and about the note in the morning mail. It sounds more farfetched than the soap and takes almost as long to tell. Judy's finished dessert by the time I've finished the story.

"Brent's right," she says with finality. "I think Ned wrote the note. It makes the most sense. He wants to make partner so bad he can taste it."

"More than we do?"

"Sure. He has a famous daddy to live up to, remember? And the firm is his whole life. It's all he has."

Judy's words echo inside my head. It's all *I* have, too. That must be why I obsess over it and she doesn't. I take a gulp of water from a smudgy glass.

"We don't know enough to say whether the car's connected to the note, but it seems more likely than not. And for some reason, call it sexism, I find it hard to believe that a woman would be stalking you in a car. So Delia's out."

"Yeah, I guess." I feel tense and confused. On the big-screen TV, a gigantic nurse looks tense and confused. My life, parodied before my eyes. I try to block out the TV, but it's as hard to ignore as the huge clock in my office window. Big, scary things seem to be everywhere I go lately, like a nightmare of Claes Oldenburg's.

"Do you ever see the car in the daytime?"

"No."

"That's consistent with someone who works during the day."

"Everybody at Stalling, in other words."

Judy thinks a minute. "Have you thought about calling the cops?"

"Brent wants me to, but I hate to do that. The last thing I need right now is an investigation in the department. I might as well kiss my career good-bye."

"Hmmm. I see your point. Let's not do the freak yet, let's see if it blows over. I'll be your bodyguard in the meantime. How does that sound?"

I consider this. "I can't afford to feed you."

"Very funny."

On the TV, two monster nurses are discussing whether somebody will live through the week. Their glossy mouths are the size of swimming pools. A commercial for a mile-high can of Crisco comes on.

"Mary?"

"Yeah?"

"You look spaced. Listen, it's okay to be upset about this. I don't blame you. It's spooky."

"It's not just the car, Jude. It's everything."

"What do you mean?" She sets down her milk-shake.

"I don't know what I mean. What I mean doesn't make sense."

"So tell me what you're thinking. It doesn't matter if it makes sense."

I look at Judy's blue eyes, so wide-set and uncluttered. I'm reminded of how different we are. There's a whole country between us. She's so free and openhearted, like the West Coast, and I'm so—well, East. Burdened with my own history, dark and falling apart. "I don't know. Forget it, Jude. It's stupid."

"Come on, Mary. Let's talk about it."

"I don't know."

"Try it."

"All right." I take another gulp of water. "It's just that lately, like after my argument for

Harbison's, I hear this . . . voice. Not that I'm hearing voices, like Son of Sam or something, not like that."

"No German shepherds," she says with a smile.

"No. Sometimes the voice sounds like Mike, you know? Not the tone of it, I mean, but what it says. It sounds just like something he would say. Something right. Am I explaining this okay?"

"You're doing fine."

I take a deep breath. "You know the expression, what goes around comes around?"

She nods patiently. Her long silver earrings swing back and forth.

"Sometimes I think that the car, and now the note, are happening for a reason. And I think it's going to get worse unless I change something. Do something different, do something better. I think Mike, or the voice—whoever, is trying to tell me that."

She frowns deeply. "You think you did something to cause the note? And the guy in the car?"

It strikes a chord. That's exactly how I feel. I nod yes, and am surprised to feel my chest blotching up.

"That's crazy. You didn't do anything, Mary. Somebody's jealous of you. It's not your fault."

I feel flushed and hot. There's no water left in my glass.

"What is this, some Italian thing? Some Mediterranean version of karma?"

"I don't know."

Judy looks sympathetic. "It's nothing you did, Mary. You did not cause this. You are not responsible for it. If it doesn't go away, which I sincerely hope it does, we'll deal with it. We'll figure it out together."

Judy gives me a bone-crushing squeeze and we leave the restaurant. We decide not to walk around after lunch, and she buys us both some shoestring licorice from a candy store on the basement level. She says it'll cheer me up, but she ends up being wrong about that.

I'm back at my desk at 1:58, wrestling with my fears and the Noone brief. After it's finished, I send it along to the partner in charge, Timothy Jameson. I do a good job because every partner gets a vote in the partnership election, and I can't afford to screw anything up at this point. I tally the votes for the third time today—I'm like an anorexic, counting the same few calories over and over. If Berkowitz votes for me, I might have the requisite votes right there, but there's a faction that hates Berkowitz, and Jameson's in it. The election will be close. My head begins to thunder.

In the afternoon, I'm in the chambers of the Honorable Morton A. Weinstein, resident genius of the district court. Judy calls him Einstein, naturally. Einstein is stoop-shouldered, with a frizzy pate of silvery hair. Steely half-moon reading glasses make him look even smarter. He's flanked by a geeky law clerk who mousses with margarine. Even the geeks want to look like Pat Riley.

We're sitting at a chestnut-veneer conference table to discuss my new case, *Hart v. Harbison's*, which, to my dismay, is a stone-cold loser. I'd spent the cab ride to the courthouse skimming the thin case file as I looked out the window for the dark car. I don't know which worried me more. I've seen bad discrimination cases in my time—evidence of the shitting upon of every minority in the rainbow—but *Hart* is the worst. I'd settle the case instantly if it were up to me, but I have a mission. Search, destroy, and petition for costs.

To make matters worse, there's a cherub posing as plaintiff's counsel. He can't be more than a year out of law school, and his face is as tender and soft as a newborn's. His hair, a wispy strawberry blond, brings out the rosy hue of his cheeks. His briefcase is spanking new; his bow tie looks clipped on. My job is to ignore all this cutehood and yank out his nuts with the roots intact.

"Young man," interrupts Einstein, "I'm sorry. I didn't catch your name."

"Oh, jeez. I'm sorry, Your Honor." He blushes charmingly. "I'm new at this, I probably forgot to say it. My name is Henry Hart. Henry Hart, Junior."

"Is the plaintiff your father, Henry?" asks Einstein.

"Yes. They call me Hank. I just got my mother to stop calling me Little Hank, if you can believe that. I have to remind her that I'm twenty-four now." He smiles, utterly without guile.

I can't believe what I'm hearing. Harbison's did this to the child's *father*? And I have to justify it?

"Twenty-four, my, my." Einstein turns to his law clerk and chuckles. "Was I ever twenty-four, Neil?"

Neil doesn't miss a beat. "Come on, Judge. You're not that old."

"No? I remember the big one. World War II. I was a navigator in the Eastern Theater. Flying B-24's out of Italy."

"The flying boxcars!" says Hank.

Einstein looks delighted. "How do you know about the flying boxcars?"

"My father flew a B-29 out of England."

"Well, I'm impressed. I look forward to meeting him, even under these circumstances." Einstein's gaze lingers warmly on Hank's face. "Now, is this your first pretrial conference, Hank?"

"Yes, sir."

Einstein touches Hank's sleeve lightly. "Well, son, it's nothing to be afraid of. All I want to do is to hear both of you out. Maybe see if we can settle this matter."

"Right, sir."

"Go ahead and outline the facts for me. You needn't rush."

"Okay, Your Honor. Thanks." Hank glances down at his notes. "The facts in this case are simple. My father worked at Harbison's for thirty-two years, as long as I can remember. He's an accountant. He started out in Harbison's book-keeping department." Hank rechecks his notes. "He got promotion after promotion and a salary increase each time. He entered management in 1982. He was promoted to chief financial officer in 1988, reporting directly to the chief executive officer, Franklin Stapleton. But as soon as he turned sixty-five, Your Honor, Mr. Stapleton told him he had to retire. In clear violation of the Age Discrimination in Employment Act." Hank glares at me accusingly.

I scribble on my legal pad to avoid his stare. I write: *I hate my job. I'm moving to New Jersey to grow tomatoes in the sun.*

"Go on, Hank," says Einstein.

"Of course, my father refused. He was at the peak of his skill and experience, and he needed the income besides. So, in retaliation, Harbison's demoted him. They stripped him of his title, his office, and his pride, Your Honor. They busted him down to office manager of their store in the King of Prussia mall. So, after serving Harbison's for thirty years, after reporting directly to the chief executive officer, they had him peddling eye bolts, Your Honor. In the mall." His boyish chest heaves up and down with outrage.

The chambers are silent. I write: *The beach would be nice. I could look for dimes in the sand with a metal detector.*

"Well, Henry, I was about to give you a lecture on the relative wisdom of representing relatives," Einstein says with a smile, "but your dad has found a very fine lawyer in you."

"Thank you, sir." Hank blushes again.

The judge frowns at me over the rimless edge of his half-glasses. "Ms. DiNunzio, you represent Harbison's in this matter?"

I nod yes. I feel like the devil in disguise.

"That's quite a story I just heard. I'm sure the jury will be as impressed with it as I am."

I clear my throat as if I know what I'm going to say, but I have no idea. "Your Honor, I just got this case today. We're new counsel."

Einstein frowns again. This frown says, You are making excuses, and that is reprehensible.

What's a girl to do? I parrot back what I read in the file on the way over. "As you know, Your Honor, there are two sides to every story. Harbison's denies that it made such statements to plaintiff and that it demoted plaintiff on account of his age. Harbison's position is that it demoted plaintiff because his management style was abrasive and, in particular, he was verbally abusive to company employees."

"That's a lie and you know it!" Hank shouts, and leaps to his feet.

An appalled Einstein clamps a firm hand on Hank's arm. "Sit down."

Hank eases back into his chair. "I'm sorry, Your Honor."

Einstein snatches off his reading glasses and tosses them onto the file in front of him. The judge plays by the rules, which don't provide for name-calling in chambers. He can barely look up, he's so offended. "It's not *me* you owe the apology to, young man," he says finally.

"That's all right, Your Honor," I break in. "I'd be upset too, if it were my father." I mean this sincerely, but it sounds condescending. Unwittingly, I've exploited the only weakness in Hank's case—that he is his father's son.

The point, however inadvertent, is not lost on Einstein. The tables turn that fast. The judge replaces his glasses and, without looking at Hank, asks coldly, "Henry, is your father interested in settling this matter?"

"Yes, Your Honor."

"Ms. DiNunzio, is Harbison's interested in settling this matter?"

"No, Your Honor."

Einstein snaps open his black Month-at-a-Glance and thumbs rapidly through the pages. "The deadline for discovery is two months from today. You go to trial July thirteenth. I'll send you both my Scheduling Order. Exchange exhibits and expert reports in a timely manner. I do not expect to hear from either of you regarding extensions of time. That's it, counsel."

We leave Einstein's chambers. Hank flees ahead of me to the elevator bank. As he forces his way into an elevator, I see that he's in tears.

"Hank, wait!" I call out, running to the elevator. But the stainless steel doors close as I reach it, and I'm left staring at the ribbon of black crepe between them. I press the DOWN button.

I hear the voice. It sounds harsher now, less like Mike. *What goes around comes around. You made an angel weep, now you're getting it back. A phone call greets you at the door. An anonymous note shows up in your mail. And a dark car is tracking your every move.*

Pong! The elevator bell rings out, silencing the voice.

The doors rattle open. The only person in the elevator is a steroid freak in a muscle shirt and mirrored sunglasses. Acne dots his shoulders and his hips jut forward suggestively as he leans against the side of the elevator. "Come on in, honey," he drawls. "The water's fine."

"Uh, no. I'm going up."

"Maybe next time, sugar."

As soon as the doors close, I punch the DOWN button again. I slip thankfully into the next elevator, packed with honest citizens wearing yellow JUROR buttons. I grab a cab back to the office and spend most of the ride as I did before, looking out the windows, peering anxiously at every dark sedan on Market Street. When I get back to the office, Brent's desk is empty. He has his opera lesson tonight; he says there's more to life than shorthand.

I go into my office to empty my briefcase.

There, sitting at my desk, bent over my papers, is Ned Waters.

Ned's green eyes flash with alarm as he looks up. The big clock glows faintly behind him. "Mary. I was just leaving you a note."

"A note?" My throat catches. Did Ned send the note I got this morning? Does he drive a dark car?

"I thought you left for the day. Your secretary was gone, so I couldn't leave a message."

"He studies opera singing."

"Opera, huh?" Ned rises awkwardly. He replaces one of my ballpoints in their mug and snatches a piece of paper from my desk.

"Is that the note?" I set my briefcase on the file cabinet.

"Yeah." He crumples it up and stuffs it into his

jacket pocket. "But you won't need it now. I can tell you what it says. I thought you might like to grab some dinner."

"Dinner?" I don't know what else to say, so I stare at him open-mouthed, like a trout.

"I heard you won an important motion. We could celebrate."

"You want to celebrate my winning a motion?"

"Sure. Why wouldn't I?"

"Maybe because we're competing with each other. You know, for partnership."

He looks stung. "I didn't even think of that, Mary."

I sigh, suddenly exhausted by the intrigue, the guessing, the strangeness of my life of late. "I don't get it, Ned. The last time we had dinner was in law school."

He looks down for a minute, studying his wingtips. When he meets my eye, his gaze is almost feline in its directness. "I wanted to call you back, but by the time I got my courage up, you were practically engaged."

It sounds genuine. I feel flattered and wary at the same time. I don't know what to say, so I don't say anything. I try not to look like a trout, however.

"Isn't that right?"

"Not exactly. I met Mike after you and I went out. And I didn't get engaged all that fast."

"No? You looked to me like you fell pretty hard. I remember seeing you doing research in the library, you looked like you were on cloud nine. Unless it was the sheer joy of working for Bitterman."

"Not likely."

"How could you stand that guy? I know he's supposed to be a legal genius, but what a jerk. I heard from Malone he was a tyrant in the courtroom."

"And out of it. He threw a fit when I wouldn't do the research for his second article. Reamed me out in his chambers."

"Why?"

"The law should be my first love, he said."

"But it wasn't."

I think of Mike.

Ned clears his throat. "Anyway, you looked like a woman in love, even to somebody as dense as me. I figured I didn't have a prayer, so I settled for being friends. What a guy, huh?"

"What a guy."

His hands shift inside the pockets of his bumpy seersucker jacket. "So. Please don't make this any harder than it is. Let me take you to dinner."

"I don't really go out, Ned. I mean, I don't know if you're talking about going out, but I—"

"Why do we have to label it anything? Let's just have dinner together. We're old friends, classmates, and we went out once. I've been remiss in not getting hold of you sooner, but— well, there was a lot going on." He shrugs uncomfortably. "Let's go eat, huh?"

I can't decide. The silence is excruciating.

"Come on. It won't kill you."

"Tell me one thing. What kind of car do you drive?"

"Talk about a non sequitur!" he says, with a deep laugh. It's a merry sound, happy and relieved, and shows his teeth to advantage. They're white and even, I bet they grew in that way. "Okay, I confess. I drive a Miata."

"What color?"

"White."

"Do you have a car phone?"

"You want to see my W-2? I can afford dinner, you know."

"That's not why I'm asking, and we'll split dinner."

"So why are you asking? And no, we won't."

"Just tell me, okay? Please."

"Of course I don't have a car phone. The Miata is as pretentious as I get."

So I agree, reluctantly.

Dinner turns out to be no fun at all in the beginning, when I'm busy worrying about whether Ned rents the car he follows me around in. Then he orders me a Tanqueray-and-tonic, and it eases my anxiety on impact. I begin to enjoy the restaurant, an elegant one overlooking Rittenhouse Square, and Ned's conversation, which comes more easily than it used to. In fact, he's changed a lot, as far as I can tell. He seems freer, more lively. We trade firm gossip, and he confides that he's always been intrigued by Judy. An enigma, he calls her. I find this funny, since she's no fan of his either. By the refill of my drink, I confess that Judy calls him Cool.

"Why does she call me that? I'm not cool at all."

"You *are* cool, Cool."

"Am not."

"Are too."

He laughs. "This is mature."

"Admit it! Look at you, you're a preppie hunk. You're like a J. Crew catalog, only alive." I realize I'm flirting, even as I speak. It not only scares the shit out of me, it makes me feel profoundly guilty. I celebrated my first motion with Mike, and here I am, celebrating my second with Ned. And I'm still Mike's wife, inside. I clam up.

Ned doesn't notice my silence and launches into his life story. He tells me about his wealthy Main Line family and his father, who's the managing partner of the Masterson firm. When he's finished his Dover sole, he changes the subject, as if he suddenly became aware that he'd been soliloquizing. "Only two months to go until P-day. June 1st, the partnership election."

I move a radish around on my plate.

"I didn't think June would be a good month for you. Isn't that when your husband—"

"Yes." The anniversary of Mike's death is June 28, but I didn't think Ned knew that. "How did you—"

"I remember. I went to the funeral."

"You did?" I'm not sure I want to talk about this.

"I didn't think you'd mind. I wanted to go. Mike seemed like a very nice guy. I'm sorry."

"I didn't think you ever met him."

"Sure I did. You introduced us when he came by school to meet you for lunch. He rode his bike over. He rode a bike, right?"

I nod yes. I line up my forks, squaring the tines off at the top.

"I'm sorry. I guess I shouldn't have mentioned—"

"No, it's fine."

"Well. Let's see, at least one good thing will happen in June."

"What's that?"

"You're making partner."

"Please. You make it sound like a done deal."

"It is. You're a shoo-in. You don't have a thing to worry about."

Then I remember what Berkowitz said about Ned's coming in to see him. "I heard they were only making two partners in litigation, not three. Did you hear that?"

"I try not to believe every rumor I hear, there are so many flying around. First I heard they were making three, then I heard it was down to two. This morning I heard that the Washington office was going to push through one of the lateral hires. It's ridiculous." He shakes his head.

"A lateral? In Washington? Shit."

"I'm sure they'll make three from Philly, Mary. The department's had a great year."

"Yeah. I guess." I note that he doesn't mention his meeting with Berkowitz on this very subject. I regard this as a material omission, and it makes me doubt him all the way through the dessert, shaved chocolate somethings.

Later, Ned insists on walking me home, since it's only a few blocks from his house. We walk in silence on this muggy night, so humid that the air forms halos around the mercury vapor lights. Rittenhouse Square is almost deserted. The runners have run home, the walkers have walked. Only the homeless remain, sleeping on the park benches as we go by. I look around for the dark car, but it's nowhere in sight.

Suddenly, before we've reached my doorstep, Ned kisses me. I'm totally unprepared for it, and his hesitant peck lands on my right eyebrow. I feel mortified. I worry about whether my neighbors saw. I worry about whether Alice saw. I even worry about whether Mike saw. I hurry inside, muttering a hasty good-bye to Ned, who looks concerned and sorry as I close the door.

I gather my mail from the floor and am about to stick it under my arm when I remember that, as of this morning, the United States mail is no longer my friend. I set down my briefcase and look through the letters, holding my breath. Bills: Philadelphia Electric, Greater Media Cable, Allstate, *Vanity Fair*. Two more catalogs, sent to DiNunziatoi and O'Nunzion respectively, and then a small white envelope, with no return address. My name is on the front, spelled correctly in block letters, and so is my home address. The stamp is an unfurled American flag.

Just like the note at work. I swallow hard.

I run my finger across the front. Laser-printed, not typed.

I tear open the envelope. Inside is a small white piece of paper:

I'M THE PERFECT ANSWER TO ALL YOUR
REAL ESTATE NEEDS!
And here's the perfect recipe:
Artichoke Dip
1 8 oz. can artichoke hearts
1 cup mayo

1 cup parmesan cheese
garlic powder optional
Mash artichokes, mix everything together.
Bake at 350 for 30 minutes. Serve with pita
bread!
Call SHERRY SIMMONS at JEFMAR REALTY!

Christ. Artichoke dip.

I crush the paper and trudge up the carpeted stairs. I'm getting so paranoid I'm losing it. What's the matter with me? Mike hasn't been gone for a year and I'm kissing another man. What's the matter with Ned? Is he trying to start up a romance, when one of us is about to be fired and the other canonized? I unlock my door with a sigh and flick on the light switch. I toss my briefcase onto the couch and plop down next to it, opening up the first bill.

Philadelphia Electric. You need a Ph.D. to break the code on your rate charges. I'm trying to decipher the tiny numbers when the phone on the end table rings. I pick it up without thinking. "Hello?"

There's no response. No static.

I'm not paranoid. It's real. "Leave me alone, you fucking asshole!"

But the only reply is a click.

"Goddamn it!"

I slam down the phone, my chest tight, and then grab it from the hook just as quickly. I hear the high whine of the dial tone. It runs interference for me, like a swift and burly lineman. See if you can get through that, you prick. Alice, who's been dozing like the Sphinx on the quilted couch, blinks slowly and goes back to sleep.

Get a grip, girl. I keep hold of the phone. The dial tone gives way to a woman's voice, speaking patiently and sweetly, like a young mother to a toddler. "If you want to make a call," she says, "please hang up and try again. If you need assistance, please hang up and dial your operator."

I lean back and breathe easier, listening to the young mother's voice. She sings her lullaby again. I let it enter and pacify me.

But she's squelched by a jarring *BRRRR-RRRRRRR.*

I sit bolt upright.

"Goddamn you!" Furious, I get up and shove the receiver between the cushions of the couch. Alice's eyes open wide, ears flat against her sleek head. Then she leaps out of harm's way.

"Goddamn you to hell!"

I smother the receiver with another cushion, and another, so that the couch looks like it's been trashed. But still I can hear the sound.

It won't leave my head.

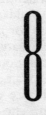

can't sleep. I adjust the light level, the covers, the air-conditioning. I take off my T-shirt and put it back on again. I gather my hair in a ponytail on top of my head, then yank it out. I try everything. Nothing works.

My head is full of visions, faces that swim up at me out of the dark. Starankovic's wounded mask. A baby-faced Hank, tears coursing down his cheeks. Ned, with his cat's eyes, lying with me like an incubus. Finally, Mike's robust face appears, with its coarse, working-class nose stuck in the middle. Framed by untamable brown curls, animated by eyes full of love. *But you love me for it,* he'd said. I bury my head under the pillow, which helps no more than the cushions over the telephone.

I feel wretched as I watch the night bleed into the dawn. Angry. Tired. Guilty. I feel the need to do penance, to make up for my date with Ned, so I get up to clean the bathroom. Penance, if you don't know, is the notion that the soul can be Martinized While-U-Wait, like a camel skirt. Probably the most bizarre concept I've ever heard, after original sin. The idea that a child's soul turns black the instant of its birth is something even Angie couldn't make me understand. But I scrub behind the toilet seat just the same. Despite my best efforts, I'm still Catholic after all these years.

I scuff into the living room in my pink slippers, dust mops for the feet, and exhume the telephone receiver. I hang it up and rearrange the cushions on the couch. Alice watches me, looking faintly suspicious.

"Who asked you?" I say.

I scuff into the kitchen and crack a pressurized can of Maxwell House. The can opens with a fragrant hiss, then the telephone rings.

"Fuck!" I send the can opener spinning across the kitchen counter. Is it the caller? At this hour? I pound into the living room, my adrenaline pumping, and tear the receiver from the cradle. "Who is this?"

"Mary? It's Ned!"

"Oh, jeez."

"I know it's early, but that's quite a greeting."

"Someone keeps calling me and hanging up. It's not you, is it?" I'm only half joking.

"Did you push star sixty-nine?"

"What's that?"

"If you push star sixty-nine after someone calls you, the phone calls them back."

"How do you know that?"

"I'm cool, remember?"

"Oh. Yeah." I cringe.

"Okay. Well. Let me say why I'm calling before I lose my nerve altogether. I wanted to tell you that I'm sorry about what happened after dinner. About pushing things like that. I couldn't sleep, I felt like such a bozo. I've always liked you, Mary. Been attracted to you. But still, I shouldn't have done that. I'm sorry."

"Uh . . . that's okay."

"I really am sorry."

"I know."

"Well, I would love to see you again. If you want to see me again, that is. I promise I won't attack you. I mean it."

I pause. I don't know how to say what I need to say. That I haven't dated in ten years? That the last man I dated before Mike was Ned? That I'm not ready yet? That I may never be?

"Okay, fine," Ned says suddenly. "Whatever you want. Maybe after June you'll change your mind. Does that sound all right to you?"

"Okay. I guess."

"We can be friends until then. Would that be okay with you?"

"Fine."

"God, I hate this talking about feelings. It can be so bloody exhausting."

"So cut it out. Be like me."

He laughs softly. "I'll see you later then, at work."

"Sure." I hang up, feeling somewhat empty. I like him, but I'm not ready for what he wants. And he's a mystery to me, still. Why didn't he tell me about Berkowitz?

Meeeooow! It's Alice, wanting to be fed. She saunters into the kitchen, tail high.

"You only talk to me when you want something," I say, and follow her in. I pour some allegedly gourmet cat food into her bowl. "You don't call, you don't write."

Alice ignores me; she's heard it all before. I squat down and watch her. She eats with her eyes closed, but still manages to find each little kibble fish. It's her best trick, I decide, stroking her silky back. She'll tolerate my touch until the kibble fish are gone; then she'll return to the windowsill. Her next feeding will be the next time she acknowledges that I pay the rent around here. I'd give her away in a second, to a science lab, if it weren't for Mike. He found her in a trash can and brought her home in the pouring rain, wrapped in his denim jacket. She didn't move the whole time, so Mike thought she was dead.

"If she's dead, why did you bring her home?" I asked, ever the pragmatist.

"I couldn't leave her there, like she was trash," he said. "I'll bury her tomorrow, before school."

He put her in a Converse shoe box and put the shoe box under the bathroom sink. The next morning, Mike found her in the bathtub, staring in wonder at the dripping faucet. He named her Alice in Wonderland; she imprinted him on her cat brain as Mommy. They were crazy about each other.

After Mike died, I got the idea that he would want to see Alice again, at least to say good-bye. I know it sounds crazy, but I drove the animal to the cemetery and made my way through the graves with the bulky cat carrier until I got to the plain gray headstone that says LASSITER. It doesn't say BELOVED HUSBAND on it, because I couldn't bear to see that chiseled so finally on his headstone.

I set Alice's carrier down at the foot of Mike's grave and opened the door of the carrier with shaking hands. Out came Alice, sniffing the summer air. I watched, teary-eyed. I didn't know what to expect, but I hoped it would be something magical and profound. It was neither. What happened was that Alice took off, springing between the monuments like a jackrabbit. I shouted for her and gave chase, leaping in my espadrilles over mounds that constituted ANTONELLI and MACARRICCI, by the flying eagle that said TOOHEY and the weeping cherub that marked FERGUSON. Alice kept going and so did I, because the last thing I wanted to do was lose Mike's cat in the frigging cemetery. I caught up with her by the CONLEY mausoleum. She scratched me all the way back to LASSITER.

Brrrnng! The telephone rings loudly, jolting me out of my daydream. I stand up and set my jaw. I'm ready for you, asshole. Star sixty-nine. I run in and pick up the receiver.

"Hello?"

No answer, then *click,* and a dial tone. No static. My heart begins to pound. No static means he's not in the car. He's at home, wherever he lives, lying in bed. Thinking about me. I pound the buttons for star sixty-nine.

I hear one ring, then another. What am I going to say to this guy? There's another ring, then a fourth, and a fifth. He's not answering.

I hang up the phone. This has got to stop. I look around the empty apartment, suddenly aware of my aloneness. I stow the coffee in the freezer and slip out of my T-shirt in the bathroom, away from any windows. I lock the bathroom door before I shower. I'm no dummy; I've seen *Psycho.*

I dress quickly and leave for the office. In the cab, I keep an eye out for the sedan, but it's not in evidence. As soon as I get in, I ask Brent to change my home number.

"Hallelujah," he says.

"Let's have my office number changed, too."

"Now you're talkin'."

"Did I get anything more evil than usual in the Evil mail?"

"No. And no calls from weirdos, either. Except the ones who work here." He hands me a packet of yellow phone messages.

"What is it with these people, they don't sleep?" I look over the messages. Martin, Jameson, a couple of clients, someone named Stephanie

Fraser. I hold up the message. "Do I know Stephanie Fraser? Is she at Campbell's?"

"No. That's Stephanie Furst. This one said she met you after your Bitterman argument. She wants you to call back."

"Oh, yeah, I remember her. She thinks Bitter Man hates women. Absurd. He hates everybody." I hand Brent back the messages.

"Did you see the car again last night?"

"No."

"We're on a roll," he says, relieved. He looks good, in a soft rayon shirt.

"New shirt?"

He looks down at it like a little kid. "Jack gave it to me. You like?"

"It's nice. Something about it looks familiar. Let me think. I got it! It's black!"

"Shows how much you know. It's midnight. And yesterday was more of a charcoal."

"Right."

"Get out of my face. I've got filing to do. Now, git!"

"Be that way. I'm going down to see Judy."

"But you have a deposition, remember? Tiziani will be here in an hour."

"Oh, shit! Shit. Shit. Shit." With all that's going on, the dep slipped my mind completely.

"You prepared him last week, didn't you?"

"Right. I gotta go. I'll be back in time." I hand him the messages.

"Did you think any more about the police?" he asks, but I'm off, down Stalling's internal stairwell to Judy's floor.

Judy's office is like a bird's nest. The desk is

littered with bits of paper, the bookshelves stuffed with messy books and files. Photos are everywhere. On the wall, there's Kurt, two black Labradors, and Judy's huge family. The Carriers are California's answer to the Von Trapps. They grin from various craggy summits, with heavy ropes, clips, and pulleys hanging from harnesses around their waists. The first time I saw these pictures, I thought the entire family worked for the telephone company.

"Anybody home?"

"Behind the desk," Judy calls out. I find her sitting on the floor in front of an array of trial exhibits. She looks up at me and smiles wearily. "I remember you. I knew you before I became consumed by the price of computer chips in Osaka."

"What are you doing?"

"The *Mitsuko* appeal. You know, the trial that Martin lost last month. The antitrust case."

"The zillion-dollar antitrust case."

She giggles in a naughty way. "I heard that the morning after he lost the trial, the litigation partners dumped a pile of dirty socks in the middle of his desk."

"I don't get it."

"Smell defeat! Smell defeat!" She laughs, then her smile fades. "What's the matter, you don't think that's funny?"

"It's funny."

"You didn't laugh."

I tell her about my dinner with Ned, which I refuse to call a date, and also that he didn't own up to his meeting with Berkowitz. We talk again about the phone calls and the note. She says she suspects Ned because he's so ambitious, or maybe Martin, because he lost the case for Mitsuko and I replaced him on *Harbison's*. Then I remind her of how Delia was fuming at me, and Judy rakes a large hand through a hank of chopped-off hair.

"It could be anyone," she says.

"That's comforting."

"Look. Kurt's sleeping at his studio tonight. Why don't you stay at my house?"

"Why?"

"You'll be safe, genius."

"I have to be able to live in my own apartment, don't I? What am I going to do, spend the rest of my life at your house?"

"It wouldn't be the worst thing. You can cook."

"Oh, sure, we'd be great roommates. I'd give us one week before we killed each other."

She looks hurt. "You always say that, I don't know why. Stay with me for a while. Just until you get your number changed."

"Nah, I'll be okay."

She shakes her head. "So stubborn."

"I appreciate it, though. I do."

"At least answer the phone. I want to be able to reach you."

"You can't. Brent's going to unlist the number, and I don't have the new one yet."

"They won't do it by tonight. I think it takes a day. I'll call you tonight with a signal. I'll let it ring twice and then call right back."

I agree, and promise to buy her two big

cookies for her trouble the next time we go to lunch.

"Wow!" she says.

9

"Tiziani got here early," Brent says, when I get back upstairs. "I set him up in Conference Room F with coffee and sandwiches for lunch."

"Aren't you the perfect host."

Brent winks. "He's hot."

"I thought you were a one-man man."

He gives me a playful shove and I take off.

Nick Tiziani is the personnel manager at Blake's, a national food manufacturer. He fired his female assistant because she dressed funny. That's the truth, and even though it's a lousy reason to fire someone, it's lawful. However, he also told her to stop dressing like a man and bought her a subscription to *Vogue*. He says he was trying to help; she says it was sex discrimination. A lot depends on how well he tells his story at this dep.

"Mary! *Come sta?*" Tiziani says, when he sees me.

"*Bene. Grazie*, Nick."

He shakes my hand warmly. A suave guy, Nick always smells better than I do. He's dressed head to toe in Gucci, which is part of the reason he's getting sued down to his silk boxers. Clothes are very important to Nick; he's a big proponent of form over substance. The day his funky assistant came in wearing camouflage pants was the last straw, especially because Blake's CEO was visiting from headquarters. Nick fired her on the spot. She's lucky he didn't kill her.

I review the incident with him and teach him the defense witness mantra: Don't volunteer, listen to the question, give me time to object. Don't volunteer, listen to the question, give me time to object. Nick nods pleasantly as I speak, which proves he's not listening to a word I say.

"Nick, you're with me on this, right?"

"Sure, Mary. Piece a cake."

"It's not that easy. You've never been deposed before."

"How hard can it be?"

"Harder than you think. Everything you say is recorded and is admissible in court. They'll use it to rough you up on cross, throw your own words back at you."

"You make it so complicated. It's business, that's all. Her lawyer is a businessman. I am a businessman." He touches a manicured finger to a custom shirt. "I'll explain it to him, we'll see eye to eye. Come to terms."

"Nick. Believe me, this guy is the enemy. He's not going to see it your way. His job is to see it any way *but* your way. Say as little as possible. Remember: Don't volunteer, listen to the question, give me time to object."

"Yeah, yeah, yeah." He fidgets in his chair. "Hey, did you hear this one? What's the difference between a catfish and a lawyer?"

"One is a scum-sucking bottom dweller and the other is a fish."

"You're no fun," he says, pouting.

The deposition is at the offices of Masterson, Moss & Dunbar—an away game. Masterson, Moss is another reason the case is dangerous. A hot-shit firm like that would ordinarily never represent a noncorporate plaintiff, but this plaintiff is the daughter of one of its sharky securities partners. As such, she rates one of the fairest-haired boys, Bob Maher. Maher's on every Young Republicans committee in the tristate area and is more of a sexist than Nick will ever be. But it's not Maher's prick that's in the mousetrap. Not this time, anyway.

Nick and I sit in the reception area at Masterson, which is the oldest law firm in Philadelphia and the largest, at almost three hundred and fifty lawyers. I think of it as the Father firm in the holy trinity because it's so traditional. Somebody has to wave the flag of old-line Philadelphia, and Masterson has pre-empted the field. The decor is early men's club, with bronze sconces and heavy club chairs everywhere. Maps of the city in colonial times adorn its wainscoted walls, wafer-thin oriental carpets blanket its hardwood floors. The place looks like Ralph Lauren heaven. Nick eats it up.

"Classy," he says.

"Prehistoric," I reply.

Soon we're met by Maher himself. A strapping Yale grad, Maher flashes Nick a training-table All-Ivy grin and leads us to a large conference room, which has a glass wall overlooking one of the firm's corridors. He pours Nick a hot cup of fresh coffee and introduces him to the luscious female court reporter, Ginny, no last name. Ginny tells Nick she loves his tie. Nick tells Ginny he loves her scarf. They both laugh. Everything's so chummy, I feel like the new neighbor at a swingers party. I decide that Maher's a fine practitioner of the Seduce-the-Shit-Out-of-'Em approach to deposition taking, and Nick's too turned on to catch on.

Maher begins the questioning with softballs about Nick's personnel history. Nick describes one promotion after another with a braggadocio indigenous to Italian men. I let it run and watch the lawyers scuttle back and forth outside the glass wall. Oblivious to the promenade is a tall, dignified lawyer with wavy silver hair. Legs crossed, he sits in a Windsor chair reading *The Wall Street Journal*. I recognize this as a typical dominance display by an alpha wolf in a corporate law firm. Berkowitz does it too, with less finesse.

"Mr. Tiziani . . . may I call you Nick?" Maher asks.

"Just don't call me late to dinner."

Maher laughs at this joke, ha-ha-ha, as if he's never heard it before. I glance up at the silver wolf. He's looking into the conference room over the top of the wide newspaper. That's unusual. Why would he watch a dep unless he had a specific interest in it? Then it clicks. He must be the plaintiff's father.

"Tell me, Nick, what is your current title at Blake's?"

"I'm Vice President of Personnel. I got the promotion a year ago. A year ago in September. As vice president, I report directly to Chicago. It's a dotted-line relationship with the CEO, as opposed to a straight line. I'm not sure if you're familiar with organizational charts, Bob, and I'd be happy to explain—"

I touch Nick's sleeve gently. "Nick, why don't we just let Bob ask his questions? It'll save time." Don't volunteer, listen to the question, give me time to object. Don't volunteer, listen to the question, give me time to object.

"Oh, sure, Mary. No problem," he replies helpfully. The man hasn't a clue.

The plaintiff's father turns a page of the *Journal* but continues to watch us over its top.

"Thank you, Nick," says Maher. "I'll ask you about that later. Now, as Vice President of Personnel, are you familiar with the federal laws prohibiting sex discrimination in the work-place?"

I ignore the plaintiff's father and lean over. Things are heating up and I want to be in Nick's line of vision during the questioning. Maybe it'll remind him that this is a deposition, not group sex.

"Let the record reflect that defense counsel is blocking my view of the witness," Maher says sharply.

Ginny's fingers move steadily on the black keys of her machine. Everything we say will be on the record. If you can imagine it in black-and-white type like a script, you can fabricate the reality:

"Pardon me. What did you say, Bob?"

"I said you're obstructing my view of the witness."

"I don't know what you mean, Bob."

"I can't see him when you do that."

"I'm sorry."

"There's something about the way you're sitting."

"What? I don't understand."

"Move away from the witness."

"How's this, Bob?" I don't move.

"Not good enough. More to the right."

"This is silly, Bob. Let the record reflect my agreement with counsel for plaintiff that the witness can stay for only three hours today. If we spend much more time discussing my posture, we won't be out of here until seven."

Maher quiets with a scowl.

Nick remembers that he's The Witness, not just-call-me-Nick.

And I sit back and meet the gaze of the lawyer outside, who's plainly glaring at me now over the *Journal*. The eyes of an outraged father. Even from a distance, they seem to drill into me.

"Nick, did there come a time when you met the plaintiff, Donna Reilly?"

"Yes."

"Did you form an impression of her at the time?"

"Objection," I say.

"Why?" Maher demands.

"What's the relevance of his impression of her? And the question is ambiguous. His impression of what?"

"You know full well that relevance isn't a proper objection during deposition. Besides, if the witness thinks the question is unclear, he can say so."

"I'm preserving my objection. And you're right, Bob. If the witness doesn't understand the question, he can say so." I kick Nick in his Gucci loafer.

"I don't understand the question," Nick says.

Suddenly, there's a violent movement outside the conference room. The plaintiff's father has leapt to his feet and thrown the newspaper onto the Kirman. Holy shit. He must have seen me kick Nick's shin, because he looks outraged. Like a football coach when the ref doesn't call clipping.

"All right, Nick, I'll rephrase the question," Maher says, unaware of the scene unfolding behind him.

The lawyer rushes toward the conference room door. My mouth goes dry. What's he going to do, report me to the Disciplinary Board? There's not one of us who hasn't done it—not one.

"Who's that?" Nick asks, pointing through the glass at the charging lawyer.

Maher turns around just as the door bursts open. "Hello, sir!" He pops up but forgets to grin.

The lawyer ignores him. He's taller than I thought, and his patrician features are limned with tiny wrinkles. Anger tinges his face. He looks too angry to report me; he looks angry enough to hit me. He struggles to maintain civility. "I'm loath to interrupt these proceedings, but I thought it an opportune time to meet the opposition. Hello, Miss DiNunzio." He extends a large hand over the conference table.

I'm not sure if he wants to deck me or shake hands. It turns out to be something in between; he squeezes my hand like a used tube of toothpaste.

"That's quite a grip." I withdraw my hand.

He nods curtly. "Court tennis."

"Right." Whatever that is.

"You seem to be having some trouble with your chair, Miss DiNunzio. If it's uncomfortable for you, I can have another brought in." He smiles, but it looks like it's held in place with a mortician's wire.

"I'm fine, thank you."

"If you feel uncomfortable again, feel free to alert young Bob. I'm certain he'll do whatever he can to make you more comfortable. Isn't that right, Bob." It's a command, not a question. The lawyer nods at Maher, who looks confused.

"After all," he continues, "the Masterson firm has always been a great friend to the Stalling firm, and I hear only the best about you, Miss DiNunzio. I understand you're a very fine litigator."

"Thank you."

"You're in my son's class at Stalling, aren't you?"

"Your *son?*"

"Yes. My son. Ned Waters."

"I'm Nathaniel Waters. You may know that I manage this firm."

"Oh. Yes." Not the plaintiff's father, *Ned's* father!

"I've seen us grow from one hundred lawyers, to one-fifty, to the full complement. I oversaw the opening of our London office. Now we're going to be the first Philadelphia firm in Moscow. Masterson maintains a tradition of excellence, Miss DiNunzio, and of unimpeachable ethics. I'm sure Stalling does the same." He peers at me directly, a menacing version of Ned's green-eyed gaze.

"Of course." No matter what he says, I know he's kicked the Nicks of the world under the table. You don't get where he is without some very pointy shoes. Even if they are made in England.

"Then we're in agreement. I shan't keep you further. It was fine to have met you. Give my regards to Ned, will you. Carry on." He turns on his heel and strides stiffly out the door.

Maher relaxes visibly, and our eyes meet. For a brief moment, we're cubs in the same pack. We become enemies again when Maher takes his seat and the questions begin. "Nick, let me make the question so clear even your lawyer will understand it. The first time you saw Ms. Reilly, did you form an impression of her wearing apparel?"

"Yes."

"What was your impression?"

"I thought she dressed like a slob."

Good for you, Nicky. I almost cheer. For the rest of the deposition, which stretches until the end of the day, I channel the anxiety created by Ned's father into constant objections. Nick cues off me and we work as a team, with him telling his side of the story forcefully and credibly. By the end of the dep, Maher may think that Nick is a stickler about clothes, but he'll be hard pressed to prove he discriminates against women. As we leave Masterson, I congratulate Nick, who tells me I did "a man's job."

I stop short. "Nick, you want some free legal advice?"

"Sure."

"Don't say stuff like that. You got away with it this time, but you might not the next. You know what I mean, Nick? What goes around, comes around."

A hurt look crosses his neat features. "I didn't mean it the way it sounded, Mary."

"Good."

We part company, awkwardly. I thread my way through the crowded street, slightly dazed, wondering why I've just insulted a major client.

It's about time, says the voice, then disappears.

People pour out of office buildings—women with melting makeup, men with unlit cigarettes. They jolt me aside to join the human traffic on the narrow sidewalks, which flows around street vendors like corpuscles through a hardened artery. It's the end of the workday in this weary city, and it occurs to me that I'd better let the rush-hour crowds carry me home before it gets dark, and the car appears.

I mix into the throng for safety but still find myself glancing over my shoulder a lot. I pause before the window of an electronics store and spot an answering machine. Mike hated answering machines, so we never bought one. But some creep is calling me, and Mike is gone. I go in and lay down some plastic for the lady behind the counter.

When I leave with the slim machine in a plastic bag, I expect to feel better, as if I'm doing what I can to protect myself. But I feel exactly the opposite. The purchase makes the threat all too real. I feel scared.

I walk through the square quickly, looking around at the office workers walking tiredly home. At this hour, relatively early for the super-professional crowd, we're talking paralegals, not lawyers. Secretaries, not bosses. Almost all of them are women, the vast underclass of pink-collar workers who keep America word-processed, executive-summaried, and support-staffed. I fall in step with one of the older women. She has a sweet, rounded face and wears a hand-knit sweater. A saleswoman, I think, or a librarian's assistant. We stop together at the edge of the square in front of the Dorchester, waiting for the traffic to give us an even break.

"There should be a light here," she says, slightly annoyed. "Or at least a stop sign."

I scan the cars whizzing by. "I agree."

"They'll kill you to get home five minutes faster."

A Cadillac driver waves us across the street. I lose the saleswoman on Twentieth Street, after the high-rises that demarcate the residential west end of town. I look behind me. The people on the sidewalk look normal. I check back again half a block later, and only two are left. One is a teenage girl with a backpack slung over her shoulder and the other is a flashy woman with lots of shiny shopping bags.

Something catches my eye at the corner of Spruce and Twenty-first. Not the people, the cars. Two white cars are stopped at a light, and after them is a brown one. A brown Cadillac, an older model, somewhat beat-up. An Eldorado or Toronado, one of those.

I squint at the car. Is it the same Cadillac that let me go by in front of the Dorchester?

I can't remember, but try not to leap to conclusions. There are a million Cadillacs in the world, I tell myself, moving quickly to cross.

I turn onto Delancey and can't help but glance back over my shoulder. The Cadillac is coming toward Delancey, cruising slowly. Close up, it looks like the same car.

Chill, as Judy would say. So what if it's the same car? Maybe it's someone looking for a parking space. I used to do it all the time, driving pointlessly around and around the same block. Now I pay a fortune to park in a garage nearby. It's worth every penny.

I stride down Delancey Street, remembering the magazine articles I've read about crime. Don't look like a victim or you'll be one. Stand tall, walk fast. I hoist the plastic bag up and barrel ahead. As I do, I hear the smooth acceleration of a powerful engine coming down the street behind me. I pick up my pace for the half block that's left and check over my shoulder at the corner.

I feel my stomach tighten.

It's the Cadillac, blocked by a station wagon that's trying to wedge itself into a parking space. I catch my breath. I feel like bolting across the street, but there's too much traffic. A limo rolls by, then a clunker and an endless parade of Hondas. I'm only a block from home.

I look back. The Cadillac has freed itself. It's moving forward, speeding to the corner without effort.

I feel panic begin to rise in my throat. "Come on, come on," I say to the traffic. I spot an opening in front of an empty school bus and run for it, my briefcase banging against my thigh. The bus driver protests with a startlingly loud *haaaannk*. I almost drop the briefcase but make it to the other side of the street, breathless.

Run, says the Mike-voice, softly. *Run*.

I glance backward at the top of my street. The traffic screens most of Delancey from view, but glinting at me from between the moving cars is the shimmer of a battered chrome grill. The Cadillac's still there. My heart begins to race. I can't see the driver. The windshield reflects a cloudy sky.

Run. Run. Run for your life.

So I do, a dead run, without looking back. Instantly, I hear the Cadillac gun its engine as it crosses onto my street. I speed up. The Cadillac speeds up. It's almost at my heels as I tear down the street like a madwoman.

Run, run.

The Cadillac's right behind me.

I hear someone screaming and it's me. "No! No! Help!" I keep running until I reach my front door.

Christ! My keys! The answering machine clatters to the sidewalk as I rummage furiously in my bag. Where are my fucking keys?

The Cadillac screeches to a stop behind me, right in front of my door.

"No!" I turn and scream at the car. My back is plastered against the front door, my breast heaving. "You fucking asshole, leave me alone!"

In my fear and panic, I see the driver.

A woman, dark-haired, Hispanic. The Cadillac is loaded with kids. The oldest one, a boy in the back seat, is in hysterics.

I can't quite believe it. I blink at the sight.

A mother and children. She looks upset, but I don't know why, since I'm the one having the coronary. Like my grandfather used to say, my heart attacked me.

The mother leans over an infant in a plastic car seat. "Ah, I scare you," she says, in highly flavored English. "I so sorry. I scare you, poor lady. I no mean."

I almost cry with relief. My briefcase falls to the ground with a leathery slap.

The mother turns to the boy in the back, who's still laughing, and says something to him I can't hear. He leans out of the open window with a smirk. The trace of a mustache covers a prominent lip.

"My mutha says she's sorry she scared you. We're lost. We got off the expressway too soon. She shoulda stayed on. I told her to stay on, but she wouldn't listen." He laughs again. "I told her not to keep after you too, but she wanted to tell you not to be scared. She don't listen to nobody." He points at his temple, and his mother cuffs him lightly on the shoulder. "Get offa me!" he shouts at her, *muy* macho.

They just wanted directions. Christ. I try to recover as they talk again.

The boy leans out of the car. "She wants to know if you're awright, you want to go to the hospital. I told her you don't go to the hospital for this, but she don't listen."

"Tell her thank you for me, will you? I'm fine. Tell her it's okay. It's not her fault."

They talk again, but the mother looks doubtful.

"It's not your fault!" I yell into the car, but she gets distracted by the little girls in the back, fighting over a troll doll. She snatches the troll from them and they begin to wail, identically. They look to be the same age. "Are they twins?"

The mother cups her ear.

"Twins? I'm a twin, too. I have a twin sister."

The mother chatters excitedly to the son and pushes him toward the window. He wrests his arm away and sticks his head out of the car. His expression is pained. "My mutha says that twins are a special blessing from God. You are a special person." Then he rolls his eyes.

I feel my eyes moisten, like an idiot. I want to hug his mother. "Tell her I said thank you. She is a special person, too."

He examines a set of filthy nails. "Great, we're all special. So, you know how to get to the South Street exit?"

"Tell your mother how special she is."

He looks up at me, a wry challenge. "Are you for real?"

I straighten my blazer and pick up my briefcase. "The realest."

He turns from me and shouts at his twin sisters, who are still whimpering. Then he says something to his mother, and she smiles at me happily. He leans back out of the window. "Awright?"

"Thank you. Take a right at the top of the street, then go left on Spruce. Take another right and follow it to Lombard. It'll go right into South Street."

"Got it, babe." He leans back into the car and

says something to his mother. The mother waves good-bye. As the Cadillac pulls away, the kid flips me the finger.

I laugh, unaccountably elated. I pick up the answering machine, wondering whether it broke when it fell, but it looks fine. I tuck it under my arm and dig, calmly now, in the bottom of my purse for my keys. I feel giddy, reminded of my father's old joke. Why are your keys always in the last place you look? To which Angie and I would moan, in stereo: Because once you find them, you don't look anymore.

I find my keys and let myself in. I pick up my mail. My heart is even lighter when I find there are no anonymous notes in the mail. I feel like I've gotten a reprieve as I climb the stairs to my door.

But halfway up the staircase, as I thumb through the key ring for my apartment key, I notice that something about the stairwell looks different.

Then I see why.

At the top of the darkening stairway, my apartment door is open.

Wide open.

freeze. Did I leave without locking the door this morning? Is that possible?

I feel my senses heighten. I strain to hear something from inside my apartment, but there isn't a sound. The air smells vaguely of cigarettes, but then it always does, since my landlords are smokers. The door is open wide and it looks dark inside. Alice is nowhere in sight. I can't believe this. Someone could be in there, right now. *He* could be in there.

I have to get out and away. I have to call the cops. I will myself into moving. I back slowly down the staircase, easing my back along the wall, my eyes riveted to the door. If he comes out, if anybody comes out, I'll scream like hell. I inch painstakingly downward, trying not to make any noise. The plastic bag rustles slightly as I move, and I curse having bought the answering machine.

My apartment door grows smaller and smaller at the top of the staircase, and I reach the landing. Only a short flight to go. For a fleeting moment I worry about Alice. Would he hurt her? Would he *kill* her? I'm surprised to feel a twinge at the thought; I didn't know I even liked the cat. Still, I'm too frightened to go back. I'm almost at the entrance hall when I hear:

Run.

And I do, bolting out the door, down the pavement, to the pay phone two blocks away. My hands are shaking as I press 911. The woman says they'll have a car there in five minutes.

I walk back and hover at the corner directly across from the top of my street, holding my briefcase, purse, answering machine, and mail.

Five minutes later, there's no police.

Ten minutes later, there's still no police, and I feel like a pack animal.

Half an hour later, the only thing that's changed is that I'm keeping company with Marv, the man who sells tree-height ficus plants on this corner. I've settled into his rickety folding chair to watch the front door to my building. My fear is gone, as is the steely cold taste of panic. Both have been replaced by a low-level tension. Whoever was in my apartment is probably gone by now. I just wonder what he took and what the place looks like. And whether Alice is safe. I squint up at my apartment windows, still dark. The cat isn't on the windowsill.

In exchange for the chair, I had to listen to Marv's life story. He's spent thirty years selling anything that doesn't move—encyclopedias, bronze baby shoes, Amway detergents, and now ficus plants. He told me how he drives a U-Haul down to a Florida nursery where he buys the plants for cheap, then how he brings them up here and sells them for cheap, and how he still makes out like a bandit. The U-Haul is parked in front of his apartment. Each of the ficus trees is chained to its own parking meter. Marv owns this corner. He says, Who better?

"They ain't comin', Mary," he says. "You shoulda told 'em he had a gun. They hear gun, they come. They don't hear gun, they don't come."

"I didn't see a gun. I didn't even see a person." I watch the door across the street, but there's no activity at all. The few passersby don't look inside, which tells me nothing unusual is going on.

"So you say it anyway." He rubs a pitted cheek and looks worriedly at the sky, which is almost dark. "I'm doin' lousy today, I tell you. Can't *give* these plants away today."

I watch the street for the cops. "Maybe I should call them again."

"Won't do you no good. They don't hear gun, they don't come."

"Not even for a burglary?"

"You tell 'em it was a burglary?"

"No, not exactly. I don't know if I was burglarized. I only know the door was open and I didn't leave that way."

He pushes up the brim of a grimy pith helmet, part of his jungle motif. "*That's* what you told 'em?"

I nod.

"Why'd you tell 'em that?"

"Because it's the truth."

He bursts into laughter. "Listen to this kid! Because it's the truth, she says! You're a lawyer, what's the truth to you?" He guffaws. "Mary, you hear the one about the elephant and the tiger?"

I'm in no mood for more lawyer jokes. My chin sinks into my hand as I look down my street.

"Mary?"

"No."

He licks his lips with anticipation. "So this elephant is walkin' along in the jungle and a tiger is walkin' behind him. And every five feet, the elephant, you know, drops a turd. Now the tiger, he's walkin' behind the elephant, and he eats it."

"Jeez, Marv." I wince.

"No, no, listen, it's a good one. So the elephant, he gets disgusted. He turns around to the tiger and he says, 'Yo! Why you eatin' my turds like that?' And the tiger says, 'Because I just ate a lawyer and I want to get the taste out of my mouth.'" Marv bursts into gales of laughter.

I shake my head. "That's disgusting."

"You like that?" he says, delighted. "Wait, wait. I got another one. What's the difference between a porcupine and a Porsche full of lawyers?"

Suddenly, a white police car turns onto my street. The cavalry. "Finally. They're here." I gather up my things and scramble to my feet.

"So they came after all."

The squad car stops in front of my building and a cop climbs out of each front door. One cop is black and one is white; they're both square-jawed enough to be from central casting. It looks like a movie is being filmed in front of my apartment, with a racially balanced cast. But it's not a movie, it's my life. My apartment. My cat. "I gotta go."

"Wait, don't you wanna hear the punch line?"

"I have to go, Marv."

"In a porcupine, the pricks are on the *outside*."

I'm too tense to laugh as I hurry across the street.

"Come back if you need anything!" he calls out.

"Thanks," I call back. I hustle over to the cops, who are standing together like the twin towers. I feel slightly in awe of them, of their authority. They're the good guys. I consider telling them the whole story. About the notes and the car.

"Do you live here?" says the black cop gravely. The nameplate on his broad chest says TARRANT.

"Yes. I'm the one who called. I came home and saw that my apartment door was open. I was too scared to go in."

"Was there any sign of a forced entry?"

"No. But the door was open. I know I didn't leave it that way. I don't know if anybody is up there still. No one's come out since I called you. I've been watching the front door."

"Is there a back door?"

"Not to my apartment. I'm on the third floor."

"No fire escape?"

"No."

"We'll check it out. Do you have a burglar alarm?" Meanwhile, the white cop, named LEWIS, is squinting up at the building. When he looks up, I can see he has braces on his teeth.

"No."

"Is the house yours?"

"No. My landlords are away."

"You live alone?"

"I have a cat."

Tarrant clears his throat. "May I have your key to the front door?"

I dig in my bag again. My father's joke is miles away. With effort, I produce the keys. "This one is to the front door. The next one is the apartment door."

He takes the key ring by the front door key. "We'll check it out. Please stand back and clear the door." He throws a brawny arm in my path and guides me away from the entrance. My stomach begins to churn. In a few minutes, I'll find out what the fuck is going on.

They leave me there and enter the building. One of my neighbors across the way, the one with the Bianchi bike, watches curiously from the window. None of the other neighbors are at the windows. The shades are drawn again in the apartment across from mine. Whoever lives there is never home. A lawyer.

Out of the corner of my eye, I see Marv crossing the street and heading in my direction. I stand away from the building and look up to see if anything's going on in my apartment. The slats in the window blinds are suddenly illuminated. The cops must be in the living room. I bite my lip.

"Did they find anything?" Marv peers up with me at the building.

"They're still up there."

"Don't worry. Anything got taken, you can get replaced. It's only money."

"Except my cat."

"You think they took your cat?"

"No. I'm just worried about her."

"Me, I hate cats."

"Me too."

Suddenly, the window blinds are pulled up and Officer Lewis's silhouette appears in Alice's window. He fusses with the screen and pokes his head out briefly, then replaces it. I crane my neck to see inside the apartment, but I can't see past the cop. He does the same to the other window.

"I wonder what he's doing," I say.

"Seeing how the guy broke in. I heard some guy broke into an apartment on Lombard last week. Climbed right up the front of the building to the third floor. Like a mountain climber. Like Spider-Man."

I look up at the apartment. Two bright windows face the street, glowing from the front of the building like the eyes of a jack o'lantern. I wonder how much longer the cops will be. I wonder what they're finding. Suddenly, Alice springs onto her windowsill and does a luxuriant stretch.

"That's Alice! That's my cat!" I can't remember being so happy to see her.

"Cute," Marv says, without enthusiasm. He frowns at the window. "You know, a girl like you, you don't need a cat. You need a dog, for protection. Cats are good for nothing."

Officer Lewis appears in the window behind Alice and picks her up. He makes her do a little wave at me in the window, until she leaps out of his arms.

"Look at that, Marv!"

"Very cute."

A couple of minutes later the cops come out the front door. Lewis is sneezing almost uncontrollably. He runs by, coughing and sneezing, and leaps into the squad car. Officer Tarrant walks over to us, grinning broadly. I can't figure out what's going on.

"Nice cat," he says to me.

"What happened?"

"My partner found out he's allergic."

I look over. The white cop is in the throes of a sneezing fit. "Is he okay?"

"Might have to shoot him." Tarrant laughs, and so does Marv.

"What did you find upstairs?"

"It's fine, ma'am. Everything is absolutely fine. It looks untouched."

"Really?"

"Really."

"No one's there or anything?"

"No."

"It's totally safe?"

"Unless you're allergic to cats." He bends

down to peer into the squad car at Lewis, still hacking away.

I can't make sense of this. "But the door was open."

"Come on in with me. We'll take a quick walk through and you tell me if anything is missing." Tarrant opens the front door for me.

"Would you mind going first?"

"Age before beauty, huh?" he says, and walks ahead of me. It all seems so strange; I've never left the door unlocked before. When we reach the door to the apartment, he swings it open wide and we go in.

Everything looks normal. A small living room, with a paisley sofa and a scrubbed-pine coffee table. The TV is in place and the VCR under it. The stereo sits on the shelf. As usual, Alice doesn't even look at me. I reach for her, but she jumps from my arms with a soft thud.

"This how you left it?" Tarrant asks.

"It looks the same."

"Let's check the bedroom." He walks in front of me and flicks on the bedroom light. The bed's unmade, my clothes are piled on top of the computer, and there's a stack of paperbacks beside the bed on the floor. Neat, it's not. But it looks like it always does.

"Take a look at your jewelry box," he says.

I walk to my bureau obediently and look into the open jewelry box. I don't have a lot of jewelry, but there are a few gold chains, a set of pearls, and my gold power earrings for client meetings. "Everything's here."

"You're lucky. You have a lot of expensive

things lying around. The TV, the VCR, the computer. You ought to think about a safety deposit box for the jewelry."

"Did you search the whole apartment? I mean, am I alone?"

Tarrant nods. "We even checked under the bed."

I think he intends this as a joke, but it sends a shudder up my spine.

"Like I said, you're lucky, ma'am. I've seen places turned over, cleaned *out*. Next time make sure you lock your door."

"You sure you looked everywhere? I mean, I'm not doubting you, it's just that lately some weird things have been happening to me."

"Like what?"

His eyes are a deep, friendly brown, and his manner is professional. I feel like I can trust him. I take a deep breath and let it rip.

12

"Wait a minute," Tarrant says. "Did you report any of this?"

"No. If I did, you'd investigate."

"That's the point, isn't it?"

"Well, what would an investigation involve?"

"We'd start with your statement. Then we'd interview anyone you suspect, any witnesses to the incidents with the car."

"There aren't any witnesses."

He purses his lips. "Do you suspect anyone?"

"I think it's someone at my firm."

"I see. What did the note say exactly?"

"It said, *Congratulations on your partnership.*"

He laughs. I see my credibility fall off the table. "That's all it said? Why do you call it a hate note?"

"It was sarcastic, because I—"

"No threats of bodily harm?"

"No."

"A note like that, it could be from a friend of yours, a practical joke."

"But the car doesn't fit, does it?"

Tarrant shakes his head. "No. So come down and file a report. Bring the note. We'll send it down to the Document Unit. They'll test the paper, analyze the handwriting."

"But I can't file a report."

"Why not?"

"I can't have an investigation of the people at work right now. It'd look terrible. I'd lose my job."

"Our hands are tied unless you do."

"It's out of the question."

He shrugs. "Then my advice is to be cautious. Don't go places alone. If you see the car again, call 911."

"Okay."

"And don't be suspecting every little thing that happens to you, like today. I think you slipped up and forgot to lock the door."

"I don't know. It's not like me."

He nods, a final nod that tells me our conversation is over. "Listen to Uncle Dave. Nine times out of ten, it's a gag. Or an old boyfriend. Some guy you jilted or didn't have time for. They get over it." He claps his hands together. "Now I got to see if my partner is still alive."

"Maybe if I took him something to drink. Water, or a soda."

"I don't usually treat him that nice, but if you want to, it's not a bad idea."

"Good." I head into the kitchen, where the light is already on, and look around briefly before getting a Coke. Nothing has been disturbed. My eyes flit automatically over to the magnetic knife rack. Four steak knives, all accounted for. Plus one lethal-looking chopping knife, Mike's favorite when he played samurai chef. It all looks fine. Maybe I did leave the door open. Maybe I wasn't thinking. I get the Coke and walk downstairs with Tarrant.

Outside, I'm surprised to see Marv still around, leaning on the squad car and talking to Officer Lewis. Lewis's face is covered with hives and his eyes are swollen almost shut.

Tarrant breaks into laughter, staggering backward comically when he sees his partner. "Oh, man. You look good, Jimmy. What are you doin' Friday night?"

"Come on, Dave. I gotta get to a drugstore before I croak."

Tarrant is laughing too hard even to respond. I hand the Coke to Lewis. "I'm really sorry. Maybe this will help."

He accepts the can miserably. "I can't see it but I can tell it's good."

"Stay cool, Jim. It's not a brew. It's a diet Coke."

"I know that," he scoffs. "Thanks, ma'am."

"Thank you for your help."

They get into the car, with Tarrant driving, and pull away. I'm left standing there with Marv. Even though I'm tired, I'm in no hurry to go back upstairs.

"You musta left the door open," Marv says.

He's taken off his pith helmet, and his hair is plastered against his head in a ring.

"I guess. Thanks for the use of the chair."

"Listen, I stuck around 'cause I want to tell you something." He leans over. "You gotta think about protectin' yourself."

"I can't get a dog, Marv. I'm never home."

He looks furtively around. "I'm not talking about a dog. I'm talking about this." He looks down and so do I. In the middle of his calloused palm is a small black gun. It has an embossed black trident on its handle. It looks like a shiny new toy.

"Is that real?"

"It's a Beretta."

"Marv, what are you doing with that? Are you nuts?" I look around wildly. The guy with the Bianchi is gone from the window. So is the Bianchi.

"Shh. Shh. I'm tryin' to tell you somethin'."

"You can't just carry that around in your pocket, for Christ's sake. Is it loaded?"

"Can't drill no holes if it ain't."

I step back. "Jesus, Marv, are you crazy? That's a concealed weapon!"

"It's legal. I got a permit."

"That doesn't mean you can carry it around! Did you have that when you were talking to the cop?"

He smiles slyly. "Right under his nose and he didn't even know it. I'm telling you, Mary, you need one of these. You live by yourself. All you got for protection is that scrawny cat. Wise up." He shoves the gun into my hand.

It terrifies me, just the feel of it. Light and deadly. "Take it back. Get it away from me." I hand it to him, but he pushes it back at me. I feel panicky. "Marv, take it back! It's gonna go off!"

He takes it back, with a chuckle. "Can't go off. It's got a safety." He slips it into his pocket as if it were loose change.

"Marv, why do you have that thing?"

"You think you can run a cash business in this city without a gun? Besides, it's my right. It says it in the United States Constitution. I have the right to bear arms."

"Don't tell me what the Constitution says. The Constitution is talking about the need for an army. It's so the army can have the guns, Marv, not guys who sell plants. You'll get yourself hurt with that thing."

"Oh please."

"You will. I read that. They'll take it from you and use it against you."

"You sure you don't want to borrow it for just one night? If you need to shoot it, you just take the safety off and hold it with two hands, like on *Charlie's Angels*. Like this." He makes a Luger with his fingers.

"No, thanks."

"Sure?"

"I couldn't use it anyway. I couldn't shoot anybody. Now I'm going to bed."

"Yes, you could. If you had to. If somebody was trying to kill you, you sure as hell could."

"See you, Marv."

His thin voice calls after me. "Don't kid yourself, Mary. You'd use it. Every one of us would. Don't kid yourself."

I leave him standing there in the yellow square of light spilling out from my window. A hustler with a toy-sized gun in the pocket of his chinos.

I get inside my apartment and check everywhere for notes, for damage, for something missing. For any kind of sign that someone has been here. I find nothing.

I try my best to feel at home. I go around and touch all of my things, rechristening them. I clean up the bedroom. I open a can of Progresso soup. Still, I can't shake the feeling that something is different about the place. I settle down on the living room floor to figure out the directions for the answering machine, but I can't concentrate.

Alice comes over and sniffs the open box. She saw the whole thing. "Did I leave the door open, Alice?"

She ignores me and walks away.

"You can be replaced!" I shout after her.

I sit in the middle of my floor with a mug of lentil soup and look around my empty apartment. I feel edgy and decide to call Judy. She thinks the whole thing is as creepy as I do but convinces me that I left the door unlocked. Everybody makes mistakes, she says, even you. Then she gets worked up about Marv's gun; it takes me ten minutes to persuade her that I wouldn't think of buying one. I hook up the machine and begin screening the calls after that. I pick up when I hear Ned's voice.

"Hey, Mary. I didn't know you had an answering machine."

"It's new."

"You going to use it instead of star sixty-nine?"

"Until my number gets changed."

"I like it, it's cute. You sound like a kid."

"Great. I wanted to sound like a hit man. Hit woman."

He laughs. "Not on your life. So how are you doing? You've been burning up the phone lines."

"Don't ask."

"Anything the matter?"

"Yes, but I'm too tired to talk about it."

"Just give me the headline."

"I thought a car was following me, but it wasn't. I thought someone broke into my apartment, but they didn't. Not a good day."

"Weird."

"Yeah. Now I'm tired. I was just about to go to sleep."

"I should let you go then."

"Oh, I almost forgot. I'm supposed to tell you. Your father sends his regards."

"My father *what?*"

"I was at Masterson. He introduced himself."

"To you? Why?" Ned sounds concerned, almost frightened.

"I don't know. He said he wanted to meet me. I guess you told him that we—"

"I haven't spoken to my father in fifteen years, Mary."

"You haven't? Why not?"

"It's a long story. I'd rather not talk about it over the phone. Can I stop by your office tomorrow?"

I offer a tentative okay and we hang up. None of this makes sense. Why would a grown man sound frightened of his father? Why haven't they spoken in a decade and a half? How does his father know anything about me? I have so many questions lately, and no answers at all. I don't like this feeling, that everything's slipping out of control. I kept it together after Mike died, and it wasn't easy. Now it's all under attack. Threatened at the foundation.

I close the living room blinds and check the dead bolt. I decide to take a hot bubble bath to calm down. I push the ANSWER CALL button on the answering machine and fill the tub. I undress quickly, throwing my clothes into a heap on the bathroom floor. I sink deep into the warm, scented water, artificially blue in imitation of the Caribbean. The box promised that the sapphire currents would wash my troubles away. Don't worry, be happy. I lie still in the tub, listening for any sound in the apartment. The only noise is the crackling of the bubbles as they pop at my earlobes. I try to enjoy high tide, but as soon as I start, the telephone rings. I stiffen and wait for the machine to answer.

The rings stop, and there's a mechanical noise as the tape machine engages. "Mary, this is Timothy Jameson. See me first thing in the morning. You know when I get in." *Click.*

At least it's not *him*.

I relax in the warm, silky water. It feels good, therapeutic. I sink deeper, so the waves lap at my chin. I close my eyes. No problem, mon.

The next time I hear the telephone ring, the water is cool. Barely conscious, I hear the answering machine pick up the call. A woman's voice says, too loudly, "This is Stephanie Fraser. We met in Judge Bitterman's courtroom after your argument. I've been calling your office, but you haven't returned my calls. We just can't sweep this under the rug, Mary. We need to send a message. So please return my call. I know you must be busy, but this is important. Thank you."

Click.

"Go away, Steph. I gave at the office."

But now the water is cold, and I'm awake. How unpleasant. And I have to shave my legs, a task that used to make me feel grown-up but now is merely a pain in the ass. Cranky, I fish under the water for the Dove and soap up the stubble on my legs. I use a new plastic razor, for that extra-close shave. This way I can let it go for three more days. I'm negotiating my ankle bone with concentration when the telephone rings again.

The rings stop and the machine engages.

Silence. No message. No static. It's *him*.
Click.

I feel a sharp pinch at my ankle. A crimson seam crosses the bone. The soap makes it burn.

"Shit!"

I hurl the razor against the tile wall, and it falls to the floor.

That's when I see it: Mike's picture, the little one of his face, in a porcelain heart frame. The only picture of him I haven't packed away. I keep it on my makeup shelf in the bathroom. It's a private place that only I can see, every morning.

But it's not on the makeup shelf tonight. It's on the floor. Shattered.

"No!" I climb out of the bathtub and pick up the frame. It lies in pieces in my hand as I stand dripping on the tile floor. The porcelain has cracked into separate shards, and the glass over Mike's face is a network of tiny slivers.

How did this happen? I don't want to think what I'm thinking.

I check the makeup shelf frantically. A tube of Lancôme foundation. A glass of eye pencils and mascara. A couple of lipsticks and a bottle of contact lens solution. None of the makeup has been disturbed. If it was Alice who knocked over the picture frame, she was pretty choosy.

I look down at my hand. I can't see Mike at all. It's as if a storm cloud has passed over his features.

If someone is trying to hurt me, they sure know how to do it.

14

I take a cab to work at the ungodly hour that Jameson gets in. My nerves feel taut, my stomach queasy. I'm losing weight, but it's not worth it.

I get off the elevator on Jameson's floor, Lust. When I reach his office, his secretary, Stella, tells me he went to the bathroom. I suggest to Stella, my *paisana,* that if Jameson didn't come to work so early, he could take his morning poopie at home like everybody else. This makes Stella laugh, so she tells me a joke too raunchy to repeat. It's for her jokes that Judy calls her The Amazing Stella.

I go into Jameson's office and sit down. The office is vaguely nautical in theme, a place for

Jameson to pretend he's the captain of something. For Jameson is short, and has the complex in spades. Suddenly he runs in like a pug off the leash and slams the door behind him. "Well, Mary, I guess what I've been hearing is true."

"What do you mean?"

Jameson remains standing, dipping his fingers into the pockets of a navy blue blazer. "What I am about to tell you is for your own good, Mary. I'm telling it to you because I know you are very interested in becoming a partner here at Stalling."

"What is it?" He's making me even more paranoid than I am already.

"I've been hearing that you're Berkowitz's girl now and that you do your best work only for him."

"But I—"

Jameson holds up a tiny paw, like a doggie pope. "At first, I thought it wasn't true. It didn't sound like the Mary DiNunzio I know. But I got the *Noone* brief yesterday and I was extremely disappointed in it."

"I—"

The paw again. "I know you can do better, Mary, because you have in the past, and for me. But if you think you can make partner in this firm just by keeping Sam Berkowitz happy, you are in error. I should not have to remind you that you have an obligation that runs directly to the client in this matter. *My* client, Noone Pharmaceuticals. Noone is almost as big as SmithKline and growing by leaps and bounds. Noone is not a client I would like to lose. You understand that, don't you?"

I nod, dry-mouthed.

"Good. I thought as much." He plucks the brief from his desk and hands it to me. "Rework this according to my comments, which you'll find in red. Spend time in the library. Get authority for your position. If you can't find the cases, I want your assurance that they don't exist." He makes a note in his day journal to bill the two minutes it took to dress me down. "I need it by the end of the day."

"I can't, Timothy. I have—"

"You'd do it by the end of the day for Sam Berkowitz, so you'll do it by the end of the day for Timothy Jameson. End of discussion."

"Okay . . . I'll postpone some things."

"Fine."

I leave his office, red-faced, with a rose garden abloom on my chest. As I hurry by Stella's desk, she hands me a Styrofoam cup of coffee on a tray. "Don't take it too hard, Mare," she whispers. "He's got no one else to piss on, you know what I mean?"

I escape to my office and collapse into my chair. I feel like crying, and not just because of the brief. My life is going haywire. The center isn't holding. My work is going downhill; I'm forgetting depositions, offending clients. The partners are bad-mouthing me. Somebody's harassing me, maybe even breaking into my apartment. What goes around comes around.

And it's coming after you, says the voice.

"Mary, you in there?" says someone at the door.

Before I can answer, the door opens a crack and a white paper bag pops through the opening, followed by Ned's handsome face. His expression darkens as he comes in, closing the door behind him. "Mary?"

It's no use, I can't hide it. I feel wretched. It has to show.

"What's the matter?"

Ned looks so concerned and his voice sounds so caring that I lose it. I start to cry and find myself in his arms, which only makes me cry harder. I cry about Mike, who's not coming back, and Jameson's brief, which I can't possibly rewrite in one day, and Angie, who would rather talk to God all day than to her twin. I cry about my apartment, my *home*, which I'll never feel safe in again. I cry like a baby, freely and shamelessly, while Ned holds me close.

In the next moment he's kissing me on my forehead and on my cheeks. It feels so comforting. I hug him back, and he lifts me onto my desk and burrows into my neck. I smell the fresh scent of his aftershave and can't even begin to think about what's happening between us, as I hear my Rolodex tumble off the desk, followed by the splash of a cup of coffee and the creak of my office door.

"Mary! The carpet!" shouts Brent, who looks in, astounded, and slams the door shut with a bang.

It breaks the spell. I push Ned away and wipe the wetness from my eyes. "Jesus. Jesus Christ, Ned. I must be out of my mind."

"Mary, there's nothing wrong with—"

"Yes, there is. I shouldn't be. I can't."

"I want to be close to you, Mary. You need

that, I can see it. I used to be just like you, keeping everything in—"

"Please, Ned."

"Tell me what's happening. I can help."

"You want to help? Then stop sending me notes. And stop following me." It's a test. I watch his face for a reaction.

"What are you talking about?"

"Did you break into my apartment?"

"What?" He looks shocked.

"Did you write the note?"

"What note?"

"The note. 'Congratulations on your partnership.' It has to be you. Nobody else makes sense."

He puts up his hands. His mouth goes dry, I can see it. "Wait a minute. Wait a minute. What are you saying? Why would I do something like that to you?"

"Tell the truth, Ned. Have you written me a note or followed me in a car? Like to my parents' house?"

He touches my shoulder. "Why would I do that, Mary?"

"Answer the question."

"No. No, of course not."

I look directly into his green eyes to see whether he's lying, but I'm thrown off by the honest feeling that I find there. The door opens narrowly and Brent slips in. He carries a stack of paper towels and a plastic jug of Palmolive dishwashing liquid. He doesn't look at me or Ned but immediately sets to work sopping up the coffee spill.

"Maybe I'd better go, Mary," Ned says.

"Maybe you'd better!" snaps Brent.

Ned's barely out the door when Brent hits the

ceiling. "Mary, are you out of your mind? Have you lost it completely? Have you gone totally fucking loco?" He scrubs the rug so vigorously the detergent lathers up like shaving cream.

"Brent—"

"Fucking on the desk!" He glares up at me, the veins on his slim neck bulging.

"Brent, slow up! We weren't—"

"Do you *know* what they would do if they caught you? If you sneeze without a hankie, they cut off your balls with a cuticle scissors! What do you think they'd do if they caught you *fucking on the desk*? Huh?"

"I would never—"

"I'm sure you're not practicing safe sex!"

"Brent, we didn't—"

"Suicide! Mary, it's suicide! I go to a funeral every weekend! Everyone I know is sick, except for me. And now Jack." He throws down the paper towel.

I feel a chill. "Jack?"

He looks up at me, his eyes full of tears.

My God. Brent is going to lose Jack. My own eyes sting. "Jesus, I'm so sorry." I kneel down and rub his back through his thin black sweater. He returns to cleaning the stain, mechanically.

"I've known for a while, Mary, so it's not sudden, like it was with you and Mike. And you don't have to worry about me. I'm HIV negative. We always practiced safe sex, even from the beginning."

"My God." I hadn't even considered losing Brent. I couldn't lose him too. We've been together for eight years. I don't know what would happen to me.

"It's no joke, Mary. It's real. Anyone can get it, even Magic Johnson, even you. You're playing with fire."

"We didn't do it, Brent."

"You were going to."

"No, I wasn't." I wasn't going that far, but I did feel something for Ned when he kissed me. And I felt something else, a flicker of physical need that I thought had been buried with Mike. It thrilled me; it frightened me. I look down at the stained carpet and Brent does too.

"All that work," he says, "and it's only gone from coffee brown to Palmolive green." He offers me a paper towel and takes one for himself.

I blow my nose. "It looks like Hawaii."

"No. It looks like Placido Domingo." He wipes his eyes and throws an arm around my shoulder. "So tell me, Mare. Why is it always the Catholic girls who are doin' it on the desks?"

"Brent!" I shove him.

"With Waters yet, who writes you poison pen letters. Who follows you around!"

"It's not him."

"He's mind-fucking you, girlfriend. That man is a mind fuck." He gets up and pulls me to my feet.

"I know what I'm doing, Brent."

"Say what?" He bursts into laughter.

I laugh with him, in spite of myself. "All right, maybe I don't. But I don't think Ned's the one. I just don't."

"Oh, really? Well, you'd better be sure about that, because you got another note in this morning's mail."

"No, really?"

"That's what I was coming in to tell you."

From his back pocket, he hands me a piece of white paper. The message is laser-printed in capital letters and reads:

WATCH YOUR STEP, MARY

The envelope, the stamp, everything is the same as last time.

My heart sinks. "Who's doing this, Brent? This is so awful."

"You have to call the cops, Mare."

"I talked to them last night."

"Hallelujah! You called them?"

"After someone broke into my apartment. Which they didn't. I hope."

Brent looks crazed. "Mary, what the fuck is going on?"

"I don't know. All I know is that when I got home, the door was open. Nothing was taken. The apartment was untouched. Except for Mike's picture, which either fell off the shelf—"

"I can't believe this. This is insane! What did the cops say?"

"They think I left the door unlocked. There was no sign of a break-in."

"What do you think?"

"Last night after I saw the picture, I was sure someone was there. Today I'm not so sure."

"You didn't report it?"

"Brent, if I file a report, they'll investigate. The cop told me. They'll interview people at the firm, people I suspect. Which at this point is everyone but you and Judy. Can you imagine that? Even if they interview a handful of people, you don't think that's going to be the kiss of death?"

"They could keep it confidential."

"Sure, like they keep the number of partners confidential. Like they keep the associate reviews confidential. You know better than that—people stand in line to give you the dirt. And as soon as the gossip mill starts up, I look like shit. Either I'm accusing them of something criminal or I'm a hysterical female."

Suddenly, the phone rings. Brent answers it and then hands it to me, mouthing "Martin."

"Hi, Martin." I stare at the note in my hand.

"You're too busy to return my calls?"

"I'm sorry, Martin. I was in a dep until late at Masterson." I read the note again. WATCH YOUR STEP, MARY.

"Bernie Starankovic called. Think you can find the time to call him back?"

"Sure, Martin."

"Capital. Do so."

I hang up slowly and hand the note back to Brent. "Will you keep this somewhere safe, with the other one?"

"Now I'm storing evidence. The cops should have this, not me."

But I'm lost in thought. "You know, what about Martin? He just sounded pissed as hell, and I can see *him* writing notes like this. He's got a motive, because I'm taking his place on *Hart*. If Berkowitz is grooming me to start doing his work . . ."

"You're just guessing, Mary. Only detectives

can do detective work. Let them help you, goddamn it! If you don't call them, I will." Brent
reaches for the telephone, but I press his hand
down onto the receiver. Our hands pile on top of
one another, like a dead-serious game of one
potato, two potato.

"No, Brent. Wait. It's my career you're playing
with. If they investigate, I'm gonna lose my job.
I can tell you that right now. As sure as you and I
are standing here."

Our eyes meet over the phone. He looks surprised at my urgency. So am I.

"I need this job, Brent. It's what I have now. I
started eight years ago, and I want to see it
through. It's been a constant. For all the faults in
this firm, I know when I come in on Monday
morning I'll see you and Judy and The Amazing
Stella, and I know where the water cooler is."

"I know that, Mare, we've been together since
day one. I love you. You're my friend."

"Then listen to me. I'll make you a deal. After
the election, if it's still going on, I'll report it. I'll
raise holy hell, I mean it. But not until after the
election."

"You don't gamble with stuff like this, Mare."

"My job?"

"Your life."

I give his fist a quick squeeze. "Don't be so
dramatic, Brent. This is not *Camille,* Act Three.
Nobody's dead."

"Not yet," he says, and his glistening eyes bore
into mine. "Not yet."

Because of my discussion with Brent, which we resolve by agreeing to disagree, I'm ten minutes late to the Friday morning litigation meeting. Nobody seems to notice except Judy, who looks at me curiously as I take a seat along the wall and put the marked-up *Noone* brief face down in my lap. The meetings are held in Conference Room A, the only conference room large enough to accommodate the whole department. Conference Room A is on the sixth floor, Avarice, but the A doesn't stand for Avarice. At least not officially.

I used to love these meetings, full of war stories about Actual Trials and Real Juries. I loved them even after I realized that their purpose was

— 138 —

self-promotion, not self-education. I loved the meetings because this group of litigators—or alligators, as Judy calls us—was my own. I felt I belonged in their swamp. I believed, on faith, that they wouldn't eat me; I was one of their young. But I believe this no longer. I've lost my religion.

I watch the alligators feed voraciously on delicatessen fish, Danish, and bagels. You'd think they haven't eaten in years. I look around the room, seeing them as if for the first time. I scrutinize each freshly shaved or made-up face. Which alligator is sending me these terrible notes? Which one broke into my apartment—or maybe hired someone to do it?

Is it Berkowitz? He starts off the meeting, smoking profusely, telling everyone about the victory before Bitterman, which seems as if it happened a decade ago. He mentions my name in a familiar way and comes dangerously close to giving me some credit. Every head turns in my direction. I hear an undercurrent of snapping jaws.

Is it Jameson? Is his one of the jaws I heard?

Is it Martin? Is he the Guy Who Likes Owls But Hates Me?

Is it Lovell, a semiretired partner who still says Eye-talian?

Is it Ackerman, a supercharged woman partner who hates other women, a bizarre new hybrid in a permanent Man Suit?

There's Ned, looking at me thoughtfully. Not him, I think.

And Judy, whose bright eyes are clear of make-up. Of course not Judy.

Then who? I look at each partner, all thirty of them in the department, racking my brain to see if any one has reason to dislike me. I look at each young associate, a nestful of hatchlings, sixty-two in all. They're free of original sin. At least they look that way.

When the meeting's over, I head straight for the library and grab one of its private study rooms. Each room is soundproof and contains only a desk and a computer. And the doors lock, a feature I hadn't taken advantage of until now. I lock the door and skim the brief for Jameson's bold-red comments.

He finds my sentences TERRIBLE and the central argument INCONSISTENT. Everywhere else he has scribbled CASE CITATION! At the risk of sounding arrogant, I'll tell you there's nothing wrong with this brief. Jameson's going to make me rewrite it just because he can, even though it'll cost Noone as much as a compact car. And I'll do it because I need Jameson's vote.

I flick on the computer and it buzzes to life. I log on to Lexis, a legal research program, and type in a search request for the cases I need. It finds no cases. I reformulate the search request, but still no cases. I change it again and again and finally start to pick up cases from a district court in Arizona. That's what legal research is like—you dig and dig until you strike a line of cases, like a wiggly vein of precious minerals. Then you strip-mine as if it were the mother lode. I'm cheered by my unaccustomed good fortune when someone knocks on the glass window of the door.

It's Brent, carrying a covered salad and a diet Coke. I unlock the door to let him in.

"You vacuum-sealed, Mare?" He sets down my lunch.

"Can you blame me?"

"No, I'm glad of it. Listen, I got them to change your extension. I told them we kept getting calls for Jacoby and Meyers—it was all they had to hear. You'll have a new number by this afternoon. I already sent a letter to the clients."

"Way to go. What about my home number? I'm still getting calls."

"Shit. They wanted your authorization to unlist it, so I wrote a letter from you and faxed it over, okay?"

"Great."

"The only problem is it will take three days to make the change, and weekends don't count. It won't be changed until Wednesday of next week."

"That's not good."

"Did I say I told you so? I must have. I'm just that kind of guy."

"All right, I hear you."

"It's not your fault, it's theirs. The phone company is so much more efficient since they broke it up." Brent rolls his eyes. "What a shame. They used to be my favorite monopoly, after Baltic and Mediterranean."

"You can't make any money on Baltic and Mediterranean."

"I know, but I like the color. Eggplant," he says, in a fake-gay voice. Brent does that sometimes to make the partners laugh. He says, The joke's on them, I *am* what a gay man sounds like. "The good news is, I got you a preferred phone number."

"What's that?"

"You know, where you pick your own four-letter word for the number," he says, with a grin.

"Brent, you didn't."

"Not that, dear. Give me some credit." He pulls a yellow message slip out of his pocket and hands it to me.

I laugh. "546-ARIA?"

"You like?"

"It's cute."

"This way, people will think you got culture."

"Right." I hand him back the slip. "Thanks. For lunch, too. I owe you."

"Forget it. Somebody's got to take care of you, don't they?"

"I got a better idea. Let me buy you dinner tonight."

"Deal. Just don't try to get fresh later." He ruffles the top of my head and is gone.

I lock the door and work through the afternoon, rewriting the brief and adding the new cases. By the time I rush the disk up to Brent to correct my typing, the papers are perfect for the second time. I remember to telephone Starankovic when I get back to my desk. 4:45. He sounds as if he's still sore at the wounds inflicted by Bitter Man and is fighting like Matlock for the one plaintiff he still represents.

"I'm gonna depose the two supervisors in the Northeast store next week, Mr. Grayboyes and Mrs. Breslin," he says. "Then I'm gonna interview each and every one of your staff employees."

"Bernie—"

"If you don't consent to the interviews, I'm gonna file a motion."

"Wait a minute, Bernie." Starankovic knows he has to send a notice to schedule a deposition. He's trying to fuck me, so I fuck back. "No notices, no deps."

"I sent the notices!"

"When? I didn't get them."

"I sent 'em to Martin. I had 'em hand-delivered. I paid extra."

It takes me aback. Martin. "I didn't know about the notices, Bernie. I haven't scheduled the deps. I haven't even called the witnesses."

"That's not my problem."

"Christ! Cooperate, would you?"

"Why should I?"

"Because I'll recommend to Harbison's that they let you do the interviews. Then you won't have to file a motion."

"So?"

"Saves you money."

"Saves *you* money," he retorts.

"You want to go see Bitterman again? Really, Bernie? You need that *acido* in your life?"

There's a short pause. "Okay, Mary. You talk to your client. You schedule the deps. But it's gotta be soon. I want the interviews."

I hang up, with the feeling I've dodged a bullet. But I don't know when the next one is coming, or who's doing the shooting. Why didn't Martin tell me about the notices? What if the note writer is Martin?

Brent brings in the finished copy of the *Noone* brief. After a quick review, I walk it over to Jameson, who has stepped away again. The Amazing Stella says, "That freak spends half his time in the little boy's room."

"That's because he's full of shit," I whisper.

She smirks and beckons me closer with a coral-colored fingernail. "You know what he's doin' in there?"

"What?"

"Whackin' off."

"Stella! Jeez!" I look around to see if anyone is in earshot. The secretaries have gone home, it's after five.

"Mary, you always think everybody's an angel. I'm tellin' youse, he's got a whole drawer full of dirty magazines in his desk. He keeps it locked, but I seen it once. There's sex toys in there, too. Really *weird* toys."

"Sex toys?"

"*Weird* toys," she repeats, with a shudder. Suddenly, she snaps to attention. "Mr. Jameson! Miss DiNunzio was just bringin' this brief to youse."

"*You*, Stella." Jameson all but adds, You ignorant dago.

I try to look at him normally, but the thought of the sex toys almost makes me gag. I have to say something, so I say, "I did manage to find some cases after all. On Lexis."

"Knew you would. I'll look it over later." He scampers past me into his office. He's telling me he didn't really need the brief by the end of the day, he just wanted to make me do tricks.

Weird tricks, I think, and almost shudder myself.

Brent howls at this later, over dinner. We eat at Il Gallo Nero, a restaurant that Brent adores because Riccardo Muti used to eat here. Brent had a heavy crush on Muti. He wore a black armband on his black shirt the day the Maestro left for Milan.

"I knew it! I knew it!" Brent shouts, laughing. "Jameson's in the closet, Mare! He's a closet queen!"

"She didn't say that, Brent." I've had too much chianti and so has he. I don't care, I'm having fun. And Brent has forgotten to nag me about the cops, for which I'm grateful, because I know I'll pay for it in June.

"Yes, she did! She said weird toys. What do you think she meant?"

"I don't know. I'm a good girl."

"Dildos! Nipple pincers! Choke chains! He pretends he's a dog! He fucks rhinos! Oh, no!" We both laugh until the tears flow.

When we leave, Brent puts an arm around my shoulders and we walk up Walnut Street. The asphalt is being repaved to eliminate the potholes, which cover the city streets like minefields. Philadelphia being the well-oiled machine that it is, nobody's working on the street even though much of it is blocked to traffic. Cars lurch to avoid the police sawhorses, although there isn't much traffic tonight. The new mayor hasn't been real successful in attracting suburbanites to the city on weekends. I can't imagine why. It's a great theater town if you haven't seen *Fiddler*, and there's always that friendly pat-down before you take in a first-run movie.

"Look at this street. What a mess," Brent says. "Here, let me walk on the outside." He do-si-dos around me so he's closer to the curb, then puts his arm back on my shoulder.

"Why did you do that?"

"It's traditional. The man walks on the street side, protecting the woman from the carriages, in case they splash mud."

"That's sexist, Brent. And besides, you're gay." I switch places with him, skipping around him so that I'm curbside.

Honk-honk! A truck blares right behind my shoulder.

I jump, startled at the loudness of it. The truck's headlights go by in a double blur. The cars, confused by the roadblocks, are moving in all directions. Suddenly, I feel afraid. I haven't been watching out for the dark car. I start to tell Brent, but he plows into me, laughing, and replaces me at the curb.

"So what if I'm gay?" he says. "I still count!"

At that moment, just as Brent is dancing toward the street, a car jumps the curb in back of him. It bounds up onto the sidewalk and hurtles directly toward him, ramming into his back with a sickening thud.

I can't believe what I'm seeing.

It's the car, the one that's been following me.

"No! Brent!" I shout, but it's too late.

Brent's face freezes in agony and shock as the car lifts him bodily on its grill, like a charging bull gores a matador. His body snaps back against the car and his mouth is a silent scream.

"Stop! No!!" I watch in horror as the car flings Brent's lithe frame up off the sidewalk. He shrieks as his body literally flies through the air and slams into the plate glass window of a bank. The glass shatters with a hideous tinkling sound and rains down on Brent in a deadly sheet. Then the only sound is the clamor of the bank alarm.

And the screech of the murderous car as it digs out onto a chopped-up Walnut Street and busts up a police sawhorse with a splintering *craaaack*.

I whirl around, squinting frantically for a license plate.

There is none.

The car careens crazily up the street and out of sight.

16

The coarse wooden toothpick in Detective Lombardo's mouth wiggles indignantly. "Cheese and crackers! Why do you have to talk that way? I work with cops that have a fifty times better mouth than you." We're sitting in the hospital corridor, waiting for Brent's operation to be over.

"What's the matter with it?"

"It's not nice, for a lady."

"You know, if you'd get as worked up about whoever hit Brent as you do about my language, we'd be in good shape."

"I don't have to get worked up to do my job. I know my job. I'm doin' it." He points at me with his spiral note pad.

"Fine."

"Good."

"Good." We've been arguing like this for hours. Lombardo arrived on the scene after the ambulance got there because I reported the incident as intentional. He asked a lot of questions and wrote the answers down slowly with a stubby pencil, which he seemed to think constituted the sum total of his job. Lombardo played football for Penn State, but I'm beginning to wonder if they gave him a helmet.

Suddenly, his heavy-lidded brown eyes light up. It looks like Fred Flintstone getting an idea. "Hey, Mary, how about gay-bashing?" Hey, Barn, how about we go bowling?

"You couldn't tell that Brent was gay."

"You can always tell."

"Now what's that supposed to mean?"

"Just what I said."

I feel my eyes well up; I didn't know there were any tears left. "I don't want to hear that, Lombardo. Keep it to yourself, because you don't know what you're talking about. Brent is a great person and so are his friends. Anything else is bigotry."

"Don't get me wrong, I didn't say I don't like gay people." He glances up and down the glistening hallway. "I got a brother, you know, who's a little light in the loafers."

"Christ."

Lombardo leans closer, and I catch a whiff of Brut. "All I'm saying is that you can tell. I knew, with my brother. I knew, right off."

"You knew."

"I knew. It was his eyebrows. Something about his eyebrows." He arches an eyebrow, with effort. "See?"

I look away. I'm glad Jack isn't here for this conversation. I called him the first thing and he arrived in tears. He poured quarters into the pay phone, calling all his friends. They came in a flash and were as loving and supportive a group as I've ever seen. I tried to explain to him about the car, but he was too upset to listen. It doesn't matter how Brent got here, Jack said, only that he gets out. They all went outside a while ago to smoke a cigarette, waiting to hear if they would be going to another funeral this weekend.

"Tom, I'm telling you, the car was meant for me. It's the same car. I'm sure of it."

He frowns at the notes on his pad. "You don't know the color."

"I said it was dark. Navy, black. One of those."

"We don't have the make."

"It's a sedan. An old one. Huge, probably American."

"We don't know if the driver's male or female. You said there was no plate."

"What about the notes? And the calls?"

"I told you, I'll take the notes from you and I'll take your statement about the calls." Lombardo flips the notebook closed and slips it into his back pocket. "Look, Mary, we'll go to the scene, we'll investigate. Christ, the uniforms are already there. They'll talk to the witnesses."

"There weren't any. There were hardly any cars. Nobody stopped."

"So maybe there's a cab still workin'. We'll

hear somethin' in a day or two from one of the cars. Meantime the uniforms will scrape some paint off the sawhorse—that might tell us somethin'. Don't look at me like that, Mary. AID's pretty good."

"AID?" The name sounds familiar, but I can't place it.

"Accident Investigation Division. They do all the workup at the scene."

I lean my head against the wall, fighting a wave of nausea. AID. Of course. They investigated Mike's accident. Witness surveys. Scene examination. Analysis of his bicycle shorts for car paint. Even a flyer sent to local auto body shops. Then came the final call, from the Fatal Coordinator Sergeant. Sorry, Mrs. Lassiter, there's nothing else we can do, he said. Oh, yeah? I thought to myself. How about changing your title?

"Where are the notes anyway?" Lombardo asks.

"Brent had them. I'm not sure where they are, probably in his desk."

"You wanna take me there?"

"No. I want to stay here and see what happens to Brent."

Lombardo sucks on his toothpick. "It's not your fault, you know."

I don't reply. My mouth tastes acrid and angry. Of course it's my fault; the driver was trying to kill me. And I didn't listen to Brent and file a report, because I was more concerned about my brilliant career. I feel sick and guilty, and most of all, in the dark and twisted pit of my stomach, I feel a powerful fear. I don't want to lose Brent like I lost Mike.

I close my eyes to the picture forming in my head, the one of the car slamming into Brent's body. It's like a nightmare, a waking nightmare, and one that I had on so many sleepless nights after Mike's death, as I pictured the car slamming into him on his bike. I close my eyes to the horrific visions, trying to squeeze them out. But they bring me to see something, something I hadn't seen before. I sit up in the plastic chair.

"You gotta go to the ladies?" Lombardo asks.

I'm amazed at what I'm thinking. I face Lombardo, but I can't say anything. What if? What if there's a connection between what happened to Mike and what happened to Brent?

"My husband was killed last year by a hit-and-run driver."

"Jesus, Mary, I'm sorry. Jeez, Mary, if I hadda known. Jeez." His beefy face flushes with embarrassment.

"What I'm saying is maybe it's connected to what happened to Brent. Brent was hit by a hit-and-run driver too."

Lombardo takes the toothpick out of his mouth.

I struggle to make my argument, to find the right words. My brain is tired, so tired, and I can't think fast enough. "Tom, couldn't it be the same driver? Let's say someone is very angry at me, hates me for some reason. They even kill my husband, hit him with a car. They write me hate notes, they call me, they stalk me. They break into my apartment, they break my husband's picture—"

"Yo, wait a minute—"

"Let me finish. Then, almost a year later, about the same time they killed my husband, they try to kill me. The same way, even. But they hit Brent by accident. Right before it happened we were dancing around on the curb."

"What did they rule your husband's death?"

"An accident. He was riding his bike by the river. It was an accident, that's what we all thought at the time."

"Why do you think it wasn't?"

"Because of what happened to Brent, Tom! The same thing!"

Lombardo blinks, dully. "He wasn't on a bike, was he?" He pops his toothpick back into his mouth and reaches for his notebook.

I grab his hand. "No, Brent wasn't on a bike. He was walking."

"You said it's the same thing. It's not the same thing."

"But it is. They were both hit by a car. A hit-and-run."

"It's not the same thing. One is on a bike and the other is walking."

"All right, it's not the exact same thing."

"You can say the exact same, you can say the same. It's not the same thing." Flustered, Lombardo smooths down his nylon windbreaker.

I feel like screaming. "But they're both hit—"

"There are other differences."

"What?"

"Different time of day. Different place. With the construction on Walnut, it was probably an accident."

"But it makes sense!"

Lombardo looks at me gravely, like I'm crazed from my recent widowhood. "Mary, you're upset. Let me take care of—"

"For Christ's sake, will you fucking *think!*"

"That's it! Stop talkin' like that!" He jabs the air between us with his toothpick. A nurse, walking by, looks back with concern.

Suddenly, the double doors to the operating room swing open and the surgeon, an older man, walks out. I stand up, and Lombardo surprises me by taking my arm. I search the doctor's eyes for a sign about Brent, but there is none. He tugs down his green half-mask and walks over to us, heaving a sigh.

The sigh, I recognize. The sigh, I know. It happened just this way the last time. Oh, no.

"I'm sorry. We did everything. The injuries were extensive. There were massive chest and skull fractures. The carotid artery was severed. There was just too much bleeding."

Oh, no. Just what they said with Mike. Chest injury. Skull fracture. Brain lacerations. The medical mumbo-jumbo that provides the background noise for the worst news of your life.

"We fought very hard. So did your husband," he says.

My husband. Not my husband. Oh, no.

"It wasn't her husband," says Lombardo. "It was her secretary. A male secretary."

"I'm sorry," the doctor says awkwardly. "Well, your secretary fought very hard. I'm very sorry."

I nod and feel Lombardo's solid grip on my arm. He leads me to the elevator, and we leave the hospital. Jack and his friends, smoking nervously at the hospital entrance, take one look at us and know Brent is dead. I go over to Jack, but he breaks down and his friends close around him. They sob openly, this pale group of too-thin gay men. The two security guards exchange glances, but there's no compassion there.

Lombardo leads me to his squad car and drives to my apartment. Neither of us says anything on the ride home. I leave Brent at the hospital, just like I left Mike at the hospital. My husband, not my husband. I hear the voice, faint and far away, from within:

I tried to warn you, but you wouldn't listen. I tried, it says, and then deserts me.

"Mary?"

It's Lombardo, opening the car door for me. He helps me out of the car and walks me up to my apartment. "You're gonna be okay, you'll see. Just get some rest."

"Would you look inside my apartment? Just to make sure?"

"Sure. Sure." I hand Lombardo the key and he walks in. He finds the light switch and I hear the floors of my apartment groan, unaccustomed to such a heavy tread. In a minute he's back at the door. "Everything's okay. There's nobody here."

"Thanks."

"I'll do some checkin' about your husband. When AID investigates, they make a report. Those guys are real thorough."

I nod. Lombardo gives my shoulder a squeeze and climbs down the stairs. Cautiously, I go into the apartment. Alice sits on the windowsill, her hidden body making a hump in the tangled blinds. I walk over to the window and peek through the blinds.

The car that killed Brent isn't on the street. I watch Lombardo's squad car pull away from the curb. When I turn around, the red light on the answering machine is flashing. I pound the PLAYBACK button with a clenched fist.

The first message is silence, then *click*.

Fuck you! Fuck you! I scream in my head.

The second message is Ned. "Are you out there gallivanting around? Call me. I'm Coooooool." There's the sound of mechanical laughter, then *click*.

It has to be him. It just has to.

He's trying to mind-fuck you, Brent says.

He's too cool, Judy says.

Nine times out of ten, it's an old boyfriend, says Officer Tarrant.

I check my watch. It's 4 A.M.

I'm going crazy.

I'm going to see Ned.

Watch your step, Mary.

I run to Ned's house without stopping, driven by a force and a strength I can't control. I reach his door in no time and pound on it with my fist. *Boom-boom-boom,* right next to the brass house number, 2355. Its jagged edge rips the side of my hand. *Boom!* Blood runs out, but I don't feel it.

Open the fucking door, Cool.

Boom-boom-boom! My blood stains the number.

The door opens. It's him in sweatpants and a T-shirt that says ANDOVER. He rubs his eyes and smiles sleepily. "Mary, this is a pleasant surprise."

So cool.

I push him back into the house and slam into

the middle of his big fat ANDOVER, bloodying it. "Where the fuck were you tonight, Cool?"

He looks astonished, his eyes wide. "Mary?"

I grit my teeth and shove him again. "Where were you tonight?" I advance on him, and he steps backward. "Answer the question, Cool! Why is it you never answer the fucking question?"

"Mary, what is—"

"Tell me!" I smack him across the face. My blood sears a perfect cheekbone. His hand flies to his face, and he edges against the stairwell.

"I . . . was here!"

"Doing what?" I smack him again, so hard the blood from my hand spatters in a tiny fan across his T-shirt.

"Mary, stop it!"

"You killed Brent! And Mike!" I start to slap him again, but he catches my wrist in midair.

"Mary, no!" He wrenches my arms together.

"You did it! You!" I scream, kicking and clawing at his arms and legs. I can't believe what's happening, that I'm struggling in his arms, that I'm raging. He wrestles me to the floor, pinning me there, pressing my wrists back into the rug.

"Stop it now!" he cries out.

"You! You!" I hear myself, shouting over and over, then the huff of my own panting. I can't seem to catch my breath. I feel I'm coming out of a fit.

"Stop it, Mary!" he shouts.

"You!"

"No!"

"Cool!"

"Ned—my name is Ned! I'm not Cool, I don't

know who that is. I don't know what you're talking about. I would never hurt you, you know that!"

"Let go of my wrists!"

"Not until you're calm."

I look up at him, on top of me, looking down. His face is barely visible in the half-light. Flecks of blood mingle with his freckles; the two are hard to distinguish. I can make out his eyes, his green eyes, oddly bright and feral. His eyes are full of pain. He's not the killer, he can't be. He's hurting for me, I see it there, in his animal eyes. "Brent's dead," I whisper.

"Your secretary?"

"A car hit him. It wasn't an accident."

"My God. And you think I did it?" He shakes his head in disbelief. "Never, Mary. Never." Still straddling me, he releases my wrists.

I don't move, I can't. I feel utterly drained, shaken to the core. I want to surrender myself to the force out there that wants to hurt me, wants to punish me for what I've done. It should have been me it claimed. Not Brent, and not Mike. "It's because of me."

"No, Mary." He leans down, supporting himself on his arms, and kisses me softly.

Without thinking about it, merely responding, as a child to the breast, I kiss him back. He kisses me again, so carefully, trying to reach me. He strokes my hair as we kiss, and eases himself on top of me. I feel like I want to lose myself in him, to heal somehow this great gaping hole that's been rent in my heart by losing Mike and now Brent. I want him to love me, to fill me up inside. I don't want to be alone anymore. I want the pain to stop.

All I can feel are his kisses, deep and sweet. And his hands, stroking my hair, then cradling me, so gently. His touch feels wonderful, my skin is hungry for it. I haven't been touched like this in so long, and it feels so good that I go toward it. I feel my body surge to him as he lifts me easily to the couch and strips down my pantyhose and panties. He pulls up my skirt, and I can feel the cool leather of the couch under me and the weight of his hips parting my legs. He keeps kissing me, as I feel him, probing me slowly and purposefully with his fingers.

It's what I want, and what terrifies me, too.

He enters me gently and I gasp, taking him in all at once. I can't say anything, though I hear his whispered words in my ear, because he's moving inside me. I can hardly catch my breath. All I can do is grab his back and hold on. And I do, clinging to him there. Suspended somewhere between heaven and hell.

18

I wake up with my cheek on Ned's chest and his arms linked loosely around me. His freckled skin feels cool, and his chest, almost hairless, looks smooth and perfect. I move slowly, not wanting to wake him, and let my eyes wander over the four walls of his bedroom, which are almost as familiar by now as my own. The walls are covered with a seemingly endless series of sailing photographs, taken at locales I've heard about but never seen. Wellfleet. Bar Harbor. Newport.

I turn over as carefully, and rest my head on the meaty part of Ned's forearm. It brings me eye level with the desk of a very hard-working lawyer. Legal pads are neatly piled there, as are photocopied cases, highlighted with pink and yellow marker. A coffee can holds a bunch of sharpened pencils. There's a file box of index cards, with homemade dividers starting with APPEALABILITY and going straight through to ZENITH CASE (EVIDENTIARY ISSUES). Next to the card file is a photo of a boat that Ned sails on weekends on the Schuylkill.

I pull the sheet up to my shoulders and hug it to my breast. I figure it's midmorning, judging from the bright sun in the window. It must be Sunday. I know it's not Saturday, because I spent much of Saturday in tears, telling Ned all about Brent. He listened patiently and kindly. He kept me in aspirin and water and even went to my apartment to fetch some clean clothes. I called Jack on Saturday too, but he was too miserable to talk. He gave the phone to a friend, who told me there would be a memorial service for Brent on Sunday night.

Saturday evening Ned and I ate Raisin Bran for dinner and went back to bed. We slept like spoons until the middle of the night, when I felt him stirring. I remember him fumbling gently behind me. I reached for him, but he felt cold and slick.

"It's a condom," he whispered. "I'm crazy about you, but I'm not crazy."

Then I turned over to face him, half asleep and half awake. We made love again, slowly and quietly in the still darkness, and I felt as far away from everything as I've ever felt. It was time-out-of-time for us both, I think. Just the two of us, moving there together. Moving into each other.

We slept until dawn, when Ned disappeared downstairs into the kitchen to get us breakfast. He returned with a *Hammond's World Atlas* heaped with American cheese, white bread, and a plastic bottle of seltzer water. We talked while we ate. Then I called my mother and told her the news about Brent. She insisted on coming to the memorial service, to pay her respects to Brent's family. I didn't tell her Brent had been estranged from his family since the day he told them he was gay. Nor did I tell her I'd been standing next to Brent when he was killed.

My eyes fall on Ned's answering machine. There are no messages showing, which means Judy didn't call back while we were asleep. I called her from the hospital as soon as it happened, but she wasn't home. It seemed odd, because I remember her telling me that Kurt would be in New York for the weekend and she'd be free. I even tried reaching her up there, with no luck. I left a bunch of messages on her machine at home and also on the voice mail at work. I asked her to call me at Ned's but didn't say why.

It feels wrong that Judy doesn't know yet. I get out of bed to call her from the downstairs phone, so I don't wake Ned. I look back at him; he's sound asleep. I ease my bare feet onto a cotton dhurrie rug and tiptoe out of the room. I stop in the bathroom first. The room is immaculate; the man is either compulsively neat or has a lot of penance to do. The sink sparkles, and there's no toothpaste glommed onto its sides like in my sink. In fact, there's nothing sitting on the rim of the sink at all—no razor, aftershave, or toothpaste. Where does he keep it all? I look up at the medicine cabinet. Its mirror reflects a very nosy woman.

No. It's none of my business.

I rinse off my face with some warm water, but there's no soap in sight. I check the shower stall, but there's none there either. Where is the fucking soap? I decide not to make a Fourth Amendment issue of it and open the medicine cabinet.

What I find inside startles me.

Pills. Lots of pills. In brown plastic bottles and clear ones, too. I recognize none of their names. Imipramine. Nortriptyline. Nardil. I pick up one of the bottles as quietly as possible and read its label quickly.

NED WATERS—ONE TABLET AT BEDTIME— HALCION.

Halcion. It sounds familiar. I remember something about George Bush being on it for jet lag. I replace the bottle and pick up another.

NED WATERS—ONE CAPSULE EVERY MORNING— PROZAC.

Prozac, I've heard of. An antidepressant. A controversial antidepressant. Isn't Prozac the one that makes people do crazy things? As I replace the bottle, the capsules inside it rattle slightly. What is all this stuff? Why is Ned taking Prozac?

"Mary? Where are you?" Ned calls out, from inside the bedroom.

I close the medicine chest hastily and grab an oxford shirt from the doorknob. I slip it on and pad into the bedroom.

"There you are," he says with a lazy grin. He turns over and extends a hand to me. I walk over, and he pulls me to a sitting position on the bed. I study his face. His eyes are a little puffy from sleep, but he looks like himself. Is he on Prozac now? Is it time for his next dose?

"Do I look that bad?" He sits up and smooths his ruffled hair with a flat hand.

"No. You look fine."

He flops back down, making a snow angel in the white sheets. "Good. I feel fine. I feel better than fine. I feel happy!" He grabs my hand and kisses the inside of it. "All because of you."

Yesterday I would have been touched by the sentiment, but now I question it. Why this sudden exuberance? Is it a side effect of the Prozac, or the reason he's on it in the first place? What are those other pills he's taking?

"Hey, you're supposed to say something nice back to me." He pouts in an exaggerated way.

"Why is it that when handsome men make faces they still look handsome?"

"I don't know, you'll have to ask a handsome man. But not dressed like that. Now gimme back my shirt." He pulls me to him and flips me over with ease. In a flash I've tumbled to the messy comforter, and he's above me.

"Hey! How'd you do that?"

"I wrestled in school." He kisses me suddenly, with feeling. I find myself responding, though with less ardor than before. I can't stop thinking about what's in the medicine chest. Maybe I don't know him as well as I thought. I pull away.

"I have to call Judy."

"She hasn't called?" he asks with a frown.

"No."

He sits back on his haunches and pulls me up easily by my hand. "If you don't reach her, we can go down to her house and look around. Doesn't she live in town?"

"Yes. Olde City."

"That's easy enough. My car's downstairs."

"You park on the street?"

"No, this house has a garage."

"Let me try her again."

Ned rubs his eyes and stretches. "I'm awake. You hungry, sweetheart? You want anything?"

"Maybe. After I call her."

He touches my cheek, gently. "How are you doing?"

"I feel better today. More normal."

"Good. It's gonna be tough telling Judy, isn't it? You three were pretty close."

I nod.

"I'll go take a shower and give you some privacy, okay?"

"Thanks."

"You want to come with me? Think of all the water we'd save." He leans over and gives me a kiss. I can feel the urgency behind it, his need for more, but I keep thinking of the row of bottles. I feel myself tense up. Ned feels it too. "Is something the matter?"

I don't know what to say. I want to be straight with him, but I shouldn't have gone into the medicine cabinet. None of it is my business, even the fact that he's taking medication. "Uh, it's nothing."

"It doesn't look like nothing. It doesn't feel

like nothing." He releases me and looks me in the eye. "You having regrets?"

"No."

"What then?"

"It's none of my business."

"You're sleeping with me. If it's about me, it's your business." He cocks his head slightly.

"Well, then." I clear my throat.

"That bad, huh?"

It's hard to face him. His eyes are so bright, and they smile when he does, showing the barest trace of crow's feet. I love crow's feet. On other people. "Okay, here's my confession. I wanted to wash my face, and I couldn't find the soap. So I went in the medicine chest. I'm sorry, but I couldn't help seeing."

His face is a blank. "Seeing what?"

I look at him; he seems so earnest. I don't want to hurt him. He's been nothing but good to me.

"My Clearasil?"

"No. The bottles. The pills."

"Ohhhhh," he says, with a slow sigh, deflating on the spot.

"It doesn't matter to me. It's not that I hold it against you or anything. It's just that . . ."

His green eyes flicker with hurt. "Just that what?"

"I was surprised, I guess. You seem so fine to me, Ned, you really do. But then I open up the medicine chest and there's a Rite-Aid in there. What do you need those pills for? You're fine. Aren't you?"

"What if I wasn't? Then you leave?"

A fair question. I'm not sure I know the answer.

"Forget it, Mary. You want to understand, right?"

"Right."

"Well, once I did need those meds. All of them. But I don't need them anymore. I'm better now. Over it. If you look at the bottles, the dates are years old."

"Okay." I feel relieved. What I've been seeing are his real emotions, not some drug-induced elation.

He draws the comforter around his waist. "You want to hear the whole story?"

"Yes."

"I don't know where to begin. Wait a minute." He screws up his face in thought. "Once upon a time, I was very depressed. I didn't even know it, in the beginning. I'd been depressed for so long, I thought it was my personality. I was never really able to stay close to anyone, especially a woman. That's why I was so reserved on our first date. I was too busy figuring out how to act."

"You *were* kind of quiet."

"Nicely put," he says, with a weak smile. "I spent most of my adult life being kind of quiet. All it got me was alone—and gossiped about. Then I hit bottom, a couple of years ago, at work. Nothing interested me. I had no energy for anything, even sailing. I could hardly get out of bed to start the day. I started missing work. I don't know if you noticed." He glances at me.

"Not really."

"No one did, except my secretary. She

thought I was a tomcat." He laughs, ironically. "I was a mess. I just lost it. Lost my way. A nervous breakdown, my mother called it, but that's a dumb term. Technically, I had a major depressive episode, according to the DSM. That's closer to it."

"DSM?"

"Diagnostic something-or-other Manual. You want to read all about me? I used to know my page number, but I forget now." He gets up as if to leave the room, but I grab his hand.

"Forget the book. Tell me the story."

He settles back down. "Where was I? Oh, yes. God, I feel like I'm on Sally Jessy."

"Sally Jessy?"

"Morning TV. A big hit with depressed people." He smiles. "Anyway, to make a long story short, it was my mother who got me help. Drove into town, pulled me out of bed, and stuck me in the car. She did the job. She got me to a shrink, Dr. Kate. Little Dr. Kate. You'd like her." He laughs softly and seems to warm up.

"Yeah?"

"She's great. Pretty. Tough. Like you." Suddenly his eyes look strained. "I would have killed myself if it hadn't been for her, I know it. I thought about it enough. All the time, in fact." He looks at me, seeming to check my reaction.

I hope my face doesn't show the shock I feel.

"The first session, I sat there on this IKEA couch she has, and the first thing out of her mouth is, 'No wonder you're depressed, you smell like shit.'" He laughs.

"That's not very nice."

"I didn't need very nice. I needed a kick in the pants. I needed to understand myself and my family. I went into therapy with her. Every day. Sometimes twice a day, at lunch and after work. She started me on meds, which ones I don't remember, but they didn't help. We tried a few others until we got to Prozac—it was new at the time. It worked well—and Halcion, to help me sleep. I could never sleep. Christ, I was a mess." A strand of silky hair falls over his face, and he brushes it away quickly.

"It sounds hard."

"It was. But it was a while ago, and I lived through it. I've thought about throwing the meds away, but they remind me of where I was. Of how far I've come. Kate says I'm supposed to be proud of that. Make an affirmation, every morning." He rolls his eyes. "Can you see it? Me, facing a mirror, saying to myself, 'I'm proud of you, Ned. I'm proud of you, Ned'." He bursts into laughter. "I don't think so."

"I'm proud of you, Ned."

He laughs. "I'm proud of you, Mary."

"No, I mean it. I *am* proud of you."

"Yeah?"

"Yeah."

"So you're not going to pack?"

I shake my head. It's hard to speak. I feel so much for him.

His green eyes narrow like a cat's in the sun. "Even though I'm not as cool as you thought?"

"You're cooler than I thought."

"Oh, therapy is cool, huh?"

"Yeah. It's the nineties. Decade of the Democrats."

"Right." He laughs. "Then you won't mind that I still see Kate."

"You do?"

"Three times a week, at lunchtime. Her office is like home now, only better. I always hated my house. My father's house, I should say."

"What's the story with your father? You were going to tell me."

"He's a tyrant. He thinks he's God. He ran our house like he runs Masterson. Produce or you're out of here!" Ned's tone turns suddenly angry. Beneath the anger I can hear the hurt.

"Is that why you haven't talked to him in so long?"

"I haven't talked to him since the day I had to keep him from strangling my mother. For changing a seating arrangement without his permission."

"My God."

"Nice guy, huh?"

"Did that happen a lot? That he'd be violent, I mean."

"I was away at school, so I didn't see it. I knew it was happening, though." He leans back on his hands. "Denial is a funny thing. You're in this place where you know but you don't know. You're keeping secrets from yourself. I think that's what my trust fund's for. He screwed me up, but at least he gave me the means to figure out how." He laughs, but it sounds empty this time.

"Why do you think your father wanted to meet me?"

"I bet he knows we went out the other night. I think he keeps tabs on me."

I sit up straight, slowly. I remember the look on his father's face when he stormed into the glass-walled conference room, his fury barely held in check. It's not hard to believe that he'd be violent with his wife. Or even that he could kill. "You mean he follows you? Or has you followed?"

Ned looks stricken as he makes the connection. "What are you saying? You think he killed Brent? You think he's trying to kill *you?*"

"Do you?"

"Why would he?"

"So that you can make partner at Stalling. To assure your position."

"No. No, I can't imagine that. It's inconceivable. Uh-uh." He shakes his head.

"But you said he keeps tabs on you."

"Not that way. I think he hears things, finds out the gossip. I don't think he follows me around. No way."

"Are you sure, Ned? If you're not, we should give his name to the police."

"Mary, he's my father, for Christ's sake. Let me talk to him first."

"You want to? After fifteen years?"

"Yes. Just give me a couple of days and I'll talk to him. If I have any suspicions at all, we'll call the cops. I'm not going to take any chances with your safety, you know that."

The telephone rings suddenly. Ned reaches past me to the night table and picks it up. "Hello? Sure, Judy. She's right here." He covers the receiver with his hand. "I'll take that shower."

I nod, and he hands me the phone. As he gets up, the comforter falls away. He walks to the closet without a second thought to his nakedness. A man thing.

Judy starts talking before I even have the phone to my ear. "Mary, what's the matter? What are you doing at Ned's?"

"I've been trying to reach you since Friday night. Where were you?"

Ned takes his bathrobe from a hook on his closet door and leaves the bedroom.

"It's a long story," she says. "My brother was going to Princeton, and I had to . . . forget it. What's going on with you? What are you doing at Ned's, of all places? I just got your messages."

"It's bad news, Judy. Very bad." I swallow hard.

"What?"

"Is Kurt around? Are you alone?" From the bathroom, I hear the metallic scrape of the shower curtain on its rod and the sound of water turned on.

"He's in New York, but he should be home any minute. Why are you at Ned's—in the *morning?*"

"I'll explain later. Judy, listen."

I take a deep breath. I have to tell her about Brent. It reminds me of when I had to tell her about Mike. My parents had called her from the hospital, but she wasn't home. I reached her later with the news. It was awful. I could barely speak; she could barely speak. She practically moved into my apartment. Judy, more than anyone, got me through the funeral.

"Mary? What's going on?"

I tell her the whole story, and that I think it was the same car that's been following me. All she says, over and over, is, "Oh, my God. Oh, my God." Her voice sounds faint and tinny on the other end of the line.

"Do you think he suffered?" she asks finally.

I remember Brent's face and the agonized expression on it when the car plowed into him. There's no reason to tell Judy that. "I don't know."

"Poor Brent. Poor, poor Brent. Oh, my God."

The water shuts off in the shower. I hear Ned banging around in the bathroom.

"What are you doing at Ned's?"

"I came here. I thought he did it."

"So why are you still there? Brent is killed and you're at Ned's?"

"It's not him, Judy."

"I can't believe you. What are you doing?"

I hear Ned scrubbing his teeth, humming to himself tunelessly.

"He's been wonderful to me, Judy. He—"

"You're fucking Ned Waters? Mary, is that what you're doing?" She sounds angry.

"It's not like—"

"You're in danger, Mary! We don't know anything about him. He has every reason to try and hurt you."

Ned switches off the water in the bathroom, and I hear him walking toward the bedroom. His off-key hum has segued into an off-key march. *H.M.S. Pinafore,* as sung by a coyote.

"He'd never do that, Judy."

"But Mary!"

Ned appears in the doorway to the bedroom, bundled up in a thick terry robe. His wet hair is spiky and uncombed; his beard is slightly stubbly. He balls up a damp towel and shoots it at a wicker hamper across the room. It goes in, barely, and he grins at me.

"Don't worry, Jude. I'm fine."

"Is he right there? You can't talk, can you."

"Not exactly."

"I think you should get out of there."

"I'm fine, Jude. You can call here if you need to. Whenever you need to."

Ned sits down on the bed behind me. I feel his hands on my back, still warm from the shower.

"But what if it's him?" Judy says.

"I'm fine. I really am."

Ned massages my shoulders, pressing into them from behind. His touch is firm, insistent. I can feel the tightness in my muscles begin to disappear.

"You're making a big mistake, Mary."

"Believe me, I'm okay."

He applies more pressure, and his fingers knead the top of my shoulders. I move my neck from side to side, and it loosens up.

"We'll talk tonight. Look for me before the service."

"Good. Take care." I hang up. I wish she wouldn't worry about me with Ned. My shoulders are warm and tingly underneath his hands.

"How does that feel?" Ned asks softly.

"Terrific."

"So Judy's worried about you."

"Uh-huh."

"She thinks I'm the bad guy."

"Honestly, yes."

"I thought so."

"I'll talk to her."

"Therapy 101. You can't control what people think."

"Lawyering 101. Yes, you can."

He laughs. "Close your eyes, sweetheart."

I close my eyes and concentrate on the gentle kneading motion of his fingers on my shoulders.

"Let your head relax. Let it fall forward."

So I do, like a rag doll, as his hands work their way to my neck. He takes it slow, inch by inch. It reminds me of the way he made love to me, in the darkness. He didn't rush anything. He felt it, that's why.

"Everything's gonna be all right, Mary," he says quietly.

I almost believe him.

19

That evening, I'm sitting between my parents and Ned at Brent's memorial service. It's at the Philadelphia Art Alliance, an elegant old building on Rittenhouse Square, not six blocks from where Brent was killed. Some of Brent's friends put flowers on the sidewalk in front of the bank today, and his death was all over the news. They called it a "hit-and-run accident," which to me is a contradiction in terms. But it doesn't matter what the TV says. The only thing that matters is what the police say. I wonder if Lombardo will be here tonight.

I look around at the crowd, which appears to be growing larger by the minute, but I don't see Lombardo. The service is full of friends from the nonintersecting circles of Brent's life. There are his gay friends, the biggest group by far, as well as his fellow voice students, and a contingent from Stalling. Judy's here with Kurt, and so are most of the secretaries from the office, sitting together in a teary clump that includes Delia, Annie Zirilli, and Stella. Even Stalling's personnel manager is here, the one who gave Brent such a hard time about the tray. She eyes the gay men with contempt. Her expression says, I knew it.

Watching her, I remember what Brent said just last week. When I die, I want my ashes ground into the carpet at Stalling & Webb. He wasn't kidding.

I look down at the program with his picture on the front. A smiling face in a black shirt, surrounded by a skinny black border. This should not be. He's not supposed to die; he's too young to be inside a skinny black border. He would have said, What's wrong with this picture?

My mother touches my hand, and I give hers a perfunctory squeeze. I don't want to feel anything tonight. I want to be numb.

The eulogies begin, and Brent's voice coach is the first to speak. She's a bosomy brunette, middle-aged and wearing lipstick that's theatrically red. Brent once described her to me as robust; actually he said robusty. But she doesn't look robust tonight: She looks broken. Her speaking voice, which has a remarkable timbre, sounds so grief-stricken I can't bear to listen. I look around the room and spot Lombardo, sitting alone on one of the folding chairs against the wall. His hair is slicked down with water and he wears an ill-fitting black raincoat. He looks like an overgrown altar boy, not somebody smart enough to catch Brent's killer. And maybe Mike's.

"He had a fine voice, mind you," the singing coach is saying. Her head is held high, her posture almost a dancer's. "But Brent was never ambitious in music. He never entered any of the competitions I told him to, even when I got him the forms. He refused to do it. 'I won't go on *Star Search*, Margaret,' he said to me. '*Dance Fever*, maybe. But *Star Search*, never.'"

There's laughter at this, and quiet sniffles.

"Brent studied because he loved music with all his heart. He sang because he loved to sing. It was an end in itself for him. I used to try to instill that in all my students, but I stopped after I met Brent. That was the lesson Brent taught me. You can't teach joy." She faces the audience in a dignified way, then steps away from the podium.

There is utter silence.

I try not to think about what she said.

Two young men appear on the dais. One is almost emaciated, obviously very sick, and is being physically supported by the other. Both wear red ribbons, which on them means more than it does on all the Shannen Dohertys put together.

I know I cannot hear this.

I screen it all out.

I go somewhere else in my mind.

I think about what Judy said before the service started. How she apologized for being sharp with me on the phone. How she really doesn't trust Ned. Nothing I said could change her mind. It was the closest we've come to a fight, and at the end she backed off. Her nerves were frayed, she said. I look over at her, weeping quietly, with Kurt at her side. She loved Brent too. That's why she's acting so crazy.

The eulogies are almost over, and someone's introducing the final speaker.

Mr. Samuel Berkowitz.

I look up in amazement.

Sure enough, it *is* Berkowitz, lumbering up to the flower-filled podium in a dark suit. He adjusts a microphone barely camouflaged by Easter lilies and clears his throat. "I didn't know Brent Polk very well, but as I listen to you all here today, I wish I had. What I do know about Brent is that he was an intelligent young man, a fine secretary, and a good and loyal friend to many people. Also, that he broke every rule my stuffy old law firm holds dear."

There's laughter at this, and renewed sniffles. I smile myself, and feel so proud of Berkowitz for being here. He has more class than any of them put together. I squeeze Ned's hand, but he's not smiling. Neither are my parents; they look somber and upset. They must be thinking of Mike. They hardly knew Brent.

"In addition, I would like to announce a donation in Brent's name, which has been authorized by my partners at Stalling and Webb. Tomorrow we give ten thousand dollars on Brent Polk's behalf to Pennsylvanians Against Drunk Driving. It is our sincere hope that we can help prevent what happened to Brent from happening to other fine young men and women. Thank you." Applause breaks out as Berkowitz steps down and disappears into the crowd.

"What are they talking about?" I whisper to Ned, over the din.

"I don't know." He looks grim.

"Drunk driver, my ass!"

My mother nudges me. Don't talk in church, says the nudge.

I wheel around and look at Lombardo. His dull eyes warn me to relax. Drunk driver? I mouth to him.

He puts a finger to his lips.

Christ! I can barely contain myself. Brent is murdered in cold blood, and they're going to say it was drunk driving? It's all I can do after the service not to pound directly over to him, but I have to take care of my parents first. Ned and I help them down the steps of the Art Alliance and wait with them for a cab. My mother's eyes are smudged and teary behind her glasses; my father looks crestfallen.

"I don't like that man from your office, Maria," she says. "The big one. You know which one I mean? The big one?"

"Yes, Ma."

"No. I don't like that man at all." She shakes her head, and her heavy glasses slip down.

"Why not, Mrs. DiNunzio?" Ned asks, with a faint smile.

She holds up a finger, mysteriously. "Thin lips. You can't even find the man's lips. Like pencil lines, they are."

"Ma. His lips aren't thin. It's just your eyes."

"Don't be fresh, I saw them. He's got the thin lips. Mark my words."

Ned seems amused by this. "He's the boss, Mrs. DiNunzio."

She drills her index finger into the hand-stitched lapel of Ned's coat. "I don't care who he is. I don't like him."

"Don't give the kids no trouble, Vita," says my father. "They got enough trouble right now. A world of trouble."

"I'm not giving them trouble, Matty. I'm taking care of Maria!" People leaving the service look over, startled at the loudness of her voice. "That's what mothers are for! That's a mother's job, Matty."

A yellow cab stops at the light, and I wave it down.

"Look at Maria, Veet," says my father, momentarily cheered. "Just like a big city girl." My mother looks at me proudly. I've hailed a cab, *mirabile dictu*.

"Please, guys. Don't embarrass me in front of Ned, okay? I'm trying to make a good impression."

My father smiles, and my mother gives me a shove. "You. Always with the jokes."

The cab pulls up and Ned opens the door for them. I lean down and give them both a quick kiss. Ned helps my father into the dark cab, but my mother is tougher to shake. She grabs me by my coat and whispers, "Call me. I want to talk to you about this young man."

"Okay, I'll call you."

She whispers loudly into my ear. "It's good to

see you with someone. You're too young to put yourself up on the shelf."

"Ma . . ."

She looks at Ned sternly. "You take good care of my daughter. Or you answer to me!"

"I will," he says, surprised.

"Time to go, Ma." I fight the urge to push her into the cab.

"We love you, doll," says my father, as my mother gets in.

"Love you too," I say, closing the heavy door with relief. I feel like I've tucked them into bed. I wave, and the cab pulls away.

Ned gives me a hug. "They're wonderful," he says happily.

"The Flying DiNunzios. They're something, aren't they?"

"You're lucky, you know."

"I know, but let's not get into it now. Help me find Lombardo." I squint at the crowd coming out of the building's narrow front doors.

"I don't know what he looks like."

"Fred Flintstone."

Judy comes out with Kurt, who has managed to find a suit jacket for the occasion. She waves good-bye over the sea of people. I wave back.

Ned points over at the far edge of the crowd. "Is that him?"

"Yes!" Sure enough, it's Lombardo. I flag him down and he finally spots me. Even from a distance, his expression tells me he wishes he hadn't.

"Don't get upset, Mary."

"I'm already upset. I feel like I want to break

his face." I plunge into the crowd of people, with Ned beside me. Lombardo threads his way toward us, and we meet in the middle.

"Drunk driver, Lombardo?" I say to him. "You have to be kidding!"

Lombardo looks around nervously. "Mary, settle down."

"That's almost as absurd as gay-basher!"

Lombardo takes me aside, and Ned follows. "Look, Mary, it's just a preliminary finding, we haven't stopped the investigation. You said the car was driving crazy when it left the sidewalk. It crashed into the sawhorse. We know it was driving crazy to go up on the—"

"Bullshit!"

"Mary, don't play cop. I'm the cop."

One of the gay men in the crowd glances back. On his short leather jacket is a pink button that says ACT UP; they tangled with the police at a demonstration last year. There's no love lost between the two groups. Lombardo says, "Let's take it out of here."

We regroup at the entrance to the Barclay Hotel, next to the Art Alliance. The canvas awning snaps in the swirling winds around Rittenhouse Square. "Aren't you gonna introduce me to your friend?" Lombardo asks.

"I'm Ned Waters, Detective Lombardo." Ned extends a hand, but Lombardo hesitates before he shakes it. He's remembering that Ned's is one of the names I gave him in the hospital as a suspect.

"He's okay, Tom," I say.

Lombardo looks from me to Ned. Whatever he's thinking, he decides not to say it. "Mary, I followed up on what you told me about your husband. I looked up the AID file on his accident. I even talked to one of the men who investigated. Your husband was hit on the West River Drive, going out of town, at that first curve."

"I know that."

"It's almost a blind curve, Mary. I went out and checked it myself. I found out your husband's not the only bicycle rider to be killed at the same spot. There was an architect, three months ago."

"I read about him. He was only twenty-six."

"Your husband and the architect were killed at about the same time—Sunday morning, bright and early. Probably by someone who'd been out partyin' the night before and was drivin' home to the subs."

"But—"

"Wait a minute." Lombardo pulls out his notebook and flips through it in the light coming from the hotel. "Wait. Here we go. A doctor was killed there too. An internist, who lived in Mount Airy. The guy was fifty-eight. Two years ago, the same curve. Now Brent was hit at a whole 'nother time and place. So I—"

"Isn't that a distinction without a difference?" Ned asks.

Lombardo looks up from his little book. "What?"

"Does it really make a difference that one is in the morning and one is at night? Just because they happen at different times and places doesn't mean it can't be the same person."

"Listen, Mr. Waters, I've been a detective a little longer than you."

"I understand that."

"My gut tells me it ain't the same guy." He turns to me. "I ran down your lead, Mary. I treated it serious, because I admit it looks strange, the two incidents bein' so close together like that. But I gotta go on what makes the most sense, and it's not homicide. I see two accidents, both involving booze. It's too bad that one of them was your husband and the other was your secretary, but it's just one of those coincidences. At least that's what I think so far."

"But, Tom, the license plate."

"Half the cars in this city got no plate. The crackheads take 'em off to sell; the thieves take 'em off for the registration stickers. Look, the way I see it, the guy who killed Brent jumped the curb, trying to avoid the construction. AID told me they had two fender-benders on Walnut Street the same day, all on account of the construction."

"Then why did he drive away?"

"Happens a lot, Mary. More than you think. Somebody's drinkin' a little too much, especially on a Friday night, and before they know it— *boom*—they're up on the sidewalk. They're juiced, they panic. We usually catch up with 'em in a couple of months. Some of 'em even come clean from a guilty conscience. That's what happened with the architect." He pauses and returns the notebook to his back pocket. "AID don't have that many open fatals, you know. The doctor, a kid in a crosswalk in the Northeast, and your husband. He's one of three."

I feel numb again. Mike's a fatal. An open fatal.

"What about the calls?" Ned asks testily.

"You get any more over the weekend, Mary?"

"I don't know. I haven't been home yet."

"And what about the notes?" Ned says.

Lombardo glares at him. "I'll come by and get 'em from Mary. I'll look 'em over and send 'em to the Document Unit, but I don't think they have anything to do with Brent. They don't sound like the kinda notes you see with a killer."

"What do you mean?"

"The notes don't say 'I'm gonna kill you,' 'I'm gonna mess you up,' 'You ain't gonna live another day,' like that. That's the kind of notes you get from a freak who kills. A freak with *cipollines*. You know what that means, buddy?"

"Educate me, Detective Lombardo."

I know what it means, little onions. But the connotation is—

"Balls!"

"Tom, Ned, please."

Lombardo hunches to replace his raincoat. "I want to see the notes, Mary, but I gotta tell you, I think they're from some weak sister who's got a thing for you. Could be someone you used to know, could be someone you know now. It could even be somebody you don't know at all, like a guy in the mailroom at work. Some jerk with a crush. That's the pattern, especially with ladies like yourself, career girls. Their name's in the paper, they're on this committee, that committee. You on committees like that?"

"Some."

"This kind of guy isn't a fighter, he's a lover. He's at home, swoonin' over your picture, tryin' to get up the nerve to talk to you. So don't worry. Call me tomorrow and we'll set up a time." Lombardo's attention is suddenly diverted by Delia, who appears out of the darkness, followed by Berkowitz.

"Thomas!" Berkowitz says heartily, grabbing Lombardo's hand and pumping it. "Thanks for all you've done."

"It's nothin', Sam." Lombardo can't tear his eyes off of Delia.

"Mary," Berkowitz says, "I'm sorry about your secretary."

"Thank you."

"Why don't you take a couple days off? I'll cover your desk."

Delia purses her glossy pink lips.

I'm surprised by the offer. Covering someone's desk is strictly associate work. "Uh, thanks. I'll see."

"You let me know if you need me, Mary. It's your call."

"Sure."

Berkowitz turns to go. "Thomas, thanks again."

"No problem."

Berkowitz strides off, his heavy trenchcoat flapping, and pauses to light a cigarette in a cupped hand. The flame from the lighter illuminates the contours of his face and Delia's.

Lombardo jerks his head in Berkowitz's direction. "He's an all right guy, for a big shot. He thinks the notes are nothin' too, Mary."

"You told him?"

"Sure, we talked a coupla times over the weekend. He was very interested in the investigation."

"Let's go, Mary." Ned squeezes my arm.

I feel tired, suddenly. I'm getting nowhere with Lombardo, I can see that. I know I'm right; I can just feel it. It all makes sense, but there's nothing I can do about it tonight. Wearily, I give in. "Okay."

"Call me, Mary," Lombardo says.

I nod, and Ned steers me home. Neither of us says anything on the short walk to my apartment. I don't know what's on his mind, but my thoughts are muffled by a thick blanket of fatigue and sorrow. As we get closer to my building, I feel a distance between Ned and me. I want to be alone with my memories of Brent, and of Mike. I'm in mourning, and it's déjà vu all over again. We reach the door to my building, near where Ned kissed me for the first time. A lot has happened since that first kiss. Brent was alive then.

"You want to pick up some clothes, Mary?"

"Actually, I think I should get some sleep tonight."

"You mean you want to stay here? By yourself?" He frowns, causing his freckles to converge at the bridge of his nose.

I nod.

"I'm worried, honey. I don't know what's going on, and I have no confidence in that detective. I don't think you're safe."

"Maybe I can call Judy or something."

"You don't want me to stay?" He looks confused.

"Ned, it's not that it wasn't wonderful . . ."

His green eyes harden. "Oh, is that it? Was it wonderful for you? Because it was wonderful for me too."

"That's not what I meant."

"I got to you this weekend, Mary. I know I did. So don't pull away from me, not now."

"I'm not, but we're only a part of what happened this weekend. I keep thinking about Brent."

"Okay," he says quickly. "Okay. I'm sorry."

"I just want to be alone for a while."

"But call me, will you? Call me if you need anything, no matter how late it is. Call me."

"Okay."

"Lock the door."

"Okay."

"Eat your vegetables. And wear your muffler."

"Thanks." I give him a quick kiss and let myself into the front door of my building. I wave to him through the leaded glass in the outer door, and I think he waves back, but I can't see him clearly. The bumpy glass transforms his silhouette into a wavy shadow.

I gather the mail and check each letter as I stack it up. I never thought I would be relieved to see a pile of junk mail addressed to Dee Nunzone, but I am. I climb up to my floor, regretting that I didn't ask Ned to check the apartment. I reach the door, which still says LASSITER-DiNUNZIO, and peek vainly through the peephole. I take a deep breath and unlock the door slowly. I open it a bit, then wider. The apartment is dark. I snap on the light with a finger and stick my head in the door. It looks just the way I left it. And it's silent. No ringing telephone. No other sound. I walk slowly inside, then shut and lock the door behind me.

"Alice?" The window blinds rustle slightly. She's on the windowsill. I walk nervously into the kitchen, refill Alice's bowl, and take Mike's samurai knife from the rack. I head into the bedroom, brandishing the knife. I figure I must look scary; I'm scaring myself. The bedroom looks absolutely normal. I take a deep breath and look under the bed. Dustballs as big as sagebrush, mounds of pink Kleenex, and a tortoiseshell barrette I'd been looking for. I grab the barrette and put it on my bed.

I leave the bedroom and walk into the bathroom. The makeup shelf, which I leave in a secret configuration now—moisturizer, foundation, eye pencil, lipstick—is still in its secret configuration. And the smell of the ripe cat box confirms that at least one other thing remains undisturbed.

I relax slightly and return to the living room.

"Alice?"

The window blinds move in reply, but Alice doesn't leave her post.

"He's not coming back, Alice," I say. I'm not sure whether I mean Mike or Brent, but Alice doesn't ask for a clarification.

I fall into a chair with my killer knife and close my eyes.

20

The next sound I hear is the ear-splitting buzz of my downstairs doorbell. I glance at my watch. It's ten o'clock. I must have fallen asleep. Groggy, I get up and press the intercom button, still holding the chef's knife. "Who is it?"

"Little pig, little pig, let me come in," shouts a strong voice. Judy's.

"Hold on." I buzz her in and she arrives in seconds, having taken the stairs two by two, like she always does. She bangs into the apartment wearing a reinforced backpack and toting a rolled-up sleeping bag. She gasps when she sees the knife. "What the hell is that for?" she asks.

"Bad guys. Are you terrified?"

"Of you?"

"Yes, of me. Of me and my big no-joke knife." I wave it around and she backs away.

"Watch it with that thing."

"You ought to see what this knife can do to a piece of celery. It's not a pretty sight."

"Is this what we've come to? You running around with a machete?" She kicks the door closed with the back of her running shoe and tosses the sleeping bag onto the floor, where it rolls into the couch. Alice arches her back.

"Who are you, Nanook of the North?"

"Are you okay?"

"Yeah."

Her eyes narrow. "Yeah?"

"Okay as I can be."

"I thought so," Judy says, frowning like a doctor confirming a child's case of tonsillitis. "I brought something to make us feel better." She swings the backpack off her shoulder and tugs its zipper open, walking into the kitchen. I follow her in and watch her unpack a bag of sugar, two sticks of butter, and a cellophane pack of chocolate chips.

"You left Kurt to come here and bake stuff?" I stick the knife back onto the rack.

"Not exactly. Your new boyfriend called and said you needed protection. You did use protection, didn't you?"

I feel terrible all of a sudden. It reminds me of Brent. I flash on him that day in my office, cleaning up the coffee stain. He was so worried about me.

"What's the matter?" Judy asks, alarmed.

"Brent, Judy. Brent." I feel myself sag and

Judy gathers me up in her strong arms. I burrow into her fuzzy Patagonia pullover, with its fresh soapy smell, and start to cry.

"I know, Mare," she says, her voice sounding unusually small. "He was a good man. He loved you." She hugs me closer, and I try not to feel funny about the fact that we're two women hugging breast to breast. In fact, Judy's squeezing me so tightly that I stumble backward, to the sound of a loud *reeaow!*

We both jump. I've crunched Alice's tail underfoot. She hisses at me fiercely.

Judy laughs, wiping her eyes. "Fuck the cookies. Let's bake Alice."

I laugh too, for a long time, and it feels good, a release. We take turns drying our eyes with a roll of paper towels that has tiny daisies marching along its border. Afterward, feeling shaky and sober, we look at each other. Judy's lips are a wavy line. "This must be how you felt after Mike, huh?" she says, leaning against the kitchen counter.

Mike. His voice is gone now, and it was the last of him. I nod.

"You came back to work so soon. I never knew how you did it."

"I had to. When something like that happens, you have to do the next thing."

"The next thing?"

"Right. Whatever's next. You go and do it. Then you do what comes next after that. File a brief. Bake cookies."

Judy smiles weakly.

I point to the base cabinet. "The cookbook's inside. You want coffee?"

"Thanks." Judy yanks her pullover off over her head, revealing one of Kurt's V-neck undershirts, and settles down on the pine floor of the kitchen. She tugs my *Joy of Cooking* from the shelf and opens the thick book, idly twisting the red ribbons glued to its spine. "What is this, the wartime edition? You should throw this thing out."

"I can't." I scoop some dry coffee into the coffeemaker. "It reminds me of a missal."

"A what?"

"Forget it." Judy was raised without a religion, which is why she has so much faith.

"So, are you in love?"

I watch the coffee dribble into the glass pot. It takes forever.

"Mary? You in love?" She looks up at me expectantly. With her shaggy haircut, there on the floor, she reminds me of a sheepdog waiting for a Milk-Bone.

"I'm in confusion."

"Tell me what's going on or I'll make the German Honey Bars."

I retrieve two mugs from the cabinet and pour us both some coffee. I take mine with extra cream and extra sugar; she takes hers black. "I don't know where to start."

"Start with his German Honey Bar." She pats the floor beside her.

"You want to sit on the floor?" I hand her the coffee.

"You had sex on the floor, didn't you?"

I sit down with a sigh. The kitchen is so cramped our shoes touch in the middle—

Ferragamo meets New Balance. I wrap my hands around my own toasty mug.

"Your Honor," she says, "please instruct the witness to answer the question." She looks happy again, bugging me to say the unsayable.

"What question?"

"Did you do it on the floor?"

I wince.

"It's okay to talk about sex, Mary. You're a grown-up now, and there are no commandments within a five-mile radius. So. On the couch?"

"Judith."

"That counts as a yes on the couch."

"You're relentless."

"All right. Forget it. You're in confusion. Are you in danger?" She stops smiling.

"From Ned? No."

"You sure?"

I tell Judy all about Ned, his therapy and his father. She listens carefully, sipping her coffee. When I'm done, she sets her mug down on the floor and leans forward intently. Uneven bangs shade her eyes from the Chinese paper lamp overhead.

"You want to know what I think?"

I bite my lip. Judy's a certifiably smart person; she was number one at Boalt. If she says it, it carries weight.

"I think Brent was murdered, and I think there *is* some connection between Brent and Mike. It's too coincidental."

"So I'm not crazy."

"No. But listen to this. I think you've been analyzing this all wrong. Forget for a minute that you think the car was aiming at you, that's just an assumption. The only facts we have are that Mike's been killed and Brent's been killed. So reason backward from that. Assume that the killer did what he intended to do—kill the two men closest to you. He wasn't after you, he was after them."

"You think?"

She yanks a hand through lemony hair. "We've been reading the notes as threats to you, but what if it's someone who's just trying to get close to you? To communicate with you the only way he can? Not someone who hates you, someone who loves you. Someone who wants you all to himself."

My gut tightens as she speaks. She's close to what Lombardo was saying after the memorial service, and I forgot to mention it to her. But it doesn't square, not entirely. "A note that says 'watch your step'? It sounds like a threat to me."

"Or a warning. Particularly since almost the next night, the man you're with gets hit by a car."

"But that assumes the killer knew I'd be out with Brent, and he couldn't have. We didn't plan to go out to dinner, I offered to take him out after I finished a brief for Jameson."

"Jameson? Yuck."

I'm reminded of the weird toys in Jameson's desk, and how Brent had laughed and laughed. I tell her what Stella said. It doesn't seem funny now.

"I don't think it's Jameson," she says, shaking her head. "He's too much of a wuss. I don't think it's Ned's father either, even though he wanted to meet you that day. He could have found out that you were in Ned's class from Martindale-Hubbell."

"But Ned said he keeps tabs on him."

"That doesn't mean he has him—or you—followed. Maybe he asked around. People know you. You've been in practice for eight years in this city. You went to Penn Law, you even went to Penn undergrad."

"Maybe."

"You know, you're resisting the most obvious conclusion, Mary, and the most logical. It's Ned."

"It can't be." I shake my head.

"Look at the facts—there's a pattern here. You date Ned in law school, then you pick up with Mike. You marry Mike, and he's killed by a hit-and-run. You begin dating Ned again, and a couple of nights later Brent's killed by a hit-and-run. Don't you think that's strange?"

"It's strange, but it doesn't mean anything."

"Why doesn't it? Ned even sends you a warning after you have dinner with him—watch your step. Read it as a threat to keep you away from other men, even Brent. Look, Ned didn't know Brent was gay. You remember the rumors that you and Brent were having an affair?"

"That was ridiculous."

"I know that, but Ned doesn't. Plus he admits he's been interested in you since law school. That's weird, Mare."

"Not necessarily. He said he'd been depressed. He's had a lot of problems."

"Which way does that cut? So he's hardly the picture of mental stability."

"I'm surprised at you, to hold that against him. He was depressed. He got help. I give him credit for that, don't you?"

"That's not the point. The man has a history of serious mental illness. I'm glad he dealt with it, but that's the fact. I mean, depressed or not, he hasn't dated anyone since law school. Pining away for you? Doesn't that strike you as obsessional? Almost sick?"

"He never said that, Judy. We didn't discuss other women. You know, if you knew him, you wouldn't say these things. He's beautiful, really."

But she doesn't seem to be listening. "Look, I don't blame you for not wanting to believe me, but think like a lawyer. Imagine that you're the client. What advice would you give?" Her azure gaze is forceful, and it angers me.

"You don't like him, Judy. You never have. He cares for me, he makes me happy. I would think you'd want that for me, for Christ's sake." My tone sounds bitter; my chest is a knot. I can't remember ever fighting with her this way. "What's happening to us, Jude?"

"I don't know." She leans back against the wall, wounded and hurt. She's my best friend; she's trying to help me.

"I'm sorry," I say. "It's hard."

She flicks her hair back, dry-eyed. "I know. I'm sorry too."

We fall silent a minute.

"You know, Mary, you asked me once if I ever worry. Well, I do. About you. I used to worry about your emotional health, after Mike died, but now we're at the point where I'm worried about your life. It scares me that something could happen to you. It makes me very . . . bitchy. Bossy. I'm sorry for that."

"Jude—"

"But that doesn't mean I'm letting you off the hook. I can't watch you walk into the lion's mouth. So I'm asking you, for me. For my sake. Follow your head and not your heart. Err on the side of caution. Cut him loose."

I feel an ache in my chest. "He said he didn't do it."

"No shit, Sherlock."

I shoot her a look.

"I'm sorry, that was unkind." She thinks a minute. "Here's an idea. Don't see him for a week. We'll know a lot more in just a week. Maybe Lombardo will find out something; maybe you'll get another note. Seven days, that's all."

Easy for her to say. I feel like I need him now. I remember the weekend together, how sweet he was, and how open with me. He made love to me, he held me. He said things, things that thrilled me. Things it hurts to remember now. Tears come to my eyes; I blink them back. "You're tough, Jude."

"The stakes are high, Mary. I want to win."

And either way, I lose. Because the ache inside me is telling me something, and it's too strong to be something else.

I'm in love.

21

I feel like everyone's watching me the next morning when I get off the elevator and walk to my desk. The secretaries in my area gaze at me bathetically, to them I'm the Young Widow Times Two. A partner glances back at me, wondering whether my billable hours will fall off. A messenger pushing a mail cart hurries by with a sideways glance. His look says, The broad must be some kind of jinx.

Why are they thinking about me? Why aren't they thinking about Brent?

I feel shaky, disoriented. Nothing seems familiar here, least of all Brent's desk. There's a blotter with floral edges where there used to be a friendly clutter of wind-up toys and a rubber-band gun. Brent's mug—WHAT DO I LOOK LIKE, AN INFORMATION BOOTH?—is gone. A calendar with fuzzy kittens has replaced a portrait of Luciano Pavarotti. The air smells like nothing at all; I can't believe I miss the tang of Obsession. What I miss is Brent. He deserved a long and happy life. He deserved to be singing his heart out somewhere, for the sheer joy of it.

Somebody's grandmother is sitting in Brent's chair. She introduces herself as Miss Pershing and refuses to call me anything but Miss DiNunzio. Her dull gray hair is pulled back into a French twist, and she wears a pink Fair Isle sweater held together at the top by a gold-plated chain. She's been a secretary in the Estates Department for thirty years. She brings me coffee on a tray.

It makes me want to cry.

I close my door and stare at the pile of mail on my desk. Without Brent, it's not organized into Good and Evil and totters precariously to the left. Mixed in with the thick case summaries and fuck-you letters are batches of envelopes in somber pastel shades. I remember them from before. Sympathy cards, dispensing a generic sentiment in every cursive iteration imaginable: *My thoughts/feelings are with you/your loved ones at this time of difficulty/of sorrow. May you have the comfort/solace of your loved ones/faith in God at this time.*

I can't bring myself to read any of the mail, especially the sympathy cards. They're only a comfort to people who don't know anyone who died.

I poke at a pink card on the top of the mail, and the tower topples over. It fans out across my desk, revealing at its center a bulky manila envelope bearing my name scrawled in pen.

Odd.

Miss Pershing's sheared the top off the envelope, and so neatly that there's barely any tearing. I open it. Inside is a piece of blue notepaper which says FROM THE DESK OF JACKIE O at the top and reads:

> Mary—
> I cleaned out Brent's desk. Thank you for everything, and for being so good to Brent. You may need this.
>
> Love, Jack

Stuck in the envelope is Brent's rubber-band gun. I smile, and am trying not to cry, when I remember the notes.

The notes! Brent kept them for me. Where are they?

I ransack my desk, but they're not there. I rush out to Miss Pershing's desk, and she watches, aghast, as I slam through the drawers. They're all empty except for typing paper and Stalling letterhead.

Where are the notes? Brent would have put them someplace safe. He took care of me.

I run back to my office and call Jack, but he's not at home. I leave a message, asking him to call back. I feel panicked. It doesn't make sense that Jack would take them, but maybe he'll know where they are. I still have my hand on the telephone receiver when it rings, jangling in my palm.

"DiNunzio?" barks Starankovic. His voice has a Monday-morning-I'm-refreshed punch to it. "You changed your number? I had to go through the switchboard."

"I'm sorry—"

"When are the interviews?"

I cringe. I'd totally forgotten. "My secretary—"

"Don't blame it on him, DiNunzio. Set 'em up today or I file the motion."

"Bernie—"

Click.

I hang up the phone by the pile of disordered mail. I should straighten it up. It's the Next Thing to do and I should do it. Dictate, return phone calls, back-fuck. I pick up an envelope, a white hand-delivery from Thomas, Main & Chandler, the third firm in the holy trinity. It must be a response to a motion I filed last week. Last week, when Brent was telling me to call the cops.

What did the Mike-voice say? *I tried. I tried.*

I put the envelope back down, feeling empty inside. Hollow. Aching. Exactly how I felt after Mike died, and how I was beginning not to feel before Brent was killed. I let the leaden sensation leech into my bones, into my soul. A little white pillowcase of a soul that turned black the instant of my birth, and even blacker when the men I love were killed on my account.

Suddenly, someone is clearing his throat directly above me. I look up into the bland visage of Martin H. Chatham IV.

"How do you tolerate it?" he says, with as much emotion as I've ever heard from him.

"Stand what?"

"That blasted clock!" Martin sits down in one of the Stalling-issue chairs in front of my desk and crosses his legs.

I look over my shoulder. 9:15. "You get used to it. Sort of."

"I don't see how. But you'll be vacating this office after June, *n'est-ce pas*? When we make our new litigation partners." His tone is oh-so-controlled, but I'm in no mood to fence.

"I hope so."

"Come on, Mary. We both know you're on track."

"I am? I guess I haven't thought about it lately."

Martin's face changes, as if he's remembered his manners. "Yes. Of course. I'm sorry about your secretary."

"Thank you."

"Damn drunk drivers. It's a terrible way to go."

I flash on the car as it explodes into Brent's body. And Mike's. I feel stunned.

Martin tosses some papers onto my desk. "Here are a couple of deposition notices in *Harbison's*. They're for the two supervisors, Breslin and Grayboyes."

I should call him on it, but I feel upset, off balance. I bear down and say the Next Thing. "I talked to Starankovic. It's taken care of."

He looks mildly surprised. "Did you postpone them?"

"Yes. Starankovic wants to take some employee interviews. I told him I'd think about it."

"I know you. You won't let him do that."

"I won't?"

"You? Voluntarily expose your employees to interviews with the enemy, without benefit of counsel? So that they can say anything? It goes against all those hot-blooded instincts of yours, even if there is precedent for it."

"He's going to file a motion if we don't consent."

"Bah! Is the man a glutton for punishment?" Martin can always tap into the our-team-kicked-ass mentality that flows like blood at Stalling.

"He might win it. Even if he doesn't, it'll cost Harbison's more to fight the motion than it will to let him do the interviews."

"Money's no object, Mary, when it's the client's."

I don't bother forcing a smile.

"By the by, I understand you'll be handling the new age case for Harbison's. The plaintiff's named Hart, right?" He gets up, tugging at suspenders needlepointed with flying owls.

"Right."

"Sam wasn't sure you were ready, but I told him it was time we gave you a case of your own. If you need a hand, let me know. I'll keep it to myself," he says with a wink.

He's about to leave when Ned suddenly sticks his head in the doorway. His jacket is off and one hand is hidden behind his back. "Mary?" he says, in the split second before he spots Martin.

"Young Waters!" Martin booms. "What brings you up to this neck of the woods?"

"I thought I'd stop in to see Mary." Ned beams at me from the doorway. His smile says, We're lovers now.

I can't help but return the smile. I feel it too. Bonded to him invisibly, by virtue of the fact that he's been that close. When there's not many who have.

Martin tugs at Ned's shirtsleeve like an insistent child. "Haven't seen much of you lately at the club."

"No. I haven't been there."

"Working hard or hardly working?"

"I just haven't had a chance to sail much yet this spring."

"Too bad. I got out on Sunday. Had a beautiful day, a beautiful day. You're welcome along anytime. Alida would love another lesson," he says, with measurable warmth. His hand rests on Ned's shoulder. "She's darn good for a sixteen-year-old, don't you agree?"

"She's good," Ned says.

Martin turns to me. "Waters here taught Alida more in one afternoon than that school in Annapolis did all last summer." He slaps Ned on the back. "How about this Sunday, my man? What are you doing this weekend? Why don't you head over for brunch? We'll spend all afternoon on the water. What do you say?"

"Uh, I'm busy." Ned flashes me a grin. His eyes are bright, and his look is undisguised. "I have big plans."

Martin looks from Ned to me. His smile fades slowly. "Do my eyes deceive me?"

"It depends on what they're telling you," Ned says, with a laugh.

"Ned—" I'm not sure how to finish the sentence. I don't want Ned telling Martin about us. Not when I'm about to break us up, at least temporarily.

"What?" Ned asks, smiling. "Don't you want to tell the world? I do."

Martin looks back and forth between us again. "Say it ain't so, Joe," he says.

I'm not sure I like Martin's tone. Neither does Ned, who bristles. "Something wrong, Martin?"

"With you and DiNunzio?" Martin asks. "Of course not. I'm surprised, that's all."

"So am I," Ned answers lightly. "She's the best thing that ever happened to me."

I shoot Ned a warning glance.

Martin pats Ned's shoulder. "Don't take offense, Waters."

"None taken," Ned says abruptly, brushing past Martin to me. "Now if you'll excuse us." He whips his hand out from behind his back, but it's covered by a gray wool jacket. The jacket conceals something huge, almost as big as his arm.

Martin clears his throat behind Ned. "Well. It looks like you won't be needing me."

"I can handle it from here," Ned calls back, and Martin closes the door. Ned beams at me. "Guess what the bulge is. And it's not that I'm happy to see you, even though I am happy to see you."

"You didn't have to do anything."

"I know that. Now guess. It's in disguise." He wiggles the jacket, and it makes a crinkling sound.

"A really big muffin?"

"You're half right." He snaps the jacket off

with a magician's flourish. Underneath is a full bouquet of rich red roses, wrapped in cellophane. "Ta-da!"

"Jeez, Ned!"

He hands the bouquet to me and kisses me on the cheek. "These are for you, sweetheart."

I take the crinkly bouquet and feel myself blushing. The flowers are beautiful. The man is charming. I am in love. How am I supposed to give this up? How am I supposed to hurt him?

"Do you like them?" he asks worriedly.

"They're lovely." I avoid his eye.

Suddenly, he takes my face in his hands and gives me a long, deep kiss. I return it over the sweet smell of the flowers, feeling touched and confused at the same time.

"I missed you last night. I really did." He kisses me again, but I pull away.

"You sent Judy."

"To take care of you. But she's no substitute, right?"

I nod. The roses are a cardinal red, and the underside of each petal has a dense and velvety texture. There are twelve in all. They must have cost a fortune.

"I did get you a muffin, by the way." He wrestles with the pocket of his suit jacket and pulls out a crumpled white bag the size of a hardball. "Blueberry." He shakes it beside his ear like a light bulb. "It's in three hundred and fifty-seven pieces at this point. Sorry about that." He sets it down on my desk.

"Thank you."

"You still don't look happy. Was Martin giving you a hard time?"

"Uh, yeah. First he holds back on the two deposition notices, the ones I told you about. Then he tells me he's the one who told Berkowitz to give me the *Hart* case, not the other way around. I think he's trying to save face."

"How do you know?"

"How do I know what?"

"That Martin wasn't the one to suggest it to Berkowitz?"

"That's not what Berkowitz said. Implied, anyway."

Ned looks skeptical. "Maybe Berkowitz wasn't telling the truth. Maybe it was Martin who suggested you get the case."

"I don't understand. Why would Martin champion my cause, Ned? You saw him just now."

"That was because he wants to fix me up with his daughter. It wasn't directed at you."

"No?"

"No. I'd take Martin over Berkowitz any day."

"I'd take Berkowitz over Martin any day."

We regard each other over the flowers. We seem to be lined up on opposing sides of a class war. It breaks the mood—which is a godsend, for what I have to do.

"Is this our first fight?" he asks, with a sad smile.

"Ned—"

"Then I have something to say." He grabs the flowers and puts them on the desk. Then he walks over to me and takes me in his arms. "I'm sorry."

I can smell his aftershave, familiar to me now, and feel the heavy cotton of his shirt. "Ned—"

"You don't need a hard time from me this morning, do you?" He hugs me tighter, rocking a little, and I feel myself relax into the comfort of his arms. My hands slip easily around the small of his back. He wears no undershirt, which I love, and his shirt is slightly damp from the walk to work.

"The notes are missing, Ned."

He kisses my hair. "No, they're not. I have them."

I pull away from him. "You have the notes, Ned? *You?*"

"Not with me. I put them in my safe at home, behind the picture of that old Lightning, at Wellfleet."

"Where did you get them?"

"The notes? I went to the office after the memorial service."

"Why?"

"I had work to do, honey. I was going to work the weekend, but we spent it in bed, remember? I stopped by your office and found them on top of your desk with a note."

"But why were you even on this floor? Your office is on—"

"I don't know. I just was."

"Why did you go in my office?"

"On impulse, I guess. I wanted to be around something of yours. Look at your handwriting, you know. It was goony." He laughs nervously. "What's with all the questions?"

Fear rises in my throat. He has no reason to be

on my floor, no right to come into my office. I imagine him rooting through my desk in the glow of the clock. I hope Judy isn't right about him, but I can't take any more chances. I steel myself. "Ned, I can't see you for a while."

"What?" He looks shocked.

"I want you to bring the notes to the office as soon as you can. Maybe you should go home at lunch."

"What are you saying? What about us?"

"I'm . . . not ready for us. Not yet. Not now."

"Wait a minute, what's happening?" His voice breaks. "Mary, I love you!"

He hadn't said that, not once the whole weekend, though I wondered how deep his feelings went. Now I know, if he's telling the truth. *I love you.* The words reach out and grab me by the heart. I want so much for it not to be him, but I'm afraid Judy's right. And now I'm afraid of him. "I need time."

"Time? Time for what?"

"To think. I want the notes back."

He grabs my arms. "Mary, I love you. I'll get you the notes. I was only trying to help. I didn't think they should be left out like that, where anybody could pick them up."

I can't look at him. "Ned, please."

He releases me suddenly. "I get it. You think it's me, don't you? You suspect me." His tone is bitter.

"I don't know what I think."

"You think it's me. You think I'm trying to kill you. I can't believe this." He throws up his hands in disgust. "We spent the weekend together,

Mary. I told you things I never told anybody else in the world!"

He falls silent suddenly. I look at him, and his face is full of anger.

"That's why, isn't it?" he asks quietly. "Because of what I told you. I was depressed, so now you have me pegged for a psycho killer. Oh, this is beautiful. This is really beautiful. Tell me again how proud you are of me, Mary."

"That's not it. I just need time, Ned."

"Fine. You just got it." He stalks to the door but stops there, his back to me. "Whoever it is, they'll still be after you. And I won't be around to keep you safe."

I feel sick inside. He hurts so much, and it hurts to see him go.

"Is this really what you want?" he asks, without turning around.

I close my eyes. "Yes."

"So be it." The next sound is the harsh *ca-chunk* of the door as it closes.

When I open my eyes, I'm alone. I cross my arms and try to keep it together, looking around my office at the books and the files and the diplomas. They're so cold, fungible. They could belong to anybody, and they do. Every lawyer here has the same rust-colored accordion files, the same framed diplomas from the same handful of schools. My eyes fall on the roses, so out of place in this cold little office with the clock staring in.

10:36.

I feel like I have to regroup, to sort out everything that's been happening. I need to think things out in a safe place, but I can't remember the last time I felt safe. In Mike's arms. Another time.

In church, as a child.

In church, what a thought. I haven't been to church in ages and had lapsed way before that. But I always felt safe in church as a little girl. Protected, watched over. The idea grows on me as I stand, frozen, facing the clock.

I think of the church I grew up in, Our Lady of Perpetual Help. I was a believer then. A believer in a God who watched over us all, the cyclists and the gay secretaries. A believer in the goodness of all men, even partners, and lovers too. A believer in our fraternity with animals, including cats who won't rub against your leg no matter what.

I grab my blazer from behind the door and stop by Miss Pershing's desk. "Miss Pershing, I'll be out of the office for a couple of hours."

"Oh?" She takes off her glasses and places them carefully on her shallow chest, where they dangle on a lorgnette. "Where shall I say you are, Miss DiNunzio?"

"You shouldn't say, but the answer is, in church."

For the first time, Miss Pershing smiles at me.

I hail a cab outside our building. The cabbie, an old man with greasy white hair, stabs out his cigarette and flips down the flag on the meter. "Where to?"

"Our Lady of Perpetual Help. Ninth and Wolf."

"Lawyers go to church?" A final puff of smoke bursts from his mouth.

"Only when they have to."

He chuckles thickly, and it ends in a coughing spasm. We take off in silence, except for the crackling of the radio. The cab swings onto Broad Street, which bisects the city at City Hall and runs straight to South Philly. Broad Street is congested, as usual. We stop in the cool shadow cast by a skyscraper and then lurch into the bright light of the sun. I crank open the window, watching us pass through light and dark, listening to the old cabbie swear at the traffic, and trying to remember the last time I was in church.

Bless me, Father, for I have sinned. It's been 3,492,972 weeks since my last confession. The Jurassic Period. When I did everything the nuns told me to, so I wouldn't get my knuckles rapped, and memorized the Baltimore Catechism. I made my First Holy Communion at age seven, during which the priest put a wafer onto my tongue that he said was the body of Jesus Christ. I didn't swallow it until right before they took my picture, and my baby face is beatific in the photo. I'd swallowed my slice of Our Savior and was overjoyed that this cannibalistic act had not sent lightning zigzagging to my head.

"Shit!" The cabbie bangs on the steering wheel, foiled in his attempt to run a traffic light. Sunlight blazes into the old cab, illuminating its dusty interior and heating its duct-taped seat covers. "You think they'd time these goddamn lights, like on Chestnut Street. But no, that would make too much sense."

I nod, half listening. As soon as the light

changes, the cabbie guns the motor and we leap forward into the tall shadow cast by the Fidelity Building. Its darkness comes as a relief and seems to quiet even the irritable driver.

As a child, I used to look at my communion picture on top of our boxy television. I wanted to be as good as the little girl in my picture, she of the praying hands and the lacquered corkscrews. But I wasn't her. I knew it inside. The church told me so. They taught me that Jesus Christ suffered on the cross and died because of me. All because of me. Blood dripped from his crown of thorns and flowed in rivulets from rough bolts hammered clear through his wrists and insteps. His agony was all my fault. I felt so sorry, as a little girl, and so ashamed. Of myself.

"Hey, asshole!" shouts the cabbie, hanging out the window. "Move that shitwagon! I'm tryin' to make a living here!" The cab bucks violently in the shade. I grab for the yellowed hand strap just as we burst free of the snarled traffic into the light.

And in my religious life, what happened next was calamitous. I grew up. It was Luke who said that whoever does not accept the kingdom of God like a child will not enter it, and I stopped being a child. I stopped accepting on faith and started to doubt. Then I started to question, which brought the heavens, in the form of school administration, crashing down upon my head. I took biological issue with the Resurrection and was suspended for three days.

Light and dark, light and dark.

That's when it started, the split between me and the church. And me and my twin. For as I began to turn away from the light, Angie began to embrace it. I resented the church, for making me feel so terrible about myself as a child and for dividing Angie and me. In time, I stopped going to mass altogether, and my parents didn't force the issue. The three of them went every Sunday, while I stayed home with the Eagles pregame show. They prayed for my soul. I prayed for the Eagles.

"Do you remember Roman Gabriel?" I say to the cabbie. We're almost there.

He looks into the rearview mirror with rheumy eyes. "Sure. Quarterback for the Birds. We got him from the Rams."

"Do you remember when?"

He squints, in thought. "'Seventy-three, I think. Yeah, in 'seventy-three."

So long ago. I can't do the math in my head.

"What a fruit he was," says the cabbie. "We shoulda kept Liske."

Bless me, Father, for I have sinned. I can't remember a thing about my last confession.

And I can't forget a thing about my abortion.

22

It was so long ago.

I never told anyone, not even Mike. I intended to tell him, but changed my mind when we found out he couldn't have kids. It would have made it worse. I know it did for me.

"This it?" says the cabbie, pulling up in front of the red-brick fortress on the corner of Ninth and Wolf. He ducks down to see it better. "It don't look like a church. What'd you say it was? Our Lady of Perpetual—"

"Motion." I get out of the cab and throw him a ten-dollar bill, with no tip. "Here. This is from a fruit I know."

"Crazy broad," he mutters. The cab lurches off.

I glance around to see if I've been followed, but the street is quiet. I turn and confront my church. From the outside, there is no way to tell what type of building it is. The windows are bricked in and the heavy oak doors are squared off at the top. But for the black sign that says the times of the masses in tiny white numbers, you would think that OLPH is a Mafia front. Except that the Mafia front is across the street.

In contrast to the bleakness of the church is the grassy lot beside it, a sheltered grotto for the statue of the Virgin Mary, Our Lady of Perpetual Help herself. I remember thinking that the grotto was a miraculous place, a baby's blanket of perfect green grass tucked away from the city sidewalks. Gazing benignly over the grass, high above the electric trolley cars, was the slim, robed figure of the Virgin, tall as a spire in white marble, with her hands out-stretched in welcome. I felt peaceful there as a child.

I have the same feeling today. The statue looks the same, and so does the grass. It's verdant and thick; it looks newly mown and raked. Tulips dip their heavy heads at the statue's pedestal. No one's around, so I sit on the bench in front of it, completing my Catholic impersonation. I'm eye level with the pedestal's inscription, but don't have to look at the Roman-carved letters to know what they say. I remember:

VIRGIN MARY
MARIAN YEAR 1954
GIFT OF MR. AND MRS. RAFAELLO D. SABATINI

Mr. and Mrs. Rafaello D. Sabatini owned the Mafia front across the street, but who cared? They were good Catholics, they supported the church and the school. That was all that mattered.

At the statue's feet are plastic bouquets of red roses, Mary's flower, and along her hem are the lipsticked kisses of the insanely faithful. Rosaries dangle from her inanimate fingers, and she wears a crown made of glitter pasted onto cardboard, as if by a child. A little girl, no doubt, for little girls love the Virgin. Was I a little girl like that once? I feel a stab of pain. What does Mary think of Mary now, since her abortion?

I squint up at Mary's eyes, there at the top of the tall statue. She doesn't answer me but gazes straight ahead. She's innocent, the Eternal Virgin. Her conception, unlike mine, was Immaculate. She knows nothing of couplings that happen to Catholic girls who are on the third date of their life, with Bobby Mancuso from Latin Club. Who, despite his braces, is terribly cute and plays varsity basketball. Who takes her to McDonald's and then, in his Corvair, kisses her hotly, ignoring her protestations. Who doesn't rape her exactly, but who complains that he's in intense pain from something called blue balls, which means either that his balls are turning blue because the blood to them is cut off, or there's too much blood getting to them. She's confused about the physiology of the blue balls but understands clearly that his pain is all because of her.

His agony is all her fault.

Which makes her sorry, so sorry.

He says if she would just let him touch

between her legs, just let him do what he wanted, his pain would be relieved and his balls wouldn't be blue anymore. And before she knows it, her new plaid kilt is up and he is inside her. It's over so fast, and the whole thing is so painful and strange, so impossibly *strange*, that she's really not sure she's not a virgin Mary anymore. Until she gets home and finds the spots on her flowered Carter's. Red splotches, shaped like infernal stars, among the delicate pink blossoms. Then she's pregnant and decides to have an abortion.

No one knew. Not even Angie, and especially not Angie. I was terrified. I was ashamed. I had committed a mortal sin and would burn in eternal fire unless I repented. But the only way to repent was to confess my sin to God and to my parents, who would die from the shock. I felt trapped between commandments: THOU SHALT NOT KILL and HONOR THY FATHER AND THY MOTHER.

Not only that, but both Angie and I had been awarded scholarships to Penn, which was my only hope of going to college. Would the university extend mine until my baby—and Bobby's, who ignored me from that day forward—was born? Of course not. Even if they did, how would I support a child? My mother couldn't; her piecework sewing barely bought my uniform and books. My father couldn't; he was already on disability.

I had no choice.

I found Planned Parenthood in the Yellow Pages and took the bus to center city one Saturday morning, with an Etienne Aigner wallet full of confirmation money. The abortion would cost the $150 earmarked for a white ten-speed, but I was putting away childish things. Of necessity.

When I got to the clinic, I filled out some forms, on which I lied about my age and changed my name. I told them I was Jane Hathaway, after Nancy Kulp in *The Beverly Hillbillies*, because she seemed like such a classy lady. Then I was taken to see a counselor, a black woman named Adelaide Huckaby, who wore an African dashiki. Her nappy hair was close-cropped, revealing a marvelously round head, and her eyes were a dark brown, like her skin. We talked for a long time, and she gave me a warm hug when I cried. "You want to think about it some more?" she asked. "You can change your mind, even now."

I said no.

Adelaide came with me into what they called the Procedure Room, and we waited for the doctor together. I was lying flat on a skinny and unforgiving table in a hospital gown, with my knees supported from underneath. On the ceiling was a circle of fluorescent light. I tried not to think of it as an all-seeing eye, looking down on me from above, witnessing everything in mute horror.

"I see you get those blotches on your chest," Adelaide said softly. "My sister gets 'em too. Only you can't see 'em so well on her."

I smiled.

"It's all right, baby. Everything's gonna be all right."

Then the doctor came in. He wore granny

glasses and gave me a brief hello before he disappeared behind the white tent covering my knees. Adelaide took my hand and held it. She seemed to know I needed a hand to hold on to, and hers was strong and generous. While the doctor worked away, Adelaide described the procedure for me, her voice quietly resonant.

"Now he's inserting the speculum, so you'll feel some coldness. You know what a speculum is, baby?"

I shook my head, no.

"That's what your doctor uses during a pelvic exam, the same instrument, to hold the walls of the vagina apart."

I had never had a pelvic exam. This was, in effect, my first trip to the gynecologist. I didn't tell Adelaide that. I was supposed to be nineteen and was already feeling bad about lying.

"Now he's going to give you two shots, into your cervix, to relax the muscle."

"Needles?"

"Don't worry. In about two minutes you'll feel two tiny little pinches, not too bad."

Adelaide was as good as her word. One. Two. Like little pinpricks.

"Now we're comin' up on the part of the procedure where the doctor's going to dilate you. He's gonna use two rods, one small and one large, to open up your cervix. This is gonna be a little uncomfortable for you, honey, and I want you to hold my hand good and tight. It's gonna feel like cramps, just like the kind you get on your period."

"I don't get cramps."

"Not even the first day?"

I shook my head, no, feeling embarrassed. At that age, I felt inferior because I didn't get menstrual cramps, which kept Angie and my classmates popping blue Midols in French class. Real women got cramps.

"Well," she said, "you're a lucky girl."

I had never thought of it that way. Suddenly, I felt a violent squeeze around my lower abdomen, then another. I bit my lip, closing my eyes to the luminous cyclops in the ceiling. The pain came again and again, bringing tears to my eyes. I held on to Adelaide, and she to me, saying, "Just a couple more minutes. Hold on to my hand, honey."

Then it stopped. No more pain, no more cramping. Adelaide explained about the curette while the doctor scraped the baby off the insides of my uterus. I felt nothing.

It was over when the scraping was done. The doctor left the room, saying a quick good-bye. Adelaide stood over me, smoothing my hair back from my face like my own mother would have. She looked so happy and relieved I felt like I had graduated from something.

"Adelaide, I have to tell you something. My name—"

"Hush, baby," she said, smiling down at me. "You think I don't watch television?"

She helped me to a recovery room. I had to leave her and was led to a chair near eight other patients. Some of them were having cookies and juice, others were resting in their seats. I stayed there awhile, leaning my head back into the cushions, feeling a mixture of relief and sadness. In time, another counselor came by and roused me. She had an intense medical-student look about her, and she told me in a technical fashion about the pads and the bleeding and the follow-up and the product of the pregnancy.

When I got home, I mumbled something about the flu and crawled into bed with my stuffed Snoopy. I felt raw inside, achy. I stayed in bed through dinner, fake-sleeping when Angie came in at night. I just lay there, bleeding secretly into a pad attached to a strappy sanitary belt. Thinking about how I went in full and came out empty.

The product of the pregnancy.

I knew it was a baby; I didn't kid myself about that. But for me, that wasn't the end of the question. We killed in war; we killed in self-defense. Sometimes killing was murder and sometimes it wasn't. I was confused. I felt that what I did was right, even though I felt just as certainly that it was wrong. My church, being a lot smarter than I, exhibited no such ambivalence. It had all the answers from the get-go, so I knew my family's prayers for me were lost for good. They would disappear on the way to heaven like the smoky trail of an altar candle.

I look up at Our Lady of Perpetual Help, searching in vain for her eyes. If anyone could understand, Mary could. She had also sacrificed her child. She had no choice either.

"Are you all right, miss?" asks a voice.

I look up, with a shock. An old man is peer-

226 - LISA SCOTTOLINE

ing into my face, not ten inches from my nose. He looks worried, and I realize, to my surprise, that I've been crying. I wipe my cheek with a hand.

"Here you go," he says. He tucks a broom under his arm and offers me a folded red bandanna from the pocket of his baggy pants. "Take it."

"No, thanks. I'm fine."

"Here." Before I can stop him, he puts the bandanna up to my nose. It smells like fabric softener. "Give 'er a blow. A good hard blow."

"Are you serious?"

"Go for it."

So for a minute I forget that I'm over ten years old, a lawyer and a sinner to boot, and let the church janitor blow my nose.

"Good for you!" He folds up the bandanna and tucks it back into his pocket. He's cute, with a wizened face and sparse tufts of white Bozo hair at each temple. His nose is small and blunted at its tip, as if by a common spade. A safety pin holds his bifocals together, but his blue eyes are sharp behind the glasses. "You got troubles?"

"I'm okay."

He eases himself onto the bench, leaning on the wiggly broom for support. "That why you're cryin'? 'Cause you're okay?"

"I don't know. I don't even know why I came here."

"For help. That's why people come, for help."

"You think the church can help?"

"Sure. It's helped me all my life—God has. He's guided me." The old man leans back and smiles. His teeth are too perfect. Dentures, like my father.

"You believe."

"Of course." He looks at the statue, his back making a tiny hunch. "When was your last confession?" It sounds odd, coming from him.

"Are you a janitor?"

"Are you?"

"I'm a lawyer."

"I'm a priest! Ha!" He cackles happily, banging his broom on the ground. "Gotcha, didn't I?"

I laugh. "That's not fair, Father."

"No, it isn't, is it? I'm undercover, like in *Miami Vice*." His eyes smile with delight.

I turn away from his bright eyes, confounded by his ruse and his warmth. I don't remember priests being like this when I was little. They were distant, and disapproving.

"I'm Father Cassiotti. I'm too old to do the masses, Father Napole does that. I assist him. I help however I can. I hear confessions. I tend the Virgin."

I don't say anything. I'm not sure what to say. I look at my navy blue pumps planted in the grass.

"See my Darwin tulips? They're doing just fine. The hyacinths should be up any day now. They're always slow in coming. They need some coaxing, but I don't push it. They come up when they're ready. I just wait."

I stare at my shoes.

"I'm good at waiting."

I can almost hear the smile in his voice. My heart wells up. He's a good man, a kind man.

He's the best of the church, of what's right about the church. I take a deep breath. "Where were you when I was a teenager?"

Into my ear, he whispers, "Waukegan."

I burst into laughter.

"Exiled," he says, without rancor. "And where were you when you were a teenager?"

"Here."

"You went to school at OLPH? So, a long time ago, you were a good Catholic. Tell me, are we gonna get you back?"

"I don't think you want me back, Father."

"Of course we do! God loves us all. He forgives us all."

"Not me. Not this." I look up at the Virgin, but she won't look at me.

He slaps his knee. "Let's make a reconciliation! Right now."

"Confession? Here?"

"Why not?"

"There's no confessional. I can see you."

"Silly! Why do we have to sit in a telephone booth! In Waukegan, I performed many confessions face-to-face, although I'll admit I've never done one outdoors." He chuckles. "You don't need a booth for a confession, my dear. All you need is to examine your conscience. If you resolve not to sin in the future, confess, and accept your penance, you've reconciled yourself with God."

I search the eyes behind the bifocals. He makes it sound so easy, but I know it isn't. There are bodies on my back, big ones and little ones, and despite the kindness in his eyes, I understand that they're mine to bear. I can't confess, not to his blue eyes, not in the yellow sunshine, not before the white Virgin on the green grass. The colors are too dense here, like a child's box of crayons, and too painfully pretty. "God won't forgive me, Father."

"I'm sure that God already has, my dear. But I don't think you have forgiven yourself."

Suddenly, we're interrupted by a flock of apoplectic *mammarellas* in flowered housedresses. "Father Cassiotti! Father Cassiotti! Thank God we found you! The church door is locked, and the mass is in fifteen minutes! We can't get in!"

Their agitation rattles him. His hands shake as he reaches into his pocket and pulls out a jingling ring of keys. "My goodness, I'm sorry, ladies." He looks at me worriedly. "I have to go open the church. Will you excuse me?"

"I should be going anyway." I rise to my feet, uncertainly.

"No, please. Stay here. Please."

"Father, your flowers look so good!" chirps one of the women, grabbing Father Cassiotti by the elbow. "Look at them, Conchetta. So pretty!"

"It's a sin!" adds a second, taking his other arm.

They surge forward like a rugby team, pound for pound outweighing the little priest, and engulf him in their enthusiasm. They sweep him to the church like a winning coach, and all I can see of him is his bony hand in the air, bearing its janitor's key ring. I shout good-bye, and the key ring jingles back.

I decide to walk back to the office. It'll clear my head, and it would be impossible to find a cab down here anyway. I realize that Father

Cassiotti is right: I have to forgive myself. But I don't know how, even so many years later. I head north toward the center of the city, leaving behind the blocks that measure my girlhood.

Once out of the neighborhood, I feel nervous again. The sun is white-hot, unseasonably so, and leaves me exposed on the bare sidewalks. My walk picks up to a run, and before I know it I'm hustling through the city blocks. I glance around for the dark sedan but keep moving, jogging past babies in strollers and teenagers hanging out on the corner.

I'm slowed by the busy lunchtime crowd at Pat's, a popular cheese-steak stand across from a playground. I thread my way through the crowd; a couple of the men in line look at me curiously. My armholes are wet underneath my blazer and blotches itch on my chest. I'm about to cross the street, still going north, when I see the figures.

About fifty feet away, at the edge of the basketball court, two big men are arguing. A crowd of basketball players and truants collects around the pair. Even at this distance, something about the men looks familiar.

I freeze when I recognize them.

It's Detective Lombardo. And Berkowitz.

23

I duck behind a minivan parked on Federal Street
and watch them through its sooty windows.
The argument escalates as Berkowitz gestures
wildly, almost out of control. Suddenly, he drives
his fist into Lombardo's cheek. Blood pours from
the detective's nose. He cups it in pain, staggering backward.

Berkowitz eyes the crowd uneasily, then stalks
off the court. The onlookers applaud as he
climbs into his black Mercedes sedan, parked ille-
gally at the curb, and drives away. Lombardo
shuffles off in the opposite direction, cradling his
nose. The crowd boos loudly. "Pussy!" they
shout. "Hit 'em back, you dumb fuck!"

I draw a breath. It feels like the first one in five minutes. What the hell is going on? What are they doing, having a fight in the middle of South Philly? I remember what Lombardo said after the memorial service—that Berkowitz was very interested in the investigation. Is the investigation what they were fighting about? What else could it be, if not something having to do with Brent's death? And maybe even Mike's?

I'm scared, and Father Cassiotti's no help now. Apparently, neither are the police. I consider busting into Lombardo's office and demanding an explanation, or busting into Berkowitz's office and demanding an explanation, but who am I kidding? I'm not a gunslinger; I'm in way over my head. My first thought is to run, to get the hell out of Dodge, but where can I go? The only person I know who lives out of the city is Angie.

Angie!

In the convent, near Baltimore. The idea appeals to me immediately. I'll bang on the convent doors, pound them until they let me in. I'll say it's a family emergency, which it is, and they'll open the doors. They have to, they're a convent. What could be safer than a convent?

I look around for a phone and spot one back at Pat's. I walk over to it, trying not to break into a dead run in front of the noisy crowd of office workers and construction jocks. Almost as soon as I pick up the greasy receiver, a rangy black basketball player gets in line behind me to use it. Behind him comes a mailman. I reach Judy and tell her what I saw, shouting into the receiver over the crowd noise.

"He *punched* him?" Judy says. "What are they doing down there anyway? What are *you* doing down there?"

The basketball player makes a pleading face for the phone, and I give him a one-minute sign.

"I'm leaving the city, Judy. For the night, anyway."

"Where are you going?"

I can barely hear her. I put a finger in my free ear. "I was going to get the notes from Ned after lunch, but I can't. Will you call him and get them?"

"*Ned* has the notes? I was wondering where they were!"

"Keep them someplace safe, okay?"

The basketball player folds his hands in mock prayer.

"Judy, I have to go, somebody wants to use the phone. He's begging already."

"But where are you going to stay tonight? You can stay with me, you know that."

An old man in a mesh cap that says OLD FART gets in line for the phone behind the mailman.

"Thanks, but I got a better idea. Call you tomorrow." I hang up.

"Thanks a lot," the ballplayer says, tucking the basketball under his arm. "I got to call my girl. We had a fight, you know what I'm sayin'?"

"I think so."

I push through the crowd, looking for a cab. One should be around soon; Pat's is like a magnet. My blotches announce themselves with a vengeance. I worry about running into Lombardo, Berkowitz, or whoever's following me. My head is spinning. I spot a yellow cab and jump in, slumping down all the way in the seat. Partly from exhaustion, partly from fear.

The cab driver is a streetwise manchild in a backwards Phillies cap. He eyes me warily over his shoulder. "Look, lady, I don't want no trouble in my cab."

"There won't be. Please, I have to go to a garage at Twenty-second and Pine. My car's there. Can we just go?"

He shakes his head. "You don't look like the type to be running from the cops, but you're sure runnin' from somethin'."

"I am. I'm running from . . . my boyfriend. We had a fight."

He breaks into a knowing grin. "Man trouble."

I nod. "We have to get out of here. Fast."

"You got it, gorgeous." He flips down the flag and guns the motor. He runs two lights as he zips up Twenty-second Street. At the same time, he manages to give me unsolicited advice on my love life, delivered to a rapper's beat: Gotta make 'em beg for it, gotta make 'em want it, gotta make 'em show respect. We're at the garage by the time he shifts into, "Gotta shop around."

"Right. Listen, would you do me a favor, please? Just wait here for two minutes until you see me drive out?"

"Ain't no way he coulda followed me, lady. I was bookin'."

I hand him a tip the size of the fare.

"All right!" he says appreciatively.

"It's a green BMW."

"A BMW? I like it! Which one, the 325 or the 535?"

"The 2002, from before you were born. It's lime green, you can't miss it." I get out of the cab.

"You gotta pick and choose, remember that now."

In ten minutes, I'm making my way through the western part of the city to the Schuylkill Expressway. I almost have an accident from driving with one eye on the rearview mirror. No one appears to be following me, and when I pull onto the expressway I begin to breathe easier. The traffic is light, and I switch lanes a couple of times to see if anyone behind me does the same. It takes only a minute for me to realize that everybody else is switching lanes in a similarly haphazard way.

Which looks normal.

I hit warp speed in the car Mike lovingly called the Snotmobile and bust through the city limits like I'm breaking the sound barrier. After a time I satisfy myself that no one's on my tail, and I feel freer, safer. Like I'm not trapped anymore, by the city and by whoever's after me there. I roll down the window and snap on the radio. I recognize the husky bass voice as George Michael's, in the middle of "Father Figure." I love that song. I turn it louder.

I remember going to visit Angie, singing along to the radio while Mike drove this car. My parents trailed us in their Oldsmobile, which meant we pulled over every ten minutes for them to catch up. It didn't bother Mike that my father poked along so. Nothing really fazed him, he was like Judy that way. He loved life, truly. He let it wash over him.

I swing the peppy BMW onto Route 1 heading south, serenaded by Prince. Route 1, the old Baltimore Pike, is more direct to the convent than I-95. If I don't get lost, I'll be there by nightfall.

Angie entered the convent just after we graduated from Penn. I majored in English, she in religion. "What kind of job will you get with that major?" I asked when she chose it, but she answered with a shrug. When she finally told us, my parents were delighted, but I was appalled. I screamed at her, told her she was throwing her life away. My mother begged me to stop, my father merely shook. I ran from the house. My last look back was at Angie. She sat there, impassive behind her coffee, dead calm at the vortex of a familial hurricane.

The traffic on Route 1 moves swiftly, fluidly. I catch barely a light. A woman I don't recognize sings a ballad. My thoughts turn to the convent.

Angie's first year as a novitiate was my first year as a law student. She wasn't allowed visitors, telephone calls, or even mail. It was to be a test of her commitment to a religious life, and we heard nothing from her. I felt an almost unendurable loss, as if she were held hostage by religious fanatics, which was my take on the situation anyway. Outside the cloister, life went on. My mother's eyes deteriorated, my father gained twenty pounds. I made law review and learned to trust men again. With Mike's help.

The sad song ends abruptly, in silence.

Which was the worst thing about Angie's life in the cloister. Her vow of silence. How could they silence Angie, who was so full of talk, of ideas? I remembered the nights we gossiped in our room, the whispered jokes in class, the shouted jeers on the walk home. So much talk, so much language. English and Italian at home, French in school, Latin at mass. No more.

The traffic thins out, the stoplights are fewer. Madonna comes on, *thumpa thumpa thumpa*, and I turn off the radio with a satisfying *click*. I hate Madonna; she's even more confused about Catholicism than I am. I barrel through the rural stretches south of Media, past dairy cows and old barns. The odor of manure wafts through the air. I step on the gas.

After Angie's first year, we were permitted to see her. The visits—four a year—were held in a small room called the Parlor, and there was a wooden screen between us, almost like the lattice in a garden trellis. I wasn't able to touch her, and there was no privacy; the room was filled with the equally excited families of the other nuns. I found the visits an exercise in frustration. I couldn't talk to Angie about anything that mattered, couldn't reach her in any meaningful way at all, so the garden trellis might as well have been made of concrete. All I could do was watch us grow apart. Over the years, her face thinned out and her demeanor grew subdued. By the time she became a professed sister five years later, I felt I hardly knew her at all. I hugged her then, after the mass, and cried most of the way home.

I speed by farm after farm, and all I see for a long time are cows and billboards. WELCOME TO

MARYLAND, says the sign when I cross the border. I wind slowly through Harford County, with its quaint farms and not-so-quaint trailer parks. The sun sets off to my left, behind a Bob's Big Boy. The car rumbles along quietly; my mind is a blank. The exit for the convent comes up. I twist the car off the highway, into a suburb near the convent. I forget the name of the town, but I recognize the landmarks. A housing development of fake English mews, then a housing development of fake French chateaux.

My anticipation sours slightly. I grow apprehensive. What if they won't let me stay? What if Angie's angry at me for coming? A hard ball begins to form in my chest. It seems to calcify as I drive by a diner where Mike and I ate lunch after he met Angie for the first time. I remember that lunch.

"I understand why you miss her so much," Mike said, fiddling with the top of a red squeeze bottle of ketchup. "It would mean a lot to me if she could be at our wedding."

"Our wedding?"

"Our wedding." He grinned and slid the ketchup bottle toward me. On the red cone of its lid hung a small diamond solitaire.

That was Mike's proposal, and I accepted, but Mike didn't get his wish. Angie wasn't allowed out of the cloister to go to his wedding.

They did let her go to his funeral, however.

24

I walk alongside the convent's high stone wall until I find the front gate. It's an ancient iron gate, painted in a color impossible to determine in the twilight: forest green, maybe, or black. I can't see through the gate—it's opaque and reaches at least ten feet high, culminating in a crucifix. Of course.

Boom! Boom! I bang on the gate. Its bubbled paint flakes off. *Boom! Boom! Boom!*

Silence.

"Is anybody there? Can anybody let me in?"

More silence.

Boom! "Please, it's an emergency! Please!"

"Wait a minute," says a thin female voice on

the other side. I hear the metallic clatter of a barrel latch being retracted, and the door opens a crack. One blue eye peers out from behind a rimless spectacle. I catch a glimpse of a white veil—a novitiate—whose face comes happily to life when she sees me. "You look exactly like one of my sisters!"

"Really?"

"Yes! Sister Angela Charles."

Her sister. I'll never get used to this. "Angela's my twin. I'm Mary DiNunzio. I need to see her. It's a . . . family emergency."

The novitiate looks alarmed. "Oh, my. Well. Good thing I was out here. Come in, please." She yanks on the iron gate, grunting with effort. I push on the gate from the outside, but even with both of us laboring, it'll only open enough to let me through sideways. "Sorry about that," she says, with an easy laugh.

"That's okay. I appreciate your letting me in."

"No problem. Follow me. I'll tell Mother you're here." She bounces ahead of me, up a flagstone path that winds through the grass to the convent. Over a hundred years old, the convent's made of Brandywine granite and covered with lush ivy. If it weren't holding my twin sister captive, I'd say it was beautiful. The roof is terra-cotta tile, like the rooftops of Florence, and the arched windows are a stained glass that seems to glow with deep colors, radiating light from within on this dusky evening.

As we approach the front door, unmarked except for the Sacred Heart at its keystone, I can hear the nuns singing in the chapel. Their voices, forty in all, carry in the still night, floating over the lawn. One of the voices belongs to Angie. An alto, like me.

"In we go," says the novitiate, as she opens the carved oak door.

It's the smell that hits me first, the smell of holy water. It's a faint and sweet scent, vaguely like rosewater. The novitiate's breath smells of it too, and I wonder how this is so, or if I'm imagining it. I hear the singing, louder now that I'm inside, and we pass the closed chapel doors, over which is stenciled:

CHAPEL
DEDICATED TO ST. JOSEPH
RECOLLECTION

Angie is inside.

The novitiate leads me to the parlor. Above the door it says:

PARLOR
DEDICATED TO ST. L. GONZAGA
DISCRETION, MODESTY

The novitiate flicks on a lamp, which barely illuminates the room. "Please wait a minute while I tell Mother that you're here," she says.

"Thank you."

She closes the door, leaving me alone. The parlor looks larger now that it's empty, but it still evokes frustration in me. I sit among the vacant wooden chairs on the civilian side of the trellis, wondering how many twin sisters have sat here in

the past century and if any of them felt like I do.
The order used to be much more isolated, and
Angie says there's talk of moving to a remote
location in the Adirondacks. That's so far away
I'd never get to see her. It makes me feel sick
inside.

"Miss DiNunzio?" says the novitiate, back at
the threshold. The singing intensifies with the
open door. "Come with me. Mother is waiting
to see you in her cabinet."

"Cabinet?"

"Office. Cabinet is the French term, but we
still use it."

"Force of habit, huh?"

She smiles.

"I got a million of 'em."

I follow her down the bare, narrow hallway.
The hardwood floors shine even in the dim light.
The novitiate pads ahead softly; I clatter
obscenely in my pumps. I look around the pale
walls, reading the writing stenciled in black let-
ters at the top. I HAVE A SAVIOR AND I TRUST IN
HIM. I KNOW NOTHING SWEETER THAN TO MORTI-
FY AND CONQUER SELF. WALK BEFORE ME AND BE
PERFECT.

The hallway ends in a white door, and the
singing stops suddenly. This is the door that
encloses the cloistered area. I live on the outside
of it; Angie lives on the inside. Over the jamb it
says: GIVE GLORY TO THE LORD OF LORDS AND HIS
MERCY ENDURETH FOREVER.

It should say: POINT OF NO RETURN.

We pass through the door in silence. I take in
everything as we go by, trying to imagine what

Angie's daily life is like. We enter another hall-way, also clean and spare, and come to a door on the left, over which is stenciled:

SUPERIORESS'S CABINET
DEDICATED TO OUR HOLY MOTHER
LONGANIMITY

"What does that mean?" I ask the novitiate. "Longan . . ."

"It's a toughie, isn't it? Longanimity. It means forbearance. This is your stop. Mother will be along in a minute. You can have a seat in her office."

"Thank you."

"Sure thing," she says and pads off.

I sit down in a hard mission chair across from a desk so clean it could be for sale. The office is empty and bare, except for a two-tier set of bookshelves and an old black rotary phone. The tinny fixture in the ceiling casts a dim pool of light over the desktop. My chest tightens around the ball at its core. I can't shake the feeling that I'm back in school, waiting in the principal's office to answer for some sin. Like an abortion.

Suddenly, with a *whoosh* of her thick habit, the Mother Superior enters the office. She's tall, bone-thin, and at least seventy-five years old. There are deep wrinkles etched into her face, which contrast with the starchy smoothness of her guimpe, the cloth covering her neck and shoulders. A heavy sterling crucifix swings from a pin in her habit. "Ah, yes, Miss DiNunzio," she says. "You look more like Sister Angela Charles every day."

I rise and smile. It occurs to me that this is a variant of pop-up-and-grin. "I'm sorry to barge in, but I need to see my sister. It's a family emergency."

"So I understand. I have sent for Sister Angela." The tall nun sits down, very erect, in a wooden chair. "Please, sit." She waves me into the chair with a bony hand.

There's a soft rapping at the door. "Come in," says the Mother Superior. The door opens, and it's Angie.

"Angie!" I blurt out happily. At the sight of her, the hardness in my chest breaks up, like ice floes on the prow of a tanker.

Angie looks guarded. "Yes, Mother?"

"Sister Angela, I understand there is an emergency."

Angie's eyes widen with fear as she turns to me. "Pop? Is it Pop?"

"No, Angie. Not Pop. They're both fine."

Her shoulders relax visibly. She steps into the room and closes the door quietly behind her. "What's the matter?"

I glance at the Mother Superior. "Is it possible for me to speak with my sister alone?"

The Mother Superior purses her lips, which are so thin that they're merely a vertical wrinkle. I wonder fleetingly if my mother ever noticed them. "As you know, we frown upon interruptions of this sort."

Suddenly Angie finds her voice, earnest and just a touch defiant. "I'm sure it's important, Mother, or my sister wouldn't have come."

"It's true." The story tumbles out, vaguely crazed. "I think someone is stalking me, I'm not sure who. They killed my secretary."

"Mary, no!" exclaims Angie.

The Mother Superior blinks in surprise; her crow's feet deepen. "Have you called the police?"

"I think the police are involved somehow. I really need to talk to Angie—and stay the night. Just tonight—please?"

Angie looks nervously from me to the Mother Superior.

"Considering your circumstances, you're welcome to do so, although I'm not sure it will alleviate your plight in the long run. I will return to Chapel and will expect you in due course, Sister Angela."

"Thank you, Mother," says Angie. She bows her head as the Mother Superior passes out through the door.

"Thank you," I say. As soon as she closes the door, I rush over to Angie. She hugs me back and I cling to her, not wanting to let go. I feel whole again. "I missed you!" I say into a mouthful of lightweight wool.

"What's going on, Mary?"

I tell her everything, in fits and starts. She listens. She touches my face. She's worried for me. She loves me still. I feel happy, and so safe. When I'm finished, she leaves and tells me she'll be right back.

But the next time the door opens, it's the Mother Superior. "Come with me, please, Miss DiNunzio," she says. She reaches into the desk for a flashlight. The oak drawer closes with a harsh sliding sound.

"Where's my sister?"

"She's completing her prayers. I'm sure you'll be in them tonight. Please follow me quietly. We have a room for you in the retreatants' area. The rest of the convent is fast asleep." She flicks on the flashlight, pointing it toward the floor, and leaves the room.

I follow her into the corridor, feeling like a kid late to a scary movie. The lights seem even dimmer than they were before, but I realize it's just gotten darker outside. We walk down one bare corridor after the next, past closed door after closed door. Over each is a stenciled description:

WORK ROOM
DEDICATED TO ST. JOSEPH
SILENCE

KITCHEN
DEDICATED TO ST. MARTIN
RECOLLECTION

REFECTORY
DEDICATED TO ST. BERNARD
MORTIFICATION

ASSISTANT'S OFFICE
DEDICATED TO OUR LADY
RETIREMENT

The Mother Superior moves quickly for a woman her age, sweeping from side to side like a whisk broom. I hustle to keep up with her as we climb a creaky staircase and walk past a series of doors that have no descriptions above them. They stretch down a long corridor as it veers off to the left. Beside each door hangs a clothes brush on a hook. "What are these rooms?" I ask.

"The sisters' cells," says the Mother Superior, without looking back.

I wonder which one is Angie's but decide not to ask. At the top of the wall it says, YOU CANNOT BE A SPOUSE OF JESUS CHRIST BUT INASMUCH AS YOU CRUCIFY YOUR INCLINATIONS, YOUR JUDGMENT, AND YOUR WILL TO CONFORM YOURSELVES TO HIS TEACHINGS. I stumble, reading the long inscription.

"Watch your step," says the Mother Superior.

I gasp. *Watch your step, Mary.*

She whirls around on her heel. "Are you all right? Did you trip?"

"No. Uh, I'm fine."

"You're safe here, dear. You have nothing to worry about tonight." She strides past a library and an infirmary, both dedicated to saints I've never heard of, as well as virtues I have. She stops before a door and opens it. In the half-light I see a single bed and a spindly night table. "It's not the Sheraton, but it's not meant to be," she says, with a slight smile.

"Thank you. I really am grateful."

"Don't be too grateful, we rise at five. Sleep well." She leaves and shuts the door behind her.

It plunges me into pitch blackness. I can't see

248 — LISA SCOTTOLINE

the bed in the dark. I wait for my eyes to adjust, but they don't. I stumble in the darkness, then find the bed's thin coverlet with my hands. I crawl onto the mattress, feeling safe and exhausted, and drift into sleep.

The next thing I know, my shoulder's being touched. I look up, blinking in the gloom. There's a shadow standing over me. Suddenly, a hand covers my mouth.

"It's me, you idiot." Angie removes her hand.

"Jesus, you scared me!"

"Shhh! Whisper. I'm supposed to be asleep." Angie flicks on a flashlight and sets it down like a lamp on the night table. She's still dressed in her habit, and her silver crucifix catches the light.

"Do you sleep in that getup?" I whisper hoarsely.

"I had Hours."

"What's that?"

"Nighttime prayers. I had from three to four o'clock."

"You mean you wake up in the middle of the night to pray?"

"We pray all night, in shifts."

"Are you serious?" Something in me snaps at the thought of these poor women—my twin included—praying all night long for a world that doesn't even know they exist. "What's the point of that? It makes no sense."

"Shhh!"

"It's crazy! It's just plain crazy, don't you see that?"

"Mary, whisper!"

"Why should I? You're an adult and I'm an adult and it's a free country. Why can't I talk to my own twin?"

"Mary, please. If you don't whisper, I'll leave." She looks grave, and her mouth puckers slightly. I know that pucker. My mother's, when she means business.

"All right, I'll whisper. Just tell me what kind of place this is. They don't let you talk. They don't let you out. They barely let you see your family. And these sayings on the walls, it's like a cult! They cut you off from the world and they brainwash you."

"Mary, please. Do we have to fight?"

"It's not a fight, it's a discussion. Can't we just discuss it? I'm whispering!"

She sighs. "It's not a cult, Mary. It's a different way of life. A contemplative way of life. A religious life. It's just as valid as the way you live."

"But it's a lie. A fiction. They pretend they're your family, but they're not. She's not your mother and they're not your sisters."

"You sound jealous."

"I am, I admit it! Mea culpa, sister. Mea culpa—*Sister.*"

Angie looks hurt.

"I'm sorry, but this makes me nuts! I'm your sister, your twin. I know you, Angie, like I know myself. And I agree with you. This is a perfectly valid way to live, but not for you." I search her round brown eyes, identical to mine. We're mirror images as we face one another in the tight cell.

"I'm here for a reason," she whispers. "You just can't accept that."

"Maybe if I understood it, I could accept it."

"You won't try."

"Give me a chance. I'm smarter than I look. What's the reason?"

"To serve God. To live a spiritual life."

"I don't believe you."

Angie averts her eyes but doesn't say anything.

"I believe it from the others, but not from you."

Still she says nothing.

"Why don't you talk? You hate silence. You love to talk."

She lifts her head abruptly. "No, Mary, *you* love to talk."

"So do you!"

"No." She points at me. "I am not you. We look the same. We sound the same. But *I am not you*." Her lips tremble.

"I know that, Angie."

"You do? Are you sure?"

"Sure I'm sure."

"What makes you so sure? What? How do you know?" She doesn't pause for my answer but says softly, "As kids, we dressed the same. We wore our hair the same. We had the same favorite sandwich—bologna with mustard on white. We got duplicate presents on our birthday and at Christmas. We went to the same schools. We sat next to each other in the same classes, all our lives."

"So?"

"So who are you, Mary? And who am I?"

Angie's tone is almost desperate. "Where do you end and I begin?"

My heart fairly breaks with the revelation. "Is *that* what this is about?"

"I need to think. I need to find out."

"But it's been so long, Angie! The prime of your life! Can't you find out on the outside?"

"I tried to, but I couldn't." She shakes her head sadly. "I couldn't as long as you were around, and Mom and Pop. And I love you all. I want you all to be happy." She shudders with the force of a hoarse sob.

I feel an anguish so deep it hurts. Now that I understand what she's asking, I know the convent is no answer. And I know because I've asked the same question. I have to get her out, to convince her. I prepare to make the most important oral argument of my life. For the life of my sister.

"Angie, I didn't know who I was either, until I *lived*. Graduated. Met Mike, lost Mike. I got knocked around and twisted every which way. Things happened to me I've never told you about. Bad things, good things, too. Those things helped me find out who I am. They made me who I am. It's life, Angie. You don't figure it out before you live it. It takes living it to figure it out."

She's crying softly, but she's listening.

"Angie, you don't have to hide yourself to find yourself!"

Suddenly the door bursts open. It's the Mother Superior, whose slash of a mouth sets grimly when she discovers Angie. "Sister Angela. To Lauds."

Angie springs from my embrace and backs away.

"Angie!" I shout, my arms empty.

But Angie runs from me, and the sound of her footfalls disappears into silence.

25

I dress before dawn in the quiet little cell. The shadows are a purple-gray, but now at least I can see around me. Not that there's much to see. There's no stenciling on the wall, and the night table is bare on top. The bed looks like a child's bunk bed, maybe donated from one of the families, and the white coverlet that felt so scratchy last night has fuzzy tufts of cotton scattered over it. Behind the table is a rectangular window. I slip into my shoes and look outside.

I think it's the back yard of the convent, but I can't orient myself. I know I've never seen it before. Huge oak trees climb to my window and even higher; some of them look a century old.

Their thick branches block the view of what's beneath them, but if I tilt my head I can see down below: a grouping of white crosses, set in rows. There are about fifty of them, white as bleached bones. It takes me a minute to realize what I'm seeing.

A cemetery.

I never thought about that. I never knew. Of course, it makes sense. The nuns who live here are buried here, in rows of crosses, like at Verdun, or Arlington.

Will Angie be buried here? I can't quite believe it. Even in death, would she stay here? I draw away from the window.

There's a soft knock at the door. "Mary, are you awake?" whispers a voice. Angie's.

I cross to the door and open it.

Angie's face looks pale, almost pasty against the raven-colored habit. There are dark circles under her eyes; I know they match mine. "You didn't sleep either, huh?" I ask.

She puts a finger to her lips. "Mother says we may take a short walk together before you go," she whispers. "Follow me."

So I do. She leads me down hallway after hallway, like the Mother Superior did last night. I have to admit that the convent looks better in the daylight. The hardwood floors that seemed dark last night are in fact a golden honey tone, a high-quality pine, and they reflect the morning light. The walls are pure white, without a scuff mark on them. The sayings seem less bizarre too, once you get over the shock of phrases like MORTIFICATION OF THE FLESH in ten-inch letters. But

I keep thinking of the cemetery in the back. Tucked away, like a secret.

We head down a flight of spiral stairs that appears to be at a corner of the convent. I don't remember going up them last night. They're narrow and there's no rail, so I run my hand along the wall as we wind down them like a nautilus shell. Angie holds a tiny door for me at the bottom. I have to stoop to pass through it.

And then we're in paradise. The door opens onto a lush garden, with a skinny brick path outlining it in the shape of a heart. The path's border is marked by low-lying plants with rich olive-colored leaves, thriving even in the shade of the pin oaks. A row of flowers grows behind the row of plants, dotting the perimeter with blossoms of pink, yellow, and white. Behind them are rosebushes, one after another, just beginning to bud. The effect is something like an old-fashioned floral valentine.

"Wow!" I say.

Angie pushes the door closed in a businesslike way and moves aside a stack of clay pots. "Thank you."

"You did this?"

She blushes. "I shouldn't take all the credit." She steps into the garden and stands at the point of the heart. "I designed it."

I follow her. "When? How? What do we know about gardens? We're city kids."

She smiles, and her face relaxes. "Which question do you want me to answer first?"

"Pick one."

"Well, I designed it about five years ago. Mother felt we needed a garden, a place for quiet contemplation. The shape, obviously, is the Sacred Heart."

"Obviously."

Angie glances back at me. "You haven't forgotten everything, have you?"

"I've tried, Lord knows I've tried."

She suppresses a smile. "Let's take a walk. There's a bench at the top where we can sit down." She leads me up the path, slipping both hands into the sleeves of her habit, like the nuns did at school.

"So tell me how you did this. It's wonderful."

"It wasn't hard. We have a library here. I read about the types of flowers. Perennials. Annuals. What grows in shade, what doesn't." Angie looks up at the sky. "I think we'll get some sun today. Good."

"You can get out the sun reflector like you used to."

She stops on the path and shakes her head. "I can't believe we actually did that. A sun reflector, of all things. With only baby oil for protection. What were we thinking?"

"We were thinking we wanted to look good. What all teenage girls think. Burn off those zits."

"Stop." She bumps me with her shoulder. "Look here. These are my favorites." She nods in the direction of a group of white flowers. The stems stand about two feet high and are covered with what appears to be soft white bells. They nod gracefully in the slight breeze.

"They're beautiful. What are they?"

She bends over and cups a dimpled bell in her fingertips. "Campanula. Bellflower. Aren't they lovely? They need some sun, but they don't like too much. Most of the varieties bloom in the summer. I have those on the north side of the heart. But this little baby, this is an early version. Aren't you, sweetie?" she coos comically into the upturned face of the flower.

"The vow of silence doesn't extend to flowers, huh?"

"Why do you think they grow so well?" Angie says, and we both laugh.

"That's the first time you ever made a joke about this place, you know."

She straightens up. "Don't start, Mary."

"All right, all right."

"Come on, let's go. We don't have much time." She walks briskly toward a weathered wooden bench. She seems more energetic than when she first met me this morning.

"You love this garden, don't you?"

"Yes." She sits down on the bench. "Step into my office," she says.

I sit down obediently.

"Look over there." She points to the right of the bench, where mounds of trailing green vines make a glossy carpet. "You know what that is?"

"Free parking?"

"No, wise guy. I planted it in our honor. It's Italian bellflower."

"I love it. Goombah foliage."

She looks over at the vines. "They're hard to grow. They're like you, stubborn. I couldn't get them to come up last year. But they're lovely when they do. I saw them in a picture." Her gaze is suddenly far away.

"What do they look like?"

"Little stars. Little bell-shaped stars. They call them Star-of-Bethlehem." She keeps looking far away. I wonder what she's looking at, what she's thinking about. I follow her gaze over the garden, past the statue of some saint. I can't see anything after that, except the wrought-iron crucifix on top of the gate.

"Remember when we used to read each other's minds?" I ask her.

She doesn't answer.

"What are you looking at, Ange?"

"The other side."

"The other side of what?"

"The other side of the rose garden. On the other side is our new gazebo. Have you seen it?" She squints, as if she were trying to see through the roses.

"No."

"It's lovely. It's made from the lightest wood, a blond color. Inside are statues of the Sacred Heart and the Immaculate Heart, both hand carved in Italy. Hand painted, too. The statues gave me the idea for the garden." She pauses a minute. "The statues are in the middle of the floor, and there's a skylight over the top. When the sun shines in, the whole room glows. The light inside is remarkable. It's full." Angie looks at me. Her eyes are bright. "Do you understand what I mean, that light can be *full*? Can you see that?"

I swallow hard. "You're never going to leave this place, are you?"

Angie smiles. "You're not a very good listener, you know that?"

"I'm a lawyer. We don't get paid to listen. We get paid to talk."

"But no one's paying you now."

"No, no, you're right. No one's paying me now." It's my turn to look past the roses.

"So. I was up last night, thinking about what you said and other things." She folds her hands neatly in her lap. She seems tense again.

"I didn't mean to upset you, hurt you. It's just that I don't want you here, Angie. I saw the cemetery out back. I don't want you here then and I don't want you here now."

"I understand that."

"I really think—"

"I know what you think. You want me to go out there." She nods over the garden to the gate beyond.

"Right."

"Because you think it's better than here. Than this lovely place." Her brown eyes move over the bright flowers of the garden.

"Not that it's better. Just that it's real. It's the real world, and you have to deal with it. You can't just ignore it. Run away from it."

"No? Why not?"

"What do you mean why not?"

"Why not?"

"Because you have to live in it. Because you learn by dealing with it, by coping with it. We're strong, Angie. Mom and Pop raised us that way.

They taught us that we can deal with whatever comes our way. I know you can resolve what you have to on the outside. I just know it."

"Do you think it's important for me to do that?"

"More than important. Vital."

She pauses. "Is it important for you to do that?"

I shrug. "Sure."

"I see. Well, then, may I ask you a question?"

"Shoot."

"Why are you here?"

I look at her. She looks back. My eyes narrow, then hers. Identically.

"What?" I ask.

"Why are you here?"

"I don't know what you mean."

"It's fairly obvious, isn't it? If what you're saying is true, then why are you here? Why did you run to the convent, from the vast and wonderful outside world?"

I have no answer for this. It doesn't seem like a fair question.

"You tell me there are dangerous people out there, stalking you. They send you notes. They enter your apartment when you're not there. They might have *killed* your secretary. Your *husband*." Her pained look flickers across her face. "You believe these things to be true."

"I do."

"So leaving aside the question of why anybody in her right mind would ever choose such a place as that over such a place as this, why was your first impulse to come here? Not even to call somebody else in the police department, some-body other than this Lombardo. But to come to a convent."

"I didn't come to a convent, Angie, I came to you. If you were in Camden, I would have gone to Camden."

"But what can *I* do? I'm a nun. I have no money, no power, no resources. I don't own a single thing, not even this garden. How can I help you?"

"By seeing me. By listening to me." I rub my forehead. "I don't get it. Why are you saying this?"

"I saw you. I listened to you. Now it's the next morning and you have to leave. You have to go beyond the walls, into the world of wonderful and terrifying things. Into *your* world, where two people close to you have been killed. And what are you going to do? What are you going to do?"

I look at her, suddenly crushed, and not understanding why.

"You see, Mary, this is very hard for me." She folds her hands again in her lap. "Because I have to let you go out there, into the world you love so much, into the world you ran from. I have to let you go. But I don't see you reaching within yourself to deal with this situation, one that threatens your very life."

I look at her wide-eyed.

"How am I supposed to let you go out there, when all I can do is pray to God to protect you and I don't see you doing anything at all to protect yourself?" Her lips look parched, her expression pained. "You said we could handle anything, and I've always thought that of you, though not of myself. Can you handle this?"

"I . . . don't know."

She looks away, quiet for a minute. "You're right about one thing. You know that light I was telling you about? That I said was full?"

"Yes."

"Well, I never will leave it. I can't. It's inside me. In here." She touches her chest with a slim hand. "Do you understand?"

I nod, yes, but she isn't watching.

"It has a kind of substance to it, it's tangible to me. It guides me, and I follow it like a river. It's what I dip into when I need to know the answer. For me, it's my faith in God." Angie turns to me. "What is inside of you, Mary?"

I shake my head. "I don't know."

"Think."

"Ever since Mike—"

She holds up a finger. "No. No. No man can give it to you. Not Mike, and not this other man. No one else can give it to you. It's inside you. It's there already."

"You think?"

"I know. Isn't that what you told me last night?"

"I guess so."

"See? I listen," she says, with a smile.

Suddenly, the chapel bells peal loudly, *bong, bong, bong,* in some indeterminant hymn. Angie turns toward the sound. "I have to go." She looks worriedly back at me. "Do you see what I'm trying to tell you?"

"Yes."

She begins to rise. "I have to let you go now, and I have to know you'll be all right if I do. I was never worried about you before, Mary, but now I am. I prayed all night for you, prayed to God to keep you safe." Her eyes are brimming with tears.

I stand up and hug her tight. "Read my mind," I whisper into her habit.

"I know. You love me," she says, her voice choked.

"Right. Want me to read your mind?"

"No." She hugs me tighter.

"You love me too."

The chapel bells fall silent as suddenly as they commenced.

She braces me by the shoulders. Her wet eyes search my face.

"I'll be okay, Ange."

"You swear?"

"On a stack of Bibles."

She laughs and wipes a cheek on her sleeve. "Swear on something else. Something *you* believe in."

I give her a quick hug. "Have faith. Now go."

"Do you know how to get out of here?"

"Do you?"

Angie rolls her eyes. "I have to go. The gate's over that way. Take care of yourself."

"I will."

She kisses my cheek, then runs off toward the convent. Midway down the garden path, she gathers her skirt into her hands so she can run faster.

"Way to go!" I call after her.

She looks back with a sly smile. Then off she runs, with her veil flying and her black wool leggings churning away.

26

Clouds of steam billow around me. The water superheats my skin. My blood pumps faster; my thoughts flow like quicksilver. I'm taking a steaming hot shower in Stalling's locker room on the second floor, Anger.

How perfect.

I'm angry at myself, for rolling over like a puppy for whatever devil is out there, trying to hurt me. But no longer.

Angie was right. I preached to her to face life, but when I got scared, I ran too. But like Brent says, that was then and this is now. I had an epiphany as I drove back to the city, hurtling into a cloudless dawn on a Route 1 empty of travelers. I found my river, but its source sure as hell isn't my faith in God. And it doesn't flow with holy water, but with something closer to bile, at least right now. Whatever it is that drives me, it's why I became a lawyer in the first place. Every day on my job I fuck back professionally for Stalling's clients, and I like it. Well, I've decided it's time to start fucking back for myself. I'm not going to run for my life anymore, I'm going to fight for it.

I twist off the water and step dripping out of the shower. I towel off and slip into a white linen dress that I keep in my locker. I dry my hair quickly, ignoring the blotches aflame on my chest. I unlock the locker room door and head for my office.

The big clock stares at me. 7:56. I stare right back. Lying abandoned on my desk is Ned's bouquet of roses. They're wilted, but still holding their perfume. I take a deep breath and toss them into the wastebasket. I try not to look back as I pick up the telephone receiver and punch in the numbers from the Rolodex. It turns out that Detective Lombardo answers his own phone.

"How's your nose this morning, Lombardo?"

"Who is this?"

"Mary DiNunzio, remember me? The crazy widow? The one you tried to convince it's all in her head? I saw Berkowitz clean your clock, Lombardo, and I want to know why."

"Mary, jeez. It's not . . . you gotta ask Sam, I can't say any more."

"Bullshit."

"It's confidential."

"What about this investigation could possibly be confidential from me? Brent was my friend. Mike was my husband."

"Let me get my jacket off, okay? I just got in. Christ, you're worse than that Amazon you sent over."

"Amazon?"

"Your friend Carrier. She came in here last night and read me the riot act. What is it, you both on the rag?"

My blood boils over. "You got a house, Lombardo? A car? You like your job? Your pension?"

"What?"

"So how come you didn't investigate this matter when I first made a report?"

"What are you talkin' about, Mary? You never made a report!"

"The hell I didn't, you must've lost it. So it's your word against mine. Which would you believe—that the young widow is a filthy liar or that a city employee lost a form? Please. It's not even close."

"You would—"

"My memory is crystal clear. I came down to the station. We met. I told you about the car that was following me and my secretary. The next day he's dead, hit by the same car I warned you about. You ever been sued, Lombardo?"

"What's this all—"

"You were negligent, pal. You denied me my civil rights. I'm gonna take your shitty little house and your car. I'll garnish every paycheck you ever get."

"Don't you threaten me!"

"I'll make your life a living hell. I know how to do it, you understand? It's my job. I'm a lawyer."

"Now wait a minute—"

"Brent was gay, maybe that's why you didn't investigate. You can always tell, that's what you said. And something else, something about your brother being 'light in the loafers.' I love that colloquial stuff. It'll look so good in the complaint. It lends realism, don't you agree?"

"You're crazy!"

"A line like that, could be the newspapers will pick it up. In fact, why leave it to chance? I'll send them a copy of the complaint—maybe ten copies, to play it safe."

"I don't have to listen to this."

"Yes, you do. You do have to listen, Lombardo, and you will if you're smart. What I need from you is protection. Low-profile confidential protection from whoever's trying to hurt me. I want you to do your job, so I can do mine. I want you to watch me at Stalling—"

"Now how am I gonna do that?" he explodes. "They'd recognize me. I couldn't pass for a lawyer!"

"Put somebody else on the inside. You figure it out."

"You're safe at work. Everyone's around."

"Waters is here, Lombardo. If he's the one—"

"Oh, this is rich! Change your mind about your boyfriend?"

"I'm taking no chances. You have to watch me here."

"No way. I'll cover you on the outside, but that's it! I'll put my buddy on Waters—on the outside. You call me on the beeper when you leave and when you go in. You work only during business hours, when everyone's around. Your Amazon friend, you stay with her. After work, you go straight home. You got it? For three days."

"Two weeks."

"Four days."

"Ten days."

"Seven," Lombardo says, finally. "That's it. That's all I'm doing. I'll be damned if I'll put a tail on every nervous Nellie in this city! *Goddamned!*"

"Did you just cuss? In front of a lady?"

"I gotta go. I got a real job to do."

"Not so fast. I need something else."

"Jesus."

"Information. Those files you told me about, the ones on Mike and Brent. Where are they now?"

"AID has 'em. I shipped 'em back. But you can't get 'em."

"Why not? They should be public record."

"Not when the investigations are open. They're not gonna give you an open file. Brent has all my notes, all the investigation notes, what leads they're following—"

"That's why I want it."

"You can't get it."

"I appreciate the vote of confidence."

"Seven days, Mary. That's it."

"And this is confidential, Lombardo. That we talked, that I'm investigating the files. All of it. I don't want Berkowitz or anybody else at this firm to know about it. Understand?"

"I have better things to do."

"Thank you. And have a happy day."

Lombardo hangs up with a bang.

I hang up and exhale. So far, so good. While I'm still on a roll, I pick up the receiver and punch in four numbers.

"Mr. Berkowitz's office," Delia says.

"Hi, Delia, it's Mary. Is he in yet?"

She hesitates. "Come on up."

I bound up the stairs to Pride. Delia isn't at her desk when I stalk to Berkowitz's office, but the door is open slightly. I grit my teeth and burst in. And come face to face with the Honorable Morton A. Weinstein, the Honorable William A. Bitterman, and the Honorable Jeremy M. Van Houten, all of whom are sitting directly across from Berkowitz and looking rather startled.

"Oh . . . my. Oh."

"Mary! Why don't you come in and meet some of the hard-working members of the Rules Committee?" Berkowitz says heartily, as if I were expected. The three judges rise to their feet. In fact, they're popping up and grinning, for me.

Bitter Man, the closest, grasps my hand with clammy fingers. "I know Miz DiNunzio, Sam. She was my research assistant on that article I published on federal court jurisdiction. I believe I sent you a reprint. It was in the *Yale Law Journal*."

Berkowitz nods sagely. "I remember, Bill." He has no idea what Bitter Man is talking about.

"In fact, I bet I know more about Miz DiNunzio than you do," Bitter Man says.

"Oh, really?"

"I know she's an alto, for example. Quite a good alto at that. Am I right, Miz DiNunzio? An alto?" Bitter Man's puffy lips break into a cynical smile.

I nod. You asshole.

"You mean like in singing?" Berkowitz asks. "How do you know that, Bill?"

My chest erupts into prickly blotches.

"I don't know if I should say, Sam. Should it remain our little secret, Miz DiNunzio?"

Einstein steps in to save me, his distaste for Bitter Man evident. "Don't let Brother Bitterman get to you, Ms. DiNunzio. We can dress him up, but we can't take him out. You and I met just the other day, didn't we? On the *Hart* case?" He clasps my hand warmly.

"Yes, Your Honor."

"You made a nice point in a tough spot."

Berkowitz places a heavy arm around my shoulders. His pinstriped jacket reeks of cigarette smoke. "I'm not surprised, Morton. Mary is one of our finest young lawyers."

I try to edge away from Berkowitz, blushing deeply. It erupts at my hairline and rushes straight down my chest, like lava down a volcano. I feel awkward and confused. I want to fuck back at him, but he's co-opting the shit out of me. Anger is almost elbowed out of the way by Pride.

"Have you met Judge Van Houten, Mary?" Berkowitz says, giving my shoulders another squeeze. "He was appointed to the bench last year to replace Judge Marston."

"I'm the rookie," quips Van Houten, shaking my hand with a self-assured grin. His features are small and even, and his hair is as smooth and tawny as butterscotch. Good-looking, if you go for those Ken types. Judy calls him Golden Rod, because the scuttlebutt is that he gets around. Now I see why. "We were just discussing the issue of note-taking by jurors," he says. "It's the sort of thing that gets the academics all excited."

"At least something does," says Berkowitz, with a loud laugh. He slaps me on the back so hard I expect my contacts to take flight. Golden Rod thinks this is a real hoot too.

Einstein looks at them with tolerance over his little half-glasses. "You see, Mary, we conducted a survey to determine the bar's view on the practice of note-taking by jurors. Unfortunately, we're having a tough time coming up with a conclusion, because the findings were so diverse."

"What a surprise," Bitter Man says.

Einstein ignores him. "We have a meeting with the chief judge at noon today, so we should have learned something by then."

"We learned one thing, right, gentlemen? Next time—don't ask!" Berkowitz explodes into laughter and so does Golden Rod.

Bitter Man shifts uncomfortably in his chair. "Miz DiNunzio, why don't you share with us your view of the practice? Do you think jurors should be permitted to take notes during trial?"

The question catches me off guard. "I . . . uh . . ."

Einstein scoffs. "Come on, Bill, you're not going to cross-examine her, are you? Court's adjourned, for God's sake."

I look stupidly from Bitter Man to Einstein, waiting to see if I'm to perform. There's so much tension between them, I don't want to take sides.

"Now, Morton, don't underestimate the woman," Berkowitz says. "I'm sure she has an opinion. Don't you, Mary?"

The three judges look at me expectantly. I do have an opinion, but it might not be the right opinion, which is Berkowitz's. A week ago I would have avoided the question, but that was before I became the New Me. Now I say what I really think, possibly committing career hara-kiri:

"I think they shouldn't. It distracts them. Their job is to hear the evidence and the testimony, then do a sort of rough justice."

Einstein smiles.

Golden Rod smiles.

And, most importantly, Berkowitz smiles.

Yes!

"They don't know shit from Shinola," mutters Bitter Man.

"That's my girl!" Berkowitz says. "We report that Mary DiNunzio thinks jurors should not be permitted to take notes during trial. Now we can get on to more important subjects."

"Like golf," says Golden Rod. They all laugh, except for Bitter Man.

I seize the moment to back toward the door. "It was a pleasure seeing all of you. I'd better get back to my office."

"Back to the yoke, eh?" says Golden Rod. "Just slip it on and go plodding around in a circle."

Berkowitz laughs. "Watch it, Jeremy. We don't want an insurrection. See you later, Mary."

"Sounds good," I say casually, like I'm not at the man's beck and call. I close the door and allow the mask to slip. I feel disgusted at myself. I was bought off too easily. And I still don't know why Berkowitz was meeting with Lombardo, much less why he slugged him.

Delia's not at her desk when I leave, and I'm sure it's no accident. She would want to evade my very important question: Why did you set me up? I wonder about this on the way to the elevator, swimming upstream against the lawyers and secretaries flooding into Stalling to start the day. I stop down on Judy's floor before I go back to my office.

Judy's in the middle of her Zen-like brief-writing ritual. The trial record, marked with yellow Post-Its, is stacked on her left, Xerox copies of cases are stacked on her right, and a lone legal pad occupies the middle of a newly immaculate desk. Judy slams down her thick pencil when she sees me. "Mary, I was worried about you! Everybody was worried about you. Where'd you go last night?"

"Angie's convent." I flop into the chair facing her desk.

"Christ!"

"Exactly."

"Tell me about it." She leans forward, but I wave her off.

"Did you get the notes from Ned?" I ignore the pang when I say his name.

"Yepper. I saw Lombardo, too."

"So I heard." We trade Lombardo stories. She applauds after mine.

"You got protection! What a good idea!"

"I know. You're smarter than I am, why didn't you think of it?"

She smiles. "You'd still better stick with me when you're in the office, like Lombardo said."

"That shouldn't be too hard. We're together all the time anyway."

"Right. So how are you going to get the files?"

"I can't subpoena them until I start suit, and I can't start suit yet because Lombardo won't protect me."

"Start suit? Who are you gonna sue?"

"The police department. Maybe the city."

"Are you serious? For what?"

"I haven't figured it out yet. It doesn't matter. The complaint will be one page of civil rights bullshit, I only need it to be able to get the files. I'll withdraw it as soon as I do."

She nods. "Quite a plan."

"And that's only Plan B, the fallback. Plan A is me going down to AID and convincing them to give me the files. As the widow. I'll get the documents sooner that way, if they'll go for it."

"What do you think you'll find in the files?"

"The killer, ultimately. But for starters I want to see what similarities there are between Brent's case and Mike's. I'm going to try to get the other two files on open fatals too. Who knows what will turn up? It's like any other case."

"And you're the client."

"No. Brent is. And Mike."

She looks concerned. "Are you going to be able to do this? Emotionally, I mean?"

"If you're asking me do I look forward to reading those files, the answer is no. But I have to."

"Okay," Judy says, with a sigh. "Let me know what AID says on the phone, okay? I'll go down with you. We can go through the files together."

"Thanks, but you look busy enough. Very industrious, with the clean desk and all. What are you working on?"

She picks up her pencil. "The *Mitsuko* brief. If this argument's accepted, it'll make new law in the Third Circuit." Judy tells me about her argument with the degree of detail that most people reserve for their children or their dreams the night before. She loves the law. I guess it's her river.

Later, as I climb the busy stairwell to my office, what Judy said begins to sink in. I can't imagine sitting at my desk reading the police file on Mike's death or Brent's. Open fatals, my husband and my friend. I'm kidding myself that it's just like any other case. It's harder than any other case, but it's also more important. I'll call AID when I get back to my office. Maybe I can get a meeting this morning.

But when I reach Gluttony, Miss Pershing is pacing in front of her desk in an absolute panic. "My goodness, where have you been? You didn't come back yesterday the whole day, and you didn't call! I left messages on your machine. I even tried your parents, but they didn't know where you were. Now they're waiting upstairs in the reception area for the deposition!"

"Who is? What deposition?"

"Your parents, they're waiting."

"My parents are upstairs?"

"They're very worried. They wanted to see you the moment you arrived. And Mr. Hart! He's upstairs with his lawyer now."

"Hart is here for his deposition? Oh, Christ." I didn't notice a deposition in *Hart* for today. I didn't see a notice in the pleadings index, so I assume that nobody at Masterson noticed a dep, either. Maybe the notice got lost when the file was sent to Stalling. Or maybe somebody deliberately took it out.

"Miss DiNunzio, they're waiting. All of them." Miss Pershing's thin fingers dance along the edge of her chin.

I steady her by her Olive Oyl shoulders. "Here's what I need you to do, Miss Pershing. Get us a conference room and have Catering Services set us up for breakfast. Then call Legal Court Reporters, the number's on the Rolodex. Ask them to send over Pete if he's available. Pete Benesante, got that?"

"Benesante." She's so nervous she's quivering, and it makes her look vulnerable. Her job is all she has. She's me in thirty years.

"After you do that, take the Harts to the conference room for me. Tell them I'll be right there. I have to see my parents first. Okay?"

She nods.

"Are they having a shit fit?"

She colors slightly.

"Excuse me. My parents. How are they?"

"They're fine. They're very nice people. Lovely people. They invited me over for coffee this Saturday. They said perhaps you'd be free as well."

"Maybe, Miss Pershing. But right now we have to get moving. Welcome to litigation. This is called a fire drill."

She looks nervous again.

"Don't worry. Everything's going to be all right."

"It's in God's hands." She walks unsteadily out the door, chanting Benesante, Benesante, Benesante, like a Latin prayer.

I go through my drawer for the thin *Hart* file and page through it quickly. As I remembered, the only papers in it are the complaint and some scribbled notes from the lawyer at Masterson who represented Harbison's. I've seen the notes before, on the way to the pretrial conference with Einstein. They're practically indecipherable, written in a shaky hand. I can make out sentences here and there—what I told Einstein about Hart's rudeness to company employees—but most of it's a mess.

Who took these notes? Who did we steal this case from, anyway? I flip through the notes, three pages long. On the last page is a notation: 5/10 CON OUT/FS 1.0 NSW. I recognize it as a billing code. Stalling's is almost identical. The notation means that on May 10, the Masterson lawyer had a conference out of the office with Franklin Stapleton, Harbison's CEO.

Their conference lasted an hour. The Masterson lawyer must be NSW.

NSW. Nathaniel Waters?

Ned's father.

27

"Everything's ready, Miss DiNunzio," says Miss Pershing, practically hyperventilating in the doorway to my office. "You have Conference Room C. Mr. Benesante's on his way."

"Thank you, Miss Pershing." I stare at the notation. Is NSW Ned's father? It would make sense, because only a megapartner would get an hour's audience with Stapleton. Even Berkowitz has never met Stapleton. He deals with Harbison's through the GC.

"Also, there's someone on the telephone." She frowns at the message slip. "It's a Miss Krytiatow . . . Miss Krytiatows. . . ." She looks up, exasperated. "Her first name is Lu Ann."

"I don't know her, Miss Pershing. Take her number. I'll get back to her when I can."

"All right. I'll be back at my desk if you need anything." She turns to go.

"Miss Pershing, the Harts, remember?"

Her hand flutters to her mouth. "Oh, my. I forgot. I'm so sorry."

"No problem. Just take them to the conference room and tell them I'll be there."

"You mean, *stall* them. Like Jessica Fletcher." She winks at me.

"Jessica who?"

"Jessica Fletcher, on *Murder, She Wrote.* She's a sleuth!" Miss Pershing's eyes light up.

"You got it. Like Jessica Fletcher."

"Right-o."

"In fact, I have a favor to ask you. Something I need to have done while I'm in the dep. The kind of favor a sleuth would like."

"Now this is my cup of tea," she says, brightening.

"Get a district court subpoena from my form files. Then call up the Accident Investigation Division—they're a part of the Philadelphia police. Don't tell them who you are. Get some information about who's in charge of their records on open investigations for fatal accidents. Put that name on two of the subpoenas. My guess is that it's the Fatal Coordinator Sergeant, but I'm not sure. Just don't tell them why."

"Got it," she says, with another wink, and hobbles off.

I return to the file and read the notation again. 5/10 CON OUT/FS 1.0 NSW. If NSW is Ned's father, does that explain why the deposition notice is missing? Did he tamper with the file to make me look bad in comparison to Ned? Is Ned's father the note writer? The killer?

I slap the file closed and tuck it under my arm. I head up the stairs slowly enough to give Miss Pershing time to get the Harts out of the reception area. My parents must have been worried sick. I wonder if they got hold of Angie and how much she told them. It had to be the whole story for them to come here. They've only been to Stalling once, when I was first hired. My father got lost on the way to the bathroom.

The Harts are gone when I reach the reception area. A CEO type, his lawyer, and his lawyer's bag carrier are engaged in a whispered confab at one end of a glass coffee table, leaning over slick copies of *Forbes, Time,* and *Town and Country.* At the other end of the table is the redoubtable team of Vita and Matthew DiNunzio. They sit together in their heavy car coats, a worsted mountain of concerned parenthood, slumping badly in the soft whiter-than-white sectional furniture. I know what my mother is thinking: This sofa, it cost a fortune, and it has no support.

"Maria!" shouts my father, with joy. He stands up, arms outstretched. "Maria! Doll!"

Every head in the place turns. The CEO and his lawyer break off their expensive conversation. The bag carrier stifles a laugh. Two young associates, running by with files, look back curiously. Stalling's veteran receptionist, Mrs. Littleton of the purple hair, just beams. I wonder if she's invited to coffee too.

I cross to greet my parents before my father shouts again. "Ma. Pop. Are you guys okay?"

They reach for me and envelop me in their scratchy coats. They smell like home, a closed-up odor of marinara and mothballs. It's crazy, all hell is breaking loose in my life, but I'm happy to see them. I hope Angie didn't tell them everything. I don't know how much more they can take, particularly my father.

"Maria, what happened? Where were you?" says my mother, half moaning. Her pancake makeup looks extra heavy, which signifies that she's come downtown. "We were so worried!"

"We called Angie," my father chimes in. "She said you went to see her. Are you in trouble, honey?"

The CEO leans closer to his lawyer and continues his conversation. The bag carrier has nothing to do but watch us, which he does. I don't like the way he looks at my parents, with a mixture of incredulity and amusement. What's the matter? I want to say. You never seen Italians before?

"Pop, I'm not in trouble. Everything's—"

"What?" He nudges my mother, agitated. "What did she say, Vita?"

"She said she's not in trouble, but I don't believe her," my mother shouts. "Look at her eyes, Matty. Look at her eyes." She grabs for my chin, but I intercept her deftly, having had some practice with this.

I look over her shoulder at the smirking lawyer.

"Come with me. Let's get out of here." I take her by one hand and him by the other and walk them out of the reception area. We gather in front of one of the conference rooms, away from the elevator bank. I stand very close to my father, so I don't have to yell too loudly. "Listen to me. Everything is fine. I am fine."

"Then why did you go see Angie?" my mother asks, blinking defiantly behind her thick glasses.

"What did Angie say?"

"Hah! You think I was born yesterday? You tell me why you went, then I tell you what she said."

"What?" asks my father.

I hug him close and talk directly into his ear. "I went to see Angie. I was worried about something, but now it's fine. I'm fine. I'm sorry if I made you worry."

"Angie said you were lonely."

"That's right, Pop. I was lonely. I was worried about her, missing her. Everything's okay now. But I have to get back to work. I have a deposition. I have to go take it."

"You givin' us the bum's rush?"

"I have to, Pop. I can't help it."

"Something's wrong, Matty. I can see it in the child's eyes. Ever since she was little, she can't hide her eyes." My mother trembles, agitated.

I touch her shoulder. "Ma. I promise you, I'm fine. If my eyes look funny, it's because I'm about to lose my job." I press the button to get them an elevator.

"No. We're not leaving until this is settled."

"What, Vita?"

"We're not leaving until my daughter tells me what is going on. And that's final!"

My father winces. "Veet, she has to do her job."

I nod. "Right. Pop's right. I have to do my job." The elevator arrives. I step inside and press the HOLD button. "Ma, please. I have to work. I have to go, they're waiting for me. There's nothing to worry about. I'm sorry I upset you, I really am."

My father shuffles into the elevator, but my mother merely folds her arms. It's easier to move the Mummers up Broad Street than it is to move my mother one inch. Especially when she folds her arms like that.

The elevator starts to buzz loudly. The noise reverberates in the elevator. Even my father covers his ears.

"Ma, please."

"Vita, please."

She wags a finger at me, her knuckle as knobby as the knot on an oak tree. "I don't like this. I don't like this at all."

"Ma, I'm fine."

The elevator buzzes madly.

She takes two reluctant steps into the elevator. I release the button and the buzzing stops abruptly. "Don't worry, Ma. I love you both." I jump out of the elevator.

"We love you," says my father. The doors close on my mother's scowl.

When I turn around, the bag carrier is standing alone in the elevator bank. He's wearing a three-piece suit and a smirk I would love to smack off.

"You look familiar to me," he says casually. "Did you go to Harvard?"

"No. I'm too stupid." I start to walk past him, but he touches my arm.

"You look like somebody I knew on law review there, in 1986. I was editor in chief that year."

"Editor in chief, huh?"

"Editor in chief."

I lean in close to him. "Let me tell you something. I saw the way you carried that bag, and I must say I've never seen a man carry a bag as well as you did. In fact, it takes an editor in chief to carry a bag that well." I chuck him one in the padded shoulder. "Keep up the good work."

I take off and head for the stairs.

Fucking back. It's getting to be fun.

I run up the stairs to the conference room, mentally switching gears on the way. I have a job to do. I have to ask Hart every question I can think of, and I have only this one shot before trial. I have to find out everything he has to support his case so I can get a defense ready. And I have to find out what the hell is going on with Ned's father and my files.

I slip inside the conference room. It smells of fresh coffee and virgin legal pads. Pete's already there, setting up his stenography machine. He gives me a professional nonpartisan-type nod. We both know this is bullshit. He's my reporter and it will be my record. He'll make me sound like Clarence Darrow before he's done, with none of the uhs, hums, and ers that I come out with in real life.

The Harts stand together at the coffee tray. I reach for Hank's hand. "Hello, Hank."

"Hi, Mary," Hank says. "I assumed the dep would be here, since you replaced Masterson as defense counsel." He looks like an English schoolboy in a plaid bow tie, which is slightly askew.

"Right. I should have called you, but I was out yesterday."

"I know, I tried to confirm."

"I'm sorry. By the way, when did you get the Notice of Deposition? I don't seem to have a copy in my pleadings index."

He thinks a minute. "We got it when Masterson filed the answer, I think. No, we got it with the other stuff."

"Other stuff?"

"You know, the discovery. Interrogatories and document requests. We answered them two weeks ago. You've seen them, haven't you?"

"No, actually. Maybe they got lost when the file was transferred to us." Discovery. Of course, the written questions that Hart would have to answer and the papers he'd have to produce. Without those papers, I'm crippled for today. "Hank, would you mind if I borrowed your copy of the discovery for the deposition?"

"Not at all." He sets his shiny briefcase on the table and opens it up. Anybody else would have denied having the documents and exploited my disadvantage, but Hank hands me a thick packet of paper. Candy from a baby. I'm almost too ashamed to take it. Almost.

"Thanks, Hank."

"The documents we produced are on the bottom," he says helpfully.

"Great." I take the papers, but there's too

much to read now. I'll do it over the lunch break, and wing it this morning. But why are the papers missing from the file in the first place? Who did this to me? "Who handled this case at Masterson, Hank? I forget. Was it—"

"Nathaniel Waters," booms a deep voice, speaking for the first time. It's Hart the Elder. "They pulled out their big gun."

NSW *is* Ned's father. Jesus H. Christ.

"Mary, this is my father, Henry Hart," Hank says.

"Hello, Mr. Hart." I extend a hand, but he ignores it. I withdraw it quickly, as Hank looks uncomfortably at me. Hart the Elder won't even meet my eye and yanks a chair out from under the table. He's an attractive man, tanned and trim. There's almost no gray in his hair; I wonder if he dyes it. It would be consistent, for he seems vain, in a European-tailored suit and a light pink shirt. I can see why he was an executive at Harbison's and can also imagine him being rude to employees, because he's breathing fire at me.

Two hours later, it's a full-fledged conflagration, and I've taken Saint Joan's place at the stake. I started out with only the most reasonable questions, mainly about his early years at Harbison's, but Hart fought me on each one. His son never objected. He couldn't get a word in edgewise.

"Mr. Hart, has anyone from Harbison's ever made a statement to you regarding your age?"

"Mrs. DiNunzio, you know full well they have."

"The purpose of this deposition is to find out your version of the facts, Mr. Hart. Now please answer the question."

"My version? It's the truth."

"Look, Mr. Hart, this is your chance to tell your side of the story. Why don't you do so?"

"It's not a story."

I grit my teeth. "Mr. Benesante, would you please read back the question?"

Pete picks up the tape and translates its machine-made abbreviations to Hart. "Mr. Hart, has anyone from Harbison's ever made a statement to you regarding your age?"

"Do you understand the question, Mr. Hart?" I ask.

"English is my mother tongue, Mrs. DiNunzio."

"Then answer it, please."

"Yes, they have."

"How many such statements have been made to you, sir?"

"Three."

"Do you remember when the first such statement was made?"

"Sure. It's a day that will live in infamy, if I have any say in the matter."

"When was the statement made?"

"February seventh, 1990."

"Who made the statement?"

"Frank Stapleton."

"Would that be Franklin Stapleton, the chief executive officer of Harbison's?"

"None other."

"Was there anyone else present when he made this statement?"

"You think they're dumb enough to have a witness there?"

"I take it your answer is no, Mr. Hart?"

"You take it right, Mrs. DiNunzio."

I sip some ice-cold coffee. "Where was the statement made?"

"In Frank's office."

"Do you recall the statement, Mr. Hart?"

"I'll never forget it."

"What was the statement, Mr. Hart?"

"Mr. Stapleton said to me, 'Henry, face it. You're not getting any younger, and it's time for you to retire. You can't teach an old dog new tricks, you know.'"

Pow! It's a fireball.

Soon it blazes out of control. Hart goes on to testify with certainty about the two other statements, each one referring to his age as it relates to his employment. Clearly unlawful, and each statement was made by Stapleton himself, so it's directly chargeable to Harbison's. *Pow! Pow!*

"Mr. Hart, do you have any documents regarding these alleged statements by Mr. Stapleton?"

"I most certainly do."

Pow!

"What might those documents be?"

"They might be notes."

"Have you brought them to this deposition?"

"Yes. My son gave them to you already."

"They're the ones at the bottom of the pile, Mary," Hank says.

"Excuse me a minute." I flip through the pages until I reach a set of documents on Harbison's letterhead. They're neatly typed and laser-printed, in capital letters. I pull them out and hold them up. "Are these the ones, Hank?"

Hank squints across the conference table. "Yes. That's them."

"Bear with me a minute, gentlemen." I arrange my face into a mask of scholarly calm as I read the notes. Frolicking across the top of each page is a conga line of ecstatic nuts and bolts, ending in the tagline HARBISON'S THE HARDWARE PEOPLE. On each page are verbatim accounts of Hart's conversations with Stapleton, which appear to have been made right after the conversations.

God help me.

The notes will be admissible at trial. They'll prove the truth of every word Hart says. The jury will rise up like an avenging angel. They'll take millions from Harbison's; it'll be the biggest age discrimination verdict in Pennsylvania history. *Kaboom!* The conflagration explodes into a city-wide five-alarmer. And the flames, crackling in my ears, are eating me alive.

Pete cracks his knuckles loudly. "Can we break for lunch now, Mary? My fingers are killing me."

"Sure."

"An hour okay?"

"Fine."

The Harts leave with Pete, who gives me a quick smile before he goes. He's never asked for a break before. I've had him on deps with no break all day. He was trying to save me. He knew I was tumbling into the inferno.

He's Catholic too.

28

I plunge my hot face into a golden basin of cool water in the ladies' room, half expecting to hear a hissing sound. Then I towel off and head back to the conference room to read over Hart's notes. They're bad, but I decide not to think about how very bad they are. I have to find out more about them and find out anything else he has. Fuck back, in overdrive.

I'm almost finished reading the stack of documents, which luckily contain no more surprises, when the telephone rings. It's Miss Pershing. "Miss DiNunzio, I'm sorry to interrupt you, but I have this Lu Ann on the line again. She's very anxious to talk to you. She says it's about Mr. Hart's deposition."

Who can this be? I take the call. "This is Mary DiNunzio."

"You're the lawyer for Harbison's, aren't you, miss?" says a young woman. She sounds upset. "Because I heard you're a lady lawyer, and I heard Henry's getting his deposition today."

"I represent the company, Lu Ann. Do you work for Harbison's?"

"Let me just ask you is the judge there?"

"There's no judge at a deposition, Lu Ann."

"Who's there? The jury?" Her voice grows tremulous. I can't place her flat accent. Maybe it's from Kensington, a working-class section of the city.

"No. Just relax, I think you're confused. A deposition is between—"

"Did he say anything about me? 'Cause if he does, you tell them I said it's not true! If my Kevin hears it, if anybody on that jury says anything, or it gets in the newspapers, he'll beat the shit out of me! Me and my kids both! So you just tell him that! If he loves me, you tell him to shut the fuck up!" The phone goes dead.

Stunned, I hang up the receiver. My conversation with Lu Ann is over, but my conversation with the devil is just beginning. I didn't think I believed in the devil, but I can't ignore the fact that I hear his hot whisper at my ear in the stillness of Conference Room C, on Lust.

So Hart's been playing hide the kielbasa with a Polish girl from Kensington. Let the jury in on that, Mare, and you win.

I can't. It wouldn't even be admissible.

Then ask Hart about Lu Ann right now. Take

him through her phone call, expose the little shit. He'll pack up his lawsuit and go home. You can win this case today, Mary. It's yours for the asking.

I can't do that. It's not fair. It has nothing to do with the case.

You can and you should. A quick victory would clinch your partnership, Mare. No more worrying, no more vote-counting, no more headaches. Relief from pain, isn't that what you want? Peace. You could buy a house. Get your life back on track.

I can't do it. His son is right here.

So what? You're Harbison's lawyer, you should be representing its interests, not Little Hank's. You're supposed to use every weapon in the arsenal to win, even the MAC-10s. Especially the MAC-10s.

I'm damned if I do and damned if I don't.

There's no time to decide, because the door opens and the Harts enter. Though the elder Hart doesn't smile, Hank's spirits are high. Undoubtedly, he'd advised his father to take notes of his conversations with Stapleton and is expecting a settlement offer after the dep. He's been planning this victory since his graduation and thinks that its sweet moment is at hand.

That's what he thinks, whispers the devil.

I take my seat in front of the notes, and Pete comes in.

Congratulations on your partnership, Mary. It's your choice.

Pete sits down behind the stenography machine. "You ready?"

I nod, but I'm not. I can't decide what to do. I look down at the notes and ask a couple of stupid questions about them. All the time, the devil pours poison in my ear, tempting me, taunting me. I look at Hank, sitting so proudly at his father's side. If I ask about Lu Ann, what will his cherubic face look like? What will happen at home that night, with his mother? And Lu Ann, will this Kevin—

Save it, Mary! You've represented worse. You've done worse. You and I know that, don't we? Mary and Bobby, sittin' in a tree, K-I-S-S-I-N-G. First comes love . . .

"Mr. Hart, were you ever rude to Harbison's employees?"

"I don't understand the question."

See, he deserves it. Give it to him. Right between the legs.

"What part of the question didn't you understand, Mr. Hart?"

"Any of it, Mrs. DiNunzio."

"Then let me change it slightly. Have you ever been reprimanded by anyone at Harbison's for being rude to its employees?"

"I have never been rude to anyone at Harbison's."

"That's not my question, Mr. Hart. My question is, Have you ever been reprimanded by anyone at Harbison's for being rude to its employees?"

"No."

"Has anyone at Harbison's ever told you that they thought you were rude to company employees?"

"Yes."

God, I hate this man. I should do it, I should. *Sure you should. But will you?*

"And who told you this?"

"Frank Stapleton."

A break for me. If Hart admits that Stapleton talked to him about his rudeness, I can prove that Harbison's had a business motive to demote him. That makes it a "mixed motive" case under the law—a tough defense for me to win, but it's the best I've got.

Hank makes a note on his legal pad.

Just breathe the little slut's name.

"How many times did Mr. Stapleton discuss this subject with you?"

"I wouldn't call it a discussion. That would be making too much of it, and I'm not about to let you do that."

"Fine. How many times did Mr. Stapleton make a statement to you about rudeness?"

"Only once."

"Was anyone else present when he made this statement?"

"No."

"Where did it take place?"

"On the golf course. Ninth hole." At this he smirks.

Hank makes another notation.

"What did Mr. Stapleton say about the subject?"

"It was just a comment between friends. Former friends, I should say."

"What did Mr. Stapleton say, Mr. Hart?"

"Just that sometimes I could be a little hard on the staff. That's all."

"Are you sure that's all you can recall?"

"Yes."

"What did you say in reply?"

"Nice drive." Hart glances at Pete to see if he appreciates the joke. Pete's face is stony.

"Mr. Hart, what did you say to Mr. Stapleton in reply?"

"Nothing. That was the end of it."

"Are you sure?"

"Sure as God made little green apples."

"Did you make any notes of any kind regarding this conversation?"

"On the golf course? With those sawed-off pencils?" Hart rolls his eyes.

"Anywhere at all."

"Why would I? It wasn't important enough."

"Is that a no, Mr. Hart?"

"Yes, it's a no, Mrs. DiNunzio."

I need more detail to sell this to the jury. "Mr. Hart, was there a specific incident Mr. Stapleton referred to when he discussed this with you?"

"No."

"Do you know what occasioned this discussion with you?"

"You'd have to ask him."

"I take it that's a no, Mr. Hart?"

"You're getting pretty good at this, Mrs. DiNunzio."

How long are you going to eat his shit?

"Mr. Hart, did Mr. Stapleton refer to any employee in particular during this conversation?"

"Just the kitchen help."

"Kitchen help?"

"The people who work in the company cafeteria. The Jell-O slingers in the hairnets."

"Anyone in particular?"

"Lu Ann, I think he said her name was."

Whoa, baby. That's a surprise.

Whoa, baby, is right, mocks the devil. He sounds less surprised.

Hank writes the name on his pad, then looks at me, expectantly, innocently, for the next question.

His father's sneer betrays nothing as he awaits the next question.

Pete waits too, his long fingers poised in midair over the black keys.

Do-it do-it do-it do-it do-it! screeches the devil.

It's out of my mouth before I can stop it.

It's the little voice inside me talking. The Mike-voice, chirping up. It hasn't deserted me after all. It's still with me, and it says, "I have no further questions."

It's over. Everybody packs up and shakes hands, except for Hart. "See you in court," he says, with a braying laugh. The derisive sound is echoed by a more distant infernal laughter.

Get thee behind me, Satan!

I wonder if I'm losing my mind. I gather up the file and practically flee the conference room.

Outside, the firm is alive with commerce and industry. Secretaries fly to the mailroom to get out that last letter. Associates beg another draft out of Word Processing. Partners rush to review briefs before they're filed, the better to leave their distinctive mark on it, like a poodle does a hydrant. Everyone's following the Stalling commandment THOU SHALT WAIT UNTIL THE LAST MINUTE, THEN GO CRAZY. The life signs at Stalling ground me, and I don't hear the devil anymore. By the time I reach Gluttony, I'm feeling normal, almost good, for the first time in a long time.

"Miss DiNunzio, here I am!" It's Miss Pershing, looking up at me from the bottom of the stairs. Her rubber pocketbook's slung over her wrist, and she's holding an Agatha Christie paperback. Secretaries flow around her to get to the stairwell, following the first in a set of counter-commandments, THOU SHALT BOLT AT FIVE O'CLOCK. Miss Pershing's too single-minded to notice the activity around her, like an aged pointer who's found her quarry.

"Miss Pershing, step over here." I take her by the elbow and she does a mincing side step out of the path of travel. The Amazing Stella sashays behind her, making the crazy sign at her forehead, but I don't laugh.

Miss Pershing looks suspiciously at the secretaries passing by. "I got that information you wanted." She leans toward me; her soft breath smells like Altoids. "You know which information I mean? *The* information."

"*The* information, Miss Pershing?"

"*The* information. The *police* information."

"Oh. Thank you."

"The papers are on your desk. Your theory is confirmed."

"My theory? You mean about who—"

"Yes."

"Good. Thank you. I appreciate it."

"That's all right. It's my job."

I suppress a smile. "Well, thank you, just the same."

"Also, Mr. Starankovic telephoned. He said—"

"Starankovic? Oh, fuck!"

Her eyes flare open.

"I'm sorry, Miss Pershing."

"No need to apologize, Miss DiNunzio. I'm getting used to it."

"Thanks."

"Mr. Starankovic said you didn't call him back about the interviews, so he had to file a motion. I put the papers on your desk. I hope this doesn't mean you need me to stay late tonight, because I can't. I have my book club tonight."

"Agatha Christie, right?"

She nods happily.

"It's okay, Miss Pershing. I don't need you to stay."

"Well, then, nighty-night," she says, and smiles. She's about to turn toward the elevator when Martin comes charging out of nowhere and knocks her over.

"My!" she yelps. She falls backward into my arms.

Martin runs down the stairs, elbowing everyone aside frantically, with a sheaf of curly faxes in his hand.

"Are you all right, Miss P?" I set her back onto her feet, like Dorothy did the scarecrow. She seems more embarrassed than anything else.

"Goodness!"

I look down the stairs after Martin, but he's long gone. He didn't even look back. He knocked down an old woman and didn't even look back. What kind of a man does that? A hit-and-run. I shudder, involuntarily.

"Wasn't that the young man who likes owls?" asks Miss Pershing.

"Martin H. Chatham IV."

"What bad manners!" She produces a flowery handkerchief from the sleeve of her sweater and dabs at her forehead. The handkerchief must be scented, for the air is suddenly redolent of lilac.

"Let me walk you to the elevator, Miss P." I offer her my arm and we hobble to the elevator together. I tuck her in, in front of the secretaries with the neon eyeshadow and the black miniskirts. She gives me a game wave with her pocketbook as the doors close.

Martin.

I wonder where he was the night Brent was killed. I wonder what kind of car he drives, where he lives. If he lives in town, it makes it more likely that it's him, since it would be easier for him to follow me. But I think he lives in the suburbs somewhere, on the Main Line. I decide to do a little research.

I head into my office and find Stalling's pig book on the shelf. It has photos of all the lawyers in the firm, with their degrees and home addresses. I flip through the first couple of pages to Martin's name. Under his head shot, which makes him look almost animate, it says Dartmouth College, B.A. 1969; Yale Law School, J.D. 1972. His home address is "Rondelay II" in Bryn Mawr. The Main Line, of course. Even the houses have Roman numerals after their names.

Damn. Who else could be jealous of me? Jameson. I wonder where he lives.

I page to the J's and find his picture. He looks like Atom Ant, only smug. He went to Penn too, graduating from the undergraduate school in

1970 and the law school in 1974. His home address is on Pine Street in Society Hill. A city dweller; I didn't know that. And the houses down there—the new ones—have built-in garages. I make a mental note to ask Judy if she knows what kind of car he drives. Kurt would remember if he'd seen it at a firm party. He's always working on old cars; he uses them in his sculpture. His last show was called Body Parts. I passed.

I flip the pages forward to look Ned up. Ned Waters, it says, underneath a picture of him that almost takes my breath away. His eyes, his face. His smile. God, he's beautiful. I think of him in bed, during the night, arousing me despite my slumber. It's hard to believe he's the killer, but Judy made sense. At least for now. I snap the book closed. The end.

I'm about to reshelve it when I remember. Berkowitz. Everybody knows where he lives, he custom-built the house two years ago in Gladwyne, one of Philadelphia's ritziest suburbs. The house is a palace, with a pool and a tennis court. But Gladwyne isn't that far from the city, just ten minutes up the West River Drive.

The West River Drive. Where Mike was killed.

I thumb quickly to Berkowitz's page. His meaty face takes up the entire picture frame. I skim over the schools. Drexel University, Temple Law School. City schools for smart kids with no money. I stop short when I reach his home address—or addresses, because to my surprise, there are two. One is in Gladwyne, like I thought. But the other is an apartment in the Rittenhouse, a new high-rise condo on Rittenhouse Square.

Rittenhouse Square. Where Brent was killed. Right near my apartment. So Berkowitz had access to both sites. He could have hit Mike and disappeared up the West River Drive to Gladwyne, or hit Brent and headed home to the Rittenhouse.

Berkowitz? Could it really be him?

Wait. I know he has a Mercedes, and it wasn't a Mercedes that hit Brent. But what if he has another car, an old car, that he keeps in town? The Rittenhouse has its own parking in the basement garage.

Christ. Berkowitz. Maybe Brent was right about him all along; he never did like him. Neither does my mother. Thin lips. I slip the book back onto the shelf.

I check the clock behind me. The huge golden dial glows brightly: 6:20. The sky looks too dark for six o'clock, as if a thunderstorm's coming. On my desk are the subpoenas. Miss Pershing has typed in the name of the Fatal Coordinator Sergeant, and the address looks right. SUBPOENA DUCES TECUM. It's one of the older forms, which I prefer. They look positively terroristic. I peel off the yellow Post-It that Miss Pershing has signed, Secret Agent Secretary. She's cute, but I don't want to like her. I miss Brent.

It's too late, but I punch in the number for AID and listen to their telephone ring and ring. I decide to go down tomorrow, first thing. Fuck the appointment. I'm the wife, for Christ's sake. And the lawyer.

I hang up the telephone and flop into my chair.

I look at the pile of mail on my desk. It's not like I don't have other things to do. There's a mountain of mail, including the expected motion from Starankovic. I open the envelope and read through the motion papers. They're not bad, an improvement over the crap he usually files. At least he didn't request oral argument, so I don't have to sing to Bitter Man again.

I look through the pile of phone messages on my desk, and there's one from Jameson. FILE THE BRIEF HE SAYS! Miss Pershing has written, with a little daisy in the exclamation point. I thumb through the rest of the pile. Judy, Judy, my mother, Stephanie Fraser again, the rest are clients that will have to wait. None are from Ned. Be careful what you wish, you might get it.

I turn to the mail. My heart begins to pound. On top is a plain white business envelope, with my name laser-printed in capital letters. But there's no Stalling address. And no stamp or postmark. It came through the interoffice mail, from somebody at Stalling. I pick up the envelope. My hand begins to shake slightly.

Berkowitz. Martin. Jameson. Ned. Not Ned's father, because it came interoffice.

I tear open the envelope.

I LOVE YOU, MARY

Ned. It has to be. I feel a sharp pain. How could I have been so thoroughly duped? I close my eyes.

When I open them, Berkowitz is standing in the doorway.

29

Berkowitz lurches into my office as if he owns it. I'm struck by his size, intimidated by his power. For the first time, his presence alone seems menacing, and I understand why a lot of people don't like him.

"Mary had a little lamb," he says. "Nice place you got here."

"It looks just like everybody else's." I slip the note and the subpoenas under my mail.

"Except for the view, of course."

"Right." I glance back at the clock, luminous against the darkening sky. Storm clouds gather behind the clock tower.

Berkowitz leans against the file cabinet by the

306 — LISA SCOTTOLINE

bookshelves. "Must be a weird feeling, having that thing over your shoulder. Like you're being watched all the time."

The comment sends a chill down my spine. He knows about the notes. What is this, a game? I say nothing.

"I don't think I would like that."

"The feeling or the clock?"

"Both. Either." He snorts out a little laugh.

"I don't like the feeling. The clock I can live with."

He doesn't reply, but his eyes scan my diplomas, my desk, and the other file cabinet. His expression is unreadable. "You don't have any pictures."

"No."

"Why not?"

"I don't know."

"But you have family. In South Philly."

"Yes." I flash on the car barreling by me down my parents' street. "How did you know that?"

"Your accent. It's a dead giveaway." He pauses before *Black's Law Dictionary* and runs a thick finger along its binding. I can't gauge his mood, I don't know him well enough. He seems distracted. Tense. "Do you ever use this thing?"

"No."

"Then why do you have it?"

"My parents gave it to me." The detail makes me feel exposed to him, increasing my nervousness. I tell myself to relax. I handled Lombardo, I can handle him. "Did you have an office like this when you were an associate?"

"When I started out, we were in the Fidelity Building on Broad Street. All the windows opened."

He laughs, abruptly, and slaps his breast pocket. "Do you smoke?"

"No."

"Shit."

"Sorry."

"So." He leans against the file cabinet. "Mind if I close the door?"

I feel my chest flush. "Uh . . . why?"

He cocks his head. "Now why do you think, Mary, Mary?" Suddenly he grabs the door and slams it shut. "Alone at last," he says, with a dry chuckle.

I find myself rising, involuntarily. I scan my desk for a pair of scissors or a letter opener. Nothing's there except a stapler and a dicta-phone. I have no protection. I back up and feel the cold window at my back.

"Aren't you standing kind of close to the window, Mary?"

I glance over my shoulder. The clock face glows fiercely at me through a thunderstorm. We're forty stories up, in a tower of black mirrors that flexes and groans in high winds. I tell myself to stay cool. "Why don't you just tell me what you're doing down here, Sam?"

His eyebrow arches in surprise. "Enough with the small talk, is that the idea?"

"Exactly."

"Fine. Two reasons. One: I'm having a recep-tion for the Rules Committee tomorrow night in Conference Room A. Eight o'clock. The litiga-tion partners and the district court judges are invited. You should be there."

"What?" I don't understand.

"There's a reception tomorrow night, and I want you there. Conference Room A. Eight o'clock."

"Me, at a partners' reception?"

Berkowitz looks at me like I'm crazy. "Yes, you. Do you go to receptions, Mary, Mary?"

"Yes." I relax slightly.

"Bring Carrier. You two are pals, aren't you?"

"Yes. We are." I breathe easier and step away from the window. I hear a thunderclap outside and step even farther away from the window.

"Good." He fingers his breast pocket again. "Well. Okay. Two: This goddamned thing with Tom Lombardo. I got a call today. He said you saw what happened."

"I did."

"Well, forget you did."

"What?"

"Forget about it."

"I'm just supposed to forget—"

"Yes. That's an order." His tone is gruff.

I'm beginning to understand what he's saying. "I get it—it's a deal. You want to trade off my partnership and Judy's for my forgetting about what happened with Lombardo? And maybe to Brent?"

"Mary, it's none of your fucking *business!*" he explodes, out of nowhere. With his face suddenly florid, he looks like a devil. But I fight the devils now and win. Fuck back, even when you're fucking with the devil himself.

"Don't you scream at me!" I lean toward him. We're almost nose to nose over the desk. Berkowitz, the King of Fucking Back, and me, a pretender to the throne.

Suddenly, he breaks into a sheepish smile. The redness in his face vanishes. "That's what my wife always says."

"You ought to listen."

He laughs loudly. "Lombardo's right. You got balls."

"No, I don't. So what was it about?"

"Would you believe me if I told you it's not your concern?"

"You mean not to worry my pretty little head?"

"Okay. Down, girl." He looks amused but still tense. Whatever it is, it's driving him nuts. "All right, it's about Delia. She's got her hand in the till. She's taken a hundred thou over five years."

"You're kidding."

"Wish I were." His face falls, he shakes his head. "I thought it was somebody in Accounting, maybe that asshole bean counter we let push us around. I didn't think it was her. It never even occurred to me it was her. I asked Lombardo to track it down for me, but I didn't want to believe him."

"So you hit him?"

He looks pained. "Hey, you know, it hurts. She betrayed me after I took good care of her. I loved that kid."

I meet his eye. Was Brent right about them?

"Don't give me that look. I know everybody says I'm running around with her. I let 'em think it. Fact is, she's my best friend's kid, her father was my sparring partner. He and I were like this." He holds up two tight fingers in a gesture I haven't seen in ages.

"For real?"

"For real. I'm her godfather. The first Jewish godfather in history."

I laugh, with relief. Part of the puzzle falls into place. "Is that why she's so mad lately?"

"Oh, yeah, Delia's mad at the world; she must've seen it coming. She won't even talk to me, even though I convinced the policy committee not to prosecute her. All she lost was her job, and we got a payment schedule worked out. She throws in one, I throw in ten. Can I drive a bargain or what?"

"You do okay."

He slaps his breast pocket again for a cigarette. "Anyway, she left this morning. Now I have no secretary. Got a good one I can steal?"

I think of Miss Pershing. "No."

"So. We all better here, Mary, Queen of Scots?"

"All better."

"Okay, I gotta go. I don't have to tell you not to mention this, do I?"

"Nope."

"Tomorrow night," he calls out, as he opens the door and walks out.

I collapse into my chair, hugely relieved. Tired. Drained. So the fight I saw wasn't about Brent after all, and Berkowitz isn't having an affair with Delia. I wonder what Brent would say to that revelation, but Brent isn't here. I miss him. And I think I know who killed him.

My eyes fall on the note, sticking out from underneath the mail. Ned, my lover. My love. I feel heartsick and scared. He must be crazy, really crazy. Maybe that stuff he told me about the

Prozac was just a story; I never did go back and check the dates on the bottles. Is the man I slept with really capable of killing Brent? And Mike, a year earlier? Maybe, if he's obsessed with me like Judy says. And am I safe from him, or will he turn on me now that I've rejected him?

I check the clock. 7:02. Too late for me to be alone in the office. Rain falls in sheets on City Hall; I feel the building sway slightly. I lock the note in my middle drawer and leave for Judy's office.

But I forget all about it when I see her.

30

"I'm fired," Judy says flatly.

"What?!"

"I fucked up." Her eyes are red-rimmed and puffy, as if she's been crying hard. She slouches in her chair. Her chin sags into a sturdy hand.

"What happened?" I sit down.

"The *Mitsuko* brief is in the hopper. The Supremes reversed a similar argument in a case decided yesterday. I didn't even know the case was up on appeal, because I hadn't checked the cites yet. Great, huh? A first-year mistake." Her jowl wrinkles into her hand like a basset hound's. "I'm not paying attention lately."

"Oh, Jude. How'd you catch it?"

"Guess."

I flash on Martin, banging into Miss Pershing on the way downstairs. "Martin?"

"Nope. Guess again."

"Not the client."

"Yes, the client. Certainly, the client. Who better to catch you in the biggest blunder of your career than the client? The GC faxed us a copy of the Supreme Court decision after we faxed him a draft of my brief. Don't you just love faxes? You can find out you fucked up when you're still in mid-fuckup. That's what I call technology!"

I groan. That must be why Martin had the faxes.

"Wait. That's not all. The Third Circuit brief is due in two days. I have forty-eight hours to produce a winning brief or I'm fired."

"Who said that, Martin? He can't do that!"

"No? I've pissed off a house client and embarrassed the firm. Mitsuko's appeal is in jeopardy—it's their legal right, not ours." She rakes her fingers through her hair, and it sticks up in funny places, making her look demented. "It was such a stupid mistake, I should resign."

"You'd better not. We can rewrite the brief."

"We?"

"We. I help. We do it together."

"You can't help, Mary. You don't know the record."

"I don't need to, you do. Besides, what you need is a new legal argument. A new angle."

She smiles wanly. "I appreciate it, but it's hopeless. I've thought about every argument. This was the best."

"Jude! Where's that pioneering western spirit? The Oregon Trail? The Louisiana Purchase? The Missouri Compromise?"

"Stop trying to cheer me up. And your geography sucks."

"Listen, I beat the devil today. I can do anything!"

"You're crazy. We don't have time."

"We have all night. It's pouring outside and I have to stick with you anyway. You're my bodyguard."

"Give it up, Mary."

"No. Tell me why we lost *Mitsuko*, besides the fact that Martin has no business being in front of a jury unless they all went to Choate."

"Mary, it's no use."

"Tell me, Judith Carrier!"

"Aaargh," she growls, in frustration. "Okay. I think the jury just didn't understand the case. There were too many facts. Too much financial data. The legal issues were too abstract—"

"Were the jurors allowed to take notes?"

"Yes. Judge Rasmussen always lets—"

"Yes!" I have an idea. I tell it to Judy and she loves it instantly, realizing that even if it goes down in flames, it'll be a blaze of glory.

She calls Kurt and makes two pots of coffee, one for her and one for me. I call Lombardo and give him the night off, but he doesn't even thank me. We lock ourselves in a study room in the library and burn up the Lexis hookup. After a couple of hours, we lock ourselves in a war room on Gluttony and start drafting. We send out for Chinese food twice, once at eight o'clock and again at ten o'clock. We order lo mein both times. After our second dinner, Stalling's decrepit security guard, whom Judy calls Mack Sennett, knocks on the door.

"You girls okay in there?" he asks, in a Ronald Reagan voice.

"We're fine now," I call back. "But keep checking."

"Roger wilco," he says.

Judy changes his nickname to Roger Wilco. I re-check the lock on the door.

At midnight, we persuade Roger Wilco to be our lookout while we stage a giddy raid on Catering Services for potato chips, chocolate cupcakes, and more coffee. Judy tries to snort the Coffeemate, and we think this is wildly funny. The coffee sobers us up and we draft until dawn in the locked war room. Finally, at the end of the night, we put the draft on Miss Pershing's desk, because she gets in earlier than Judy's secretary. We shower in the locked locker room, me for the second day in a row. When we get out of the shower, we realize we have no clean clothes.

"Let's just switch clothes," Judy says.

"What?"

"At least it's a change."

I pop Judy's tent of a peasant dress over my head. It billows to my ankles like a parachute. When I emerge from the embroidered hole in its top, Judy is still wrapped in a towel, holding up my tailored white dress.

"Do you need a bra with this dress?" she asks.

"Of course."

"I don't have a bra."

"What do you mean you don't have a bra?"

"I never wear a bra."

"You don't wear a bra to work? At Stalling and Webb? That's a federal offense!"

"You can't tell, my breasts are so small. You want to see?"

"No! Jesus Christ, will you cover up?"

"We're both women, Mary." She teases me by starting to unwrap the towel.

"I know that. That's why." I unhook my bra and slip it out through the wide sleeves of the smock. "Here, take mine. It's one size fits all. Nobody can tell if I'm wearing one in this dress."

"The bra off your back? What a pal!"

While Judy slips into the bra, I go over to the mirror and try to do something with my limp hair. A project for St. Rita of Cascia, Saint of the Impossible.

"Well, what do you think?" Judy asks.

I turn around. The dress, which is boxy on me, is too small for Judy, and it hugs each curve of her body. She looks dynamite. "Sell it, baby."

She gives the hem a final tug. "Can it, baby."

After we're ready, we troop out to see if Miss Pershing has arrived. She's closing up her clear plastic umbrella when I spot her, in jelly boots and a cellophane rain bonnet, at the secretaries' closet.

"Good morning, Miss Pershing."

She looks me over and smiles sweetly. "You look very pretty today, Miss DiNunzio. Very feminine."

Judy slaps a hearty hand on my shoulder.

"Doesn't she though? I helped her pick out that dress."

I give Judy a look. "Thank you, Miss Pershing. How was your book club last night?"

"Wonderful. Next week is Mary Higgins Clark."

"Sounds great. Now I have to warn you, today is going to be a tough day, because Judy and I are working on an appellate brief. We need to finish it by the end of today. It's on your desk, so could you start on it right away? We don't have time to deal with Word Processing."

"What about that other matter? The one we discussed yesterday." She meets my eye significantly.

"It will have to wait, Miss P."

"Got it!" She squares her shoulders.

"Call me as soon as you finish each page. I'll come get it. Meantime, please hold my calls. And don't tell anyone where I am, especially Ned Waters. We have to rewrite the whole day, because the brief has to be filed tomorrow."

"Not to worry." And she's off, marching to her desk in her rain helmet and jelly boots.

31

We christen it the Shit from Shinola Brief and work on it all day in the war room. We run through draft after draft and eat everything that Catering Services carts up to us. We're alternately dizzy, nauseated, euphoric, and cranky. By the end of the day, we have a terrible case of indigestion and a terrific brief. We place the final draft on Martin's desk. His office is dark, and the empty eyes of the owls follow us as we leave. "I hate those fucking owls," I say to Judy.

"They're the only friends he has."

My fatigue is catching up with me. "Think he'll like the brief?"

Judy nods happily. "He has to. It's brilliant. Thanks to you."

"No."

"Yes. You, Mary." She gives me a playful push, which sends me crashing into the wall.

"What do you eat for breakfast?" I ask, as she skips ahead.

Back at the conference room, we pull up identical swivel chairs. I collapse into mine while Judy plays in hers, spinning in a circle. Miss Pershing appears in the doorway and steals a glance at Judy, going around and around. "Miss DiNunzio, aren't you ladies through for the day?"

"No, we have a reception to go to upstairs."

"Wheeeeeeee!" says Judy.

"I would think you'd be too tired for a reception. You both worked so hard."

"We are, at least I am. But we have to go."

"We must, we must! We must increase our bust!" Judy sings, spinning. Miss Pershing looks away.

"Miss Pershing, thank you for everything you did today. I appreciate it very much, and so does my co-counsel the lunatic."

Judy stops spinning and grins, gaps on display. "God, I'm dizzy." She holds her forehead. "Miss Pershing, I want to thank you for putting up with us, especially Mary. She can be so difficult when she's under pressure."

"I don't know, I haven't found that to be the case." She smiles warmly.

"Thank you, Miss P."

"I noticed you didn't send out the . . . messages we discussed." Miss Pershing looks nervously in Judy's direction.

"It's all right, Miss Pershing. Judy knows about the subpoenas."

She seems disappointed. "Oh. Well. Why didn't you mail them? Was something wrong with the way I filled them out?"

"No, they were fine, but I'm going to wait on them."

"Well then," Miss Pershing says. "Nighty-night, girls."

"Nighty-night," I say.

Judy's eyes widen comically. "Nighty-night?"

"Say nighty-night to Miss Pershing, Judy."

But Judy's in hysterics, and Miss Pershing is long gone.

Before we leave for the reception on Avarice, we go to the locker room to freshen up. Judy offers me my clothes back, but I decline. I'm starting to like her artsy smock, and even my own bralessness. It makes me feel looser, freer. I splash water on my face to bring me back to life. Holy water, I think crazily. "Look, Jude, I'm reborn."

"You're not reborn, you're exhausted." She taps the soap dispenser. "You've been up for two days, kid. Remember your call to Lombardo? That was yesterday morning."

I rinse my face with warm water. I think of Lombardo, then Berkowitz, and finally Ned. My heart turns bitter. "You know, you were right. It was Ned who sent the notes. I can't believe it, but I think he killed Brent. And maybe even Mike." I twist off the taps with a sigh.

Judy looks surprised. "How do you know?"

"I got another note. A love note, this time. It

has to be from him. It came in the interoffice mail." I bury my face in a nubby hand towel. Maybe I'll never come out.

"Stay with me tonight. Kurt's at the studio."

I throw the towel at the hamper. It misses, but I don't bother to retrieve it. "Thanks, but I don't need to. I'm safe now. No more subpoenas, no more lawsuit. I'll call Lombardo after the reception and have him question Ned."

"What if you can't find Lombardo? You're not going home."

"Alice hasn't eaten in days. She'll starve."

"So what's your point?"

We finish up, and take the elevator to Avarice. Roger Wilco greets us when we get off and waves us grandly into Conference Room A. I hardly recognize it; it's been transformed. A string quartet plays Vivaldi in a corner. Lights glow softly on dimmer switches I never knew existed, and tuxedoed waiters pass through the crowd. The horseshoe table, covered with a pristine linen tablecloth, is laden with silver trays of jumbo shrimp, fresh fruit, and crudités. It looks like an expense account version of the Last Supper.

"Christ Almighty," I say, under my breath.

"They're just men," Judy whispers.

But the men are another story. The room reeks of their power. The apostles on the Rules Committee are here, along with a full complement of judges from the district court. I spot Chief Judge Helfer with Einstein, being fawned over by Golden Rod and a flotilla of Stalling alligators. The Honorable Jacob A. Vanek, who practically made the law in my field, yuks it up with

Berkowitz and the Honorable John T. Shales, who's rumored to be the next choice for the Supremes. The Honorable Mark C. Grossman and the Honorable Al Martinez, newly appointed from the counties, talk earnestly with Martin, who listens and listens. Bitter Man hovers over the jumbo shrimp like a blimp at the Superbowl.

"I have a job to do," Judy says, and edges into the crowd.

I float over to the bar and watch Judy mingle with Einstein and Golden Rod. She's perfect for the job, which is to collect affidavits for the Shit from Shinola Brief. Our main argument is that the jurors' note-taking contributed to their confusion about the evidence and caused a defective verdict. The record supports the argument; the jurors returned from their deliberations six times with questions from their notes. There're no cases to support our argument, but that's where the affidavits come in. That's the beauty part.

I watch Judy as she strikes up a conversation with Einstein, wherein she'll get him to tell her what a lousy idea it is for jurors to take notes. Then she'll speak to as many other judges as she can, parlaying Einstein's opinion into a consensus. Later, we'll write affidavits saying that the consensus is that jurors should not be permitted to take notes, and we'll file the affidavits with the brief. They're not a part of the trial record, but the Third Circuit isn't afraid to make new law. If it disapproves of note-taking by jurors, as the intellects like Einstein do, it'll find a way to give Mitsuko a new trial. And Judy her job back.

I raise my champagne in a silent toast to the

Shit from Shinola Brief and then to Martin, who'll file it because his back is to the wall. I take deep gulps from the fizzy drink, toasting Judy and Berkowitz. The champagne is gone too soon. I grab another from a passing waiter. It goes straight to my head. I feel dizzy and happy. I ask the bartender for a third and drink a toast to Ned, whom I loved and lost, then to Brent and to my beloved Mike. I begin to understand the expression "feeling no pain."

"Don't drink that too fast now," says the young bartender, handing me a refill. Even though his face is blurry, I see that he's a parking valet from the basement garage, disguised in a tux.

"You can't fool me, I know who you really are. Anthony from the garage, right?"

He laughs. "I can't fool you, Miss Dee."

"Doing double-duty, huh?"

"I got a choice, Miss Dee. I can look at pretty ladies or I can park a bunch of big cars. It's a no-brainer."

"We're traveling incognito, Anthony."

"In what, Miss Dee?"

Suddenly, there's a deep voice beside me, murmuring almost in my ear. I look over and it's Golden Rod, glass in hand. He looks blurry too, even though he's standing very close. "What did you say, Judge Gold . . . Van Houten?" Hearing the sloppiness of my own words, I set down my glass.

"I said, that's a very nice dress."

"Thank you."

"It's a peasant dress, isn't it? Did you get it in

Mexico, or someplace else more exciting than Philadelphia?"

"There is no place more exciting than Philadelphia, Judge."

He laughs and traces the gathered edge of the dress with an index finger. "I like the embroidery at the top."

Dumbly, I watch his finger touch my chest, just above my bare breasts. "You shouldn't do that. I'm Mike's wife, and I'm not wearing a bra," I blurt out.

Golden Rod looks stunned. Simultaneously, I realize that I'm too drunk to be here. I look around the room for Judy, but it's out of kilter. All I see are cockeyed three-piece suits. I mumble a good-bye to the startled judge and make my way to the door.

But my escape route is blocked. Bitter Man's standing right in front of the door, talking to Jameson. The mountain talking to the molehill. I walk as steadily as I can toward them. "Excuse me," I say slowly. It's an effort to talk. My head is spinning.

"Miz DiNunzio," says Bitter Man. He holds a plate with a mound of shrimp carcasses on the side. "I'm surprised to see you here."

Jameson tips forward on his toes. "You shouldn't be, Judge Bitterman. Mary's our star. Her rise in the past year has been positively meteoric." His voice is full of undisguised jealousy. He must be drunker than I am.

"I really should go, Timothy."

"Don't be so antisocial, Mary." Jameson reaches out and grabs my arm roughly. "Tell

Judge Bitterman how you're going to make partner this June. Tell him how your mentor is going to ram you down our throats."

"Timothy, I don't know what—"

He squeezes my arm. "Isn't that a nice word, Judge Bitterman? Mentor. It could mean anything, couldn't it? Teacher. Friend. Confidant. Counselor. Do you know the origin of the word *mentor*, Judge?"

For once, Bitter Man is speechless. He shakes his head.

"Mentor was the friend of Odysseus, to whom the hero entrusted the education of his son, Telemachus. Isn't that interesting? Did you know that Mary has a very special mentor too? A very powerful mentor. Sam Berkowitz is Mary's mentor. He takes very good care of Mary. Right, Mary?"

"Timothy, stop it." I try to wrest my arm away, but Jameson's grip is surprisingly strong.

"What do you think, Judge? Do you think it's Mary's sharp analytical skills that Mr. Berkowitz so admires? Or do you think it's her superb writing ability? *I* had both of those things, Judge, but our fearless leader did everything he could to block *my* partnership. So tell me, what do you think she's got that I haven't?"

Bitter Man looks from me to Jameson.

"You know, don't you, Judge? You're a brilliant man, but I'll give you a hint anyway. Mary's a merry widow. A *very* merry widow."

Bitter Man's mouth drops open.

I can't believe what Jameson's saying. It's outrageous. "I worked to get where I am, Timothy."

Jameson yanks me to his side. "I know you

did, Mary. A big, strong man like Berkowitz, I bet you take quite a pounding—"

"Fuck you!" I shout at Jameson. I wrench my arm free.

Bitter Man's eyes narrow. His face is red, inflamed with anger. "Mary, you didn't!"

I can't take the fury from his face, I couldn't convince him in a million years. I feel dizzy and faint. Heads turn behind Bitter Man, looking at us. I have to get out. I lunge for the door and run to the stairwell. I stagger down it in tears, leaning heavily on the brass banister past Lust and Envy. By the time I reach Gluttony, I'm feeling sick. From embarrassment. From alcohol. From sleep deprivation. I collapse into my chair, and my head falls forward onto a cool pillow of stacked-up mail.

32

He is seething.

His lips are moving, though I can't hear what he's shouting at me. He's shaking, he's so infuriated. His face, almost womanish in its softness, is twisted by rage.

We are alone, he and I. It's dusk, and his office is empty and dim. The secretaries have gone home, as have the others. The room is cold; he keeps the thermostat low. He has to set an example, he says.

There are photos of him, with other men who set examples. Richard Nixon. Chief Justice William Rehnquist. Clarence Thomas. Beside the photos are bookshelves filled with books, lots of books, all about the law. Legal philosophy, legal writing, legal analysis. One book after another, in perfect order. And rows and rows of golden federal casebooks, their black volume numbers floating eerily in the half-light: 361, 362, and 363. He has an entire set all to himself. He is a man of importance, a legal scholar.

But he is so angry. Raging, quite nearly out of control. I've never seen him this angry. I've never seen anyone as angry as Judge Bitterman on the day I quit.

Why is he so mad? I did one article, that was all we agreed to, I say to him. I don't have time to do another.

You used to have time! he shouts.

I don't anymore. Things have changed.

It's a young man, isn't it?

I don't answer him. It's none of his business. I am in love, though, with Mike.

Miz DiNunzio, let me quote you one of the most profound legal thinkers there was. The law is a jealous mistress, and requires a long and constant courtship. It is not to be won by trifling favors but by lavish homage. The quotation is Professor Story's, Miz DiNunzio, not mine. A jealous mistress. It means you can't have it both ways. It's your young man or the law. You have to choose.

I already have, I say to him.

That's when it dawns on me, half in a dream and half out of it. I know why Bitter Man was so angry. His speech about the law being jealous was bullshit. He was hiding behind the law, using it as a smokescreen. I didn't see through it then, but I do now. It was Bitter Man who was jealous, crazy jealous, of Mike. It's almost inconceivable, but it makes sense.

I awake with a start.

Bitter Man is standing over me, stroking my hair with a peaceful smile. "Hello, Mary," he says softly.

"Judge?"

"You are so precious to me, my dear." His cheeks look like they're about to burst with happiness, like an overfed baby.

I look around, panicky. My office door is closed. Everyone's at the reception, three floors above.

His swollen underbelly presses against my chair. "I've cared for you ever since the first day you came to work for me. Do you remember?"

I'm too stunned to answer.

"We spent the whole year together, you and I. I watched you grow, watched you learn. I know I was hard on you at times, but it was for your own good. I was your mentor then, wasn't I, Mary? I was the only one." His voice is unnaturally high.

I nod mechanically. My gorge rises at his touch.

"I tried to forget about you for many years, after you left me, but I couldn't. No other woman would do. Imagine how happy I was when a case of yours finally got assigned to me. I could barely wait until the day of oral argument. It was your first argument, wasn't it, Mary? I could tell. I thought, She has so much more to learn, and there's so much more I can teach her. She still needs me."

Oh no. I won that motion, and Mike was there, watching me with his class. Mike.

"I got the *Harbison's* case a year later almost to the day. As if fate had planned it. I scheduled argument just to see you before me, and you looked so professional in your dark blue suit. As soon as I entered the courtroom, you jumped up and smiled at me in the prettiest way. That's when I knew you felt the same way I did. After all this time."

Of course. I won that motion too. Then came the first note: CONGRATULATIONS ON YOUR PARTNER-SHIP, MARY. Bitter Man knew the win would help me make partner. Why didn't I think of him? I squeeze my eyes shut.

"I was silly to make you sing. Forgive me, but I wanted to test your love. And the other day in Sam's office, when I asked for your opinion, I was just giving you a chance to shine. But you seemed upset with me, so I sent you another note. I put it in Sam's box after our noon meeting. Did you get my note, Mary? I was worried you wouldn't get it."

My heart is pounding. My chest is flushed with blood.

"A penny for your thoughts." His hand reaches under my chin and he wrenches my face up to him. His eyes, almost engulfed by the flesh around them, look out of control.

Suddenly, the door to my office bursts open and Judy bounds in. "Mary, what happened?" she says. "I heard that Jameson—"

"Close the door!" Bitter Man shouts. He steps away from me and whips a silver revolver from his jacket, pointing it at Judy.

She looks wildly from me to him. "What the—"

"I said close the door! And lock it!"

Judy obeys quickly, staring at the gun in fear.

"Who is this woman, Mary?" Bitter Man's hammy hands train the gun expertly at Judy's chest. There's a metallic click as he cocks the trigger.

My heart leaps up at the sound. "No!" I shout.

Bitter Man looks at me sharply, a silent reprimand.

I swallow hard. "Please don't hurt her, Bill. She's my best friend. My dearest friend. Please don't."

Judy nods emphatically, her eyes wide.

Bitter Man eases off the trigger. "Your best friend? Good. We'll need her. She'll be our witness."

"Yes, that's right," I say evenly. "Now let her go, Bill. She has to go home now."

"She can't go, she's the witness. For our wedding. I'm performing it tonight. Get up, Mary!"

"Wedding?"

"There's no time to waste. I know the truth now. I have to get you away from the Jew. That blustering fool, he's no lawyer. He's nothing but a horse trader. So get up!"

I don't move. I can't.

"Get up, you whore!" He swings the gun crazily over to me.

I can barely breathe. The gun is two inches from my forehead. It's a dull silver color, like a shark, and bigger than I thought. Bigger than Marv's gun. The end of the barrel points directly at me, a lethal black circle.

"Get up!" His shout reverberates in the tiny

office. Suddenly, he shoves the gun against my forehead.

I hear Judy gasp.

The cold metal digs into my skin. I feel paralyzed in my chair, terrified to move an inch. I will myself to speak. "Bill, please. Let's talk—"

"There's no time for talk." He pushes the gun into my head.

My gut tightens. "I don't understand. I need you to . . . teach me."

"What?"

"I don't understand you, your feelings."

"My feelings?" he says, testy.

"Yes. About me."

"We don't have time for this, Mary. What about my feelings? Be precise!"

"Do you really love me? I'm not—"

"Of course I love you, of course I do." His head shakes slightly. The gun barrel jiggles against my forehead.

"I wasn't sure, Bill. I didn't know . . . how you felt. You never told me."

"Well, I do love you. I love you more than any of them."

"But how can I trust your love, when you—"

"Trust my love!" he roars. "Trust my love! I've risked everything for you. It's all been for you. All of it!"

I catch my breath. I can hear the blood throbbing in my ears. "What have you done for me, Bill?"

"I killed him! Your husband, the schoolteacher. He took you away from me, away from the law. He brought those brats into my courtroom. So ignorant. They *clapped,* by God. In *my* court-room!"

My heart stops. Mike. I hear myself moan.

"He didn't deserve you, Mary. He couldn't offer you what I can. He taught spelling, for God's sake, to small children. He knew nothing about the law. Nothing!"

"Did you kill my secretary, Bill?" I can barely utter the words.

"He had his arm around you. I thought he was your date from the night before. The one you had dinner with. The one who kissed you at your doorstep. He had no right!"

I close my eyes. Brent. A mistake. "So you followed me in the car. And called me."

"I had to."

"Why? Why did you have to?"

"To be near you. And to check up on you, I admit it. I had to make sure you were working hard, applying yourself. You get distracted by men, Mary, we both know this. I couldn't let it happen again. You have a brilliant career ahead of you. I'll teach you everything I know. You'll write, publish. You're going to be one of the best!"

The gun barrel bores into my temple.

"Now do you see how much I care for you? Now do you understand?"

The office is dead quiet. Judy is frozen in front of the door, her eyes full of horror.

"I see now . . . that you've done a lot for me, Bill. But if you really love me, you'll give me the gun. That will prove you really love me."

"I'm not stupid, Mary," he says coldly.

"But how can I believe you love me when you're threatening to kill me? It's not . . . logical, Bill. It doesn't stand to reason. You taught me that, how important it was to test—"

"Why is it so hot in here? Why?" Bitter Man looks angrily around the room. "They keep it too hot!"

The gun moves on my head. I try to squeeze back my fear. "As soon as you give me the gun, we can be married. But I won't go as your prisoner. I'll go freely. As your wife."

"No, no. This is all wrong." Tears begin to gather in his eyes, but he shakes them off. "All wrong. I need the gun. I can't give it to you."

"I'll be your wife, Bill. Finally and forever. Think of it."

"It's not going to work." He starts to sob. "You want *him* now. You don't want me anymore. You betrayed me." He drills the gun into my forehead, shoving me backward with it.

I feel panic rising in my throat, almost choking me. "No, I didn't, Bill. It wasn't true, what Jameson said. I want you. I'll work hard, I'll make you proud of me. We'll be the best, Bill. The two of us."

Bitter Man starts to whisper furiously, incomprehensibly, to himself. Tears stream down his face. I look over at Judy, who looks terrified. The judge is a madman, and he's falling apart like a demented Humpty Dumpty. "Bill, give me the gun. I want to be the best. I can't do it without you. I need you!"

"Mary," he says, crying. "Mary." It's the only understandable word he utters; the rest are whispered ravings. His eyes are so tear-filled he can't see. He moves to wipe them on his sleeve and the gun drops away slightly from my temple.

It's my only chance. And Judy's.

I reach for the barrel and yank the gun away from him with all my might. It comes free in my hand.

Bitter Man looks at me in shock, then in fury. "Mary, what are you doing!" His eyes are like glittering slits.

"Get back! Get away from me!" I scream. I point the heavy gun at him and rise to my feet, weak-kneed. I hold the gun with two hands, like Marv said.

"I'll get help!" Judy shouts. She opens the door and runs out. As fast as she is, two stairs at a time, it'll take her just minutes to get to Avarice and back to Gluttony.

"Back up, Judge!"

"You can't be serious," he says, in a voice suddenly dark with malevolence. His tears have stopped completely, as have his mutterings.

"Get back!" I aim the gun higher, right at his eyes. "Now!"

He backs up against the bookcase, sneering at me.

"Stay there! I mean it!" I lock my arms out straight. The gun wobbles slightly as I grip its grooved wooden handle.

"You would never hurt me."

"Stay back!" I try to hold the gun still. There's engraving on its steel barrel. S&W .357 MAGNUM. Jesus, it's terrifying to have something like that in your hand. To hold something that packs so much power. It can kill in the blink of an eye. *I* could kill in the blink of an eye. The realization hits me with as much impact as any bullet. There are no witnesses. I could get away with murder.

"You couldn't hurt me. You love me."

"No. I love Mike."

Bitter Man flinches. "The teacher? Forget him, he was dog shit. That's why I killed him. He died like a dog, too. Road kill." He laughs softly.

I can't hear this. I look down the barrel of the gun. At the end is an orange sight. I line it up with the small American flag that is Bitter Man's tie tack. My hand shakes slightly, but it's easier to aim the gun than I thought.

"He was nothing. Insignificant. Weak. If you had seen his face—"

"Stop it!" I use the flag like a bull's-eye. I focus on it and breathe deeply. Once, then again. An absolute calm comes over me. Bitter Man is three feet away, a large target. I have the weapon, I can use it. He killed two innocent men, men I loved. They didn't deserve to die. He does, and I can kill him. All I have to do is pull the trigger. The ultimate in fucking back.

"He whimpered like—"

"Shut up!" I spit at him, in a voice I've never heard before. I have a split second before Judy gets back.

"Mary—"

"Shut up, I said! Shut up!" I look down the barrel at his expression of contempt and disgust. I ease the trigger just a fraction. The hammer, with its corrugated pad, falls back ever so slightly. There's the loud, metallic click I heard before as the chamber rotates a millimeter. It's all very mechanical. A very handsome killing machine, precision engineered in the United States of America. If I pull the trigger a fraction of an inch more, Messrs. Smith and Wesson will kill Bitter Man for me. I don't even have to do it myself.

I raise the gun and get the flag in my sight. And then my hand isn't shaking anymore.

"Give me one good reason," I say to him.

33

That's when I hear the voice. I recognize it
suddenly. I know now who it is.

I thought it was Mike's voice, but it's not
him at all. And it's not the devil's voice, or an
angel's either. It's my soul's own voice, gamely
trying to climb out of the hole I've been digging
for it steadily, daily, since the hour of my birth.

It's me, trying to save my own soul.

Thou shalt not kill.

But I have killed. And I want to now. So
much.

Spare him. Redeem yourself.

Redeem yourself. It resonates inside me, at the
core.

Redemption.

I can't change the past, but I can make the future. I know what it cost me to kill before. This time I have a choice. I choose no.

I release the trigger. The hammer snaps forward with a final click.

At the same moment, a terrified Judy appears at the doorway, followed by Berkowitz, Einstein, Golden Rod, and a crowd of appalled judges. In the instant that I look back, Bitter Man hurls himself into my arms. "Give me that gun!" he roars.

His weight sends me crashing back onto my desk. I feel his hands scrambling at my breast for the weapon. Suddenly, the gun goes off, with an earsplitting report. I hear myself scream. The force of the explosion reverberates in my ears and vibrates up my arm. For a minute I'm not sure who's been hit.

One look at Bitter Man tells me the answer. His face is twisted in pain and surprise. He falls slowly backward, then slumps heavily to the floor. His shirt, in tatters, is black with smoke; his tie is shorn into two ragged halves. A crimson bud appears over his heart, then bursts into full vermillion bloom as he lies, contorted, on the carpet. The air stinks of fire and smoke.

Berkowitz rushes over to Bitter Man, stretched out on the floor, his blood staining the carpet. "Jesus," Berkowitz says, looking up at me. "He's dead."

The judges, all of them assembled, look at me in disbelief. In shock. In revulsion.

I freeze at the judgment in their eyes. I'm stunned, shaking, in shock. I want to explain, but

I can't. All I can do is look back at them. It's Judgment Day. I knew it was coming. It was just a question of time.

"Jesus, Mary!" Berkowitz cries out. He takes the revolver from me and gathers me up in his arms. I feel an enormous weight in my chest, the wrench of my heart breaking. I start to cry, first in great hiccups, then out of control. I'm not crying for Bitter Man. I'm crying for Mike and for Brent.

That night, after a chastened Lombardo has come and gone, Berkowitz drives me home himself. I feel utterly drained as I sit in the gleaming Mercedes-Benz, with its odor of fine leather and stale cigarettes. Berkowitz opens the car door for me and offers to walk me upstairs, but I turn him down. There's no need. I'm safe now. No more telephone calls, no more notes. My empty apartment is my own again.

The door closes behind me, and I lean against it in the dark. I stand there for the longest time, thinking of Mike, who brought me from fear into love, using only his patience and his heart. I can't believe he's gone; it's so awful that he died, and in so much pain. I feel newly grief-stricken; it makes me wonder if I ever let myself truly mourn him. Maybe I did the Next Thing too soon.

My thoughts run to Brent, who was so innocent. A wonderful friend, a loving man. His voice coach was right; he was full of joy. He's gone now, cut down by the same man, mistakenly. Somehow that makes it much worse.

Bitter Man. He was bitter and evil for a reason no one can ever fathom. The devil, truly. Their deaths were his doing. It was his fault, not mine. Now he's gone too. That much is my doing, that much I'm responsible for. No more.

Soon I'm crying, sobbing hard, and I can't seem to make it stop. I feel overwhelmed by grief; it brings me to my knees in front of the closed door. I can't believe that Mike is gone, that Brent is gone. That I'll never see either of them again.

I wish I could stop crying, but I can't, and soon I hear a loud *boom boom boom* against the door. Only it's not someone else pounding on the door.

It's my own skull.

34

FEDERAL ATTRACTION! screams the three-inch headline in the morning edition of *The Philadelphia Daily News.*

FEDERAL JUDGE ATTACKS WOMAN LAWYER: D.A. FINDS SELF-DEFENSE, reads the smaller headline in *The Philadelphia Inquirer,* its calmer sister publication.

I don't read the newspaper accounts, don't even want to see them. I just want to know if Berkowitz kept my name out of the papers, so I can practice law again in this city. Someday.

"I don't see it anywhere," Ned says, skimming the articles at my kitchen table. His tie is tucked carefully into a white oxford shirt. He stopped by on the way to work to see how I was, bearing blue-berry muffins. He didn't try to hug or kiss me. He seemed to sense that I needed the distance.

"Good."

"You should take your time going back to work, Mary." The muffins lie crumbled on the plate between us.

"I will, this time."

"I'll take care of your desk. Don't worry about a thing."

"Thanks. I'll return the favor."

Ned smiles mysteriously.

"What?"

"I'm not telling you now. You've had enough surprises." He folds up the newspaper and sets it down on the table.

"Tell me, Ned."

"Actually, it's a good surprise. You really want to hear it?" His green eyes shine.

"Sure."

"I'm leaving the firm. As soon as you come back."

"What?" It's so unexpected, it draws me out of myself for a minute.

"There's no future for me there. I'm not going to make partner."

"How do you know that?"

"Berkowitz told me."

Now I'm totally confounded. I sit up in the chair.

"He told me one day in his office, when I went in to ask him how many partners they were making."

I remember, the conversation he materially omitted at dinner that night.

"Berkowitz told me I wasn't going to be one of them, no matter how many they made."

"Why?" I feel hurt for him.

"He said I didn't have what it takes. The fire in the belly. The *cipollines*, I think he meant." He smiles crookedly.

"That's ridiculous."

"No, it's not. He's right, Mary. I didn't realize it until he said it, but he's right. I don't have the heart for it. I don't even like being a lawyer. I was only doing it to prove something to my father."

I don't know what to say. Silence comes between us.

"I did talk to him, you know," he says.

"Your father?"

"Yes. I told you I would. I called you about it, but you weren't returning my calls." He winces slightly.

"Ned—"

"That's okay, you explained it. With the last note, even I would have suspected me. Anyway, my father never had you followed, but he did do a lot of research on you. He searched your name in Lexis and pulled all the cases you worked on."

"Why?"

"To see what the competition was like. To size up my chances of making partner. That's why he watched you at your dep."

"Jesus."

"He researched Judy, too, and me. He said he wanted to know what I was working on. I guess it never occurred to him to pick up the phone." He picks idly at a blueberry crumb.

"Did he say anything about tampering with files?"

"No. I don't think he'd do that, he'd think it was unethical. Wife-beating is okay, but tampering with case files, no."

"How was it, seeing him again?"

"He looks older. His hair is all silver."

"Are you two going to—"

"No, we're not going to be pals, if that's your question. We'll talk from time to time, but that's it. Nothing's changed but his hair, I can see that. I asked him if he wanted to go into therapy with me. That went over real big." He smiles, but it's sour.

"So what are you going to do now? For a job?"

Ned pops a blueberry into his mouth. "I don't know yet. Teach law, teach sailing. Get married, stay home with the kids. All ten of them. What do you say?"

"Am I supposed to answer that?"

"I drive a Miata, what more do you want?"

"A continuance."

"Just like a lawyer, DiNunzio. Just like a lawyer." He laughs loudly, throwing his head back. He looks happy and free.

"So do I get it?"

"Motion granted," he says.

And Alice, who has been sitting under the kitchen table, rubs up against his leg.

It's June 28, the first anniversary of Mike's death.

I cruise up the smooth asphalt road that leads to the pink magnolia tree. I think of it as Mike's tree, even though it shelters at least sixty other graves. They fan out from the trunk of the magnolia in concentric circles, ring upon ring of headstones.

I pull over at the side of the road, where I always park. I cut the ignition, and the air-conditioning shuts down with a wheeze. Outside the car, the air is damp and sweet. The radio called for thundershowers this afternoon, and I believe it. The air is so wet you know the bottom's got to tear open, like a tissue holding water.

The cemetery is silent. The only sounds are the cars rushing by on the distant expressway and the intermittent quarreling of the squirrels. I make my way to Mike's grave. Only a year ago, it was on the outermost ring, but now it's somewhere toward the middle. More graves are being added, more people are passing on. Like the rings of the magnolia tree itself, it's just time moving on, life moving on.

Death moving on, too.

I walk past the monuments with names I don't recognize until I reach the ones I do. I feel as if I know these people. They're Mike's neighbors in a way, and they seem like a good lot. ANTONELLI has a new DAD sign; his family is very attentive to him. LORENZ's grave is bare, though her monument bears its chipper epitaph: ALWAYS KIND, GENEROUS, AND CHEERFUL. I love Mrs. Lorenz, how could you not?

I pass BARSON, which stands alone, off to the right. It's a child's grave, and its pink marble headstone has a picture of a ballerina etched into it. There's a Barbie doll there today, sitting straight-legged in tiny spike heels. I can never bring myself to look at BARSON for long and hurry by it to MARTIN. Something's always going on at MARTIN. It's a hubbub of activity, for a final resting place. Today I note that the showy Martin family has added yet another bush to the border that surrounds their mother's monument. I wonder about these people. I don't understand how they can bring themselves to garden on top of someone they loved.

I reach Mike's monument and brush away the

curly magnolia petals that have fallen on its bumpy top. I pick a candy wrapper off his grave, like I used to pick cat hair off his sweaters. Just because I'm not planting shrubs on his head doesn't mean I don't care how he looks. I bunch up the debris in my hand and sit down, facing his monument.

LASSITER, MICHAEL A.

It's a simple granite monument, but so striking. Or maybe I feel that way because it's Mike's name cut into the granite with such finality and clarity, and I hadn't expected to see his name on a gravestone. Not yet. Not when I can still remember doodling on a legal pad during our engagement.

Mrs. Mary Lassiter.

Mrs. Mary DiNunzio Lassiter.

Mary DiNunzio-Lassiter.

I eventually stuck with my own name, but I confess to a politically incorrect thrill when the mail came addressed to Mrs. Michael Lassiter. Because that's who I was inside, wholly his.

I still am.

I've learned that you don't stop loving someone just because they die. And you don't stop loving someone who's dead just because you start loving someone else. I know this violates the natural law that two things can't occupy the same place at the same time, but that's never been true of the human heart anyway.

I breathe a deep sigh and close my eyes.

"Look!" squeals a child's voice at my ear.

"Look what I have!"

I look over and find myself face to face with a blue-eyed toddler in a white pinafore. In her dimpled arms is a wreath of scarlet roses and a couple of miniature American flags. Plainly, the child has gone shopping on the graves. "You have a lot of stuff."

"I have a lot of stuff!" says the little girl. "I found it! That's okay!" She jumps up and down and a flag falls to the ground. "Uh-oh, flag."

A woman in a prim linen suit rushes up and takes the child by the arm. "I'm sorry that she bothered you," she says, flustered. "Lily, wherever did you get those things?"

Lily struggles to reach the fallen flag. "Flag, Mommy. Flag."

"She's no bother. She's sweet." I pick up the flag and hand it to Lily.

"Tank you," Lily says, quite distinctly.

"Where do you suppose these things belong? I'd hate to put them on the wrong . . . places."

"The flags go with those soldiers, in the bronze flag holders. The VFW gives them the flag holders, I think. That one over there, HAWLEY, he was in Vietnam."

"Oh, dear. Poor man." She turns around worriedly. "Where do you think the wreath goes?"

I take a look at it. I have no idea where it belongs. "I'll take the wreath."

"Thank you. I'm so sorry." She hands it to me gratefully and hoists Lily to her hip. "Can you make sure I find the soldiers?"

"Sure. Just look for the flag holders."

Lily howls with frustration as her mother drops

the flags into the flag holders at MACARRICI, WAINWRIGHT, and HAWLEY. I give her the thumbs up.

I stand and examine the wreath. The roses are a velvety red, fastened to the circular frame with green wire. There's even a little green tripod to make the wreath stand up. I take it and set it at the head of Mike's grave, right under LASSITER.

On its white satin sash, it says in gold script:

BELOVED HUSBAND

I look at it for a long time.
It looks good.

36

A month later, I'm in my new office at Stalling & Webb. On the wall hangs an antique quilt that I bought in Lancaster County, from the Amish. It's called a friendship quilt and has the names of the quilters and their best friends sewn onto spools of a dozen bright colors. The other day I read all the names. Emma Miller, from Nappanee, Indiana. Katie Yoder, of Brinton, Ohio. Sarah Helmuth, from Kokomo, Indiana. I like to think about these women, whose lives were so different from my own but who valued each other so much. That much we have in common, and it ties me to them.

I'm thinking about this as Judy sits on the

other side of my new desk, an Irish farm table that cost Stalling more than an Irish farm. She sports the latest example of Kurt's handiwork, a spiky haircut that looks like Jean Seberg's. If only by accident, the cut brings out the richness of her blue eyes and the curve of a strong cheekbone. She looks beautiful in it, especially when she laughs. She's a good woman; I feel blessed in knowing her. In having her in my life.

"Why are you looking at me like that, Mary?" she asks, with an amused frown.

I try to swallow the lump in my throat. How can I say *I love you*? Her eyes meet mine, and for once she doesn't bug me to say the unsayable. She knows it anyway. She wasn't number one for nothing.

"So what do you think?" Judy asks, with a grin. She gestures to the mound of filthy men's socks in the middle of my costly rustic desk. "I bet they expect you to wash them."

I clear my throat. "I think it's a good sign. They're treating me as shitty as they treat each other."

She smiles. "So you only lost fifty grand. Not too bad."

"Play money."

"Pin money."

"Mad money." I laugh. "You know, it was a lot less than Hart asked for. They must not have liked him. Particularly the forewoman, from Ambler. She could tell he was a pig." I'm smelling defeat, but it doesn't hurt half as much as I thought it would. I think this is called perspective, but I'm not sure. I never had it before.

"They should have taken notes, then you'd have grounds for appeal." She giggles.

"Right. We're zero for two, since we lost *Mitsuko*. We have to be the only lawyers chastised as a team by the Third Circuit and in record time. What did they say again?"

She straightens up and tries to look judicial. "I quote—'A bald attempt by a duo of overzealous counsel to circumvent the Federal Rules of Appellate Procedure by the deliberate inclusion of affidavits not of record.'"

"They can't take a joke."

"Bingo."

We both laugh. "So we lost two, Jude. We're doin' good."

"But we're partners now. We can screw up with impunity."

"You know, it doesn't matter that we lost *Mitsuko*. The Shit from Shinola Brief was a thing of beauty. Martin had to admit it, even though he was too gutless to sign it." I shift on the needlepointed chair that Martin is lending me; every morning I have to stick my butt into an nest of tiny owlets.

"True. And even though you lost your trial, the case went in well, it really did. You handled Hart on cross, too. Didn't ask too much, stopped at just the right time."

"Tell me again how good my closing was. I like it when you say it was good, damn good."

"Your closing was good, Mary. Damn good!" Judy shakes her wiggy little haircut.

"You don't say!"

Her blue eyes glitter. "You know, you and I

could be two halves of a very tough whole."

"You want to get married?"

She grins, gap-toothed. "In a way."

Finally I realize what she's driving at. "You serious?"

"Yepper. You could do the trial work and I could do the paperwork. We could make a go of it, run a first-class little spinoff. A boutique practice, everyone calls it now."

"Wait a minute, Judy. We'd get some referral work from Stalling, but I'd worry about where the business would come from."

"You'd worry anyway. It's in you and it's gots to come out. We'll start out small, for sure, but I don't need half the money I make here. Do you?"

"Not really. I don't have time to spend it."

"Me neither. Even with the catalogs, there's only so much damage you can do. Except for Victoria's Secret."

"Hah! What do you buy from them? You don't even wear a bra. In our new firm you'd have to wear a bra. I won't stand for—"

Judy throws a black sock at me, but I duck. "Joke all you want, but it's a good idea. You could do discrimination work, but plaintiff's side. Think about it. Do well *and* do good."

"Work for the angels, huh?" The thought strikes a chord.

"There you go! You've represented defendants for years. You can anticipate every move, right?"

"Maybe."

"So you want to do it? Let's do it. Let's just fucking *do* it!" Judy says, brimming with excitement.

The woman can go from zero to sixty in two minutes. "We don't need Stalling, Mare, we're just two more mouths to feed here. We apprenticed for eight years, it's our time now. Let's go! Onward and upward!"

I look at her. She feels none of the doubt that I do. Judy loves a challenge. She climbs mountains for fun. "You think it's that easy?"

"Yes."

I squint at her, and she grins.

Who better to jump across an abyss with than someone who climbs mountains? says the voice.

I smile, reluctantly at first, but then it grows into laughter of its own momentum. It feels like my heart opening up. "Okay. Okay. Okay!"

"Okay!" Judy launches herself into the air, arms stretched up high, and dances around my bookshelves. "She said okay!"

I can't stop smiling. "What should we call ourselves?"

She shakes her butt in a circle. "DiNunzio and Carrier! If not that, Bert and Ernie!"

"No, it has to be girls! Lucy and Ethel?"

"Thelma and Louise!"

"Forget them, they die in the end. Wait, we forgot one thing. We gotta take Miss P, agreed?"

"Of course. We need someone to wish us nighty-night."

Suddenly, Miss Pershing appears at the door, interrupting our party. "Speak of the devil," I say, as Judy boogies by and takes her for a spin.

"Ohh!" she yips. "My, my!"

"Unhand that secretary," I say, since I'm not sure Miss P's into the lambada.

"Aw," Judy says.

Her cheeks flushed, Miss Pershing smooths her hair needlessly into its twist. "Sakes alive. Well, my goodness. That was . . . exciting."

Judy curtseys. "Thank you, Miss P."

Miss Pershing looks slightly confused. "Miss DiNunzio, I thought I heard your voice, but I'm surprised to see you here."

"You didn't think I'd come in today, after I smelled defeat at the hands of that mean old jury?"

"No, it's not that. But didn't I just see you upstairs?"

"No. I haven't been upstairs at all."

Her back to Miss Pershing, Judy makes a face that says: Miss Pershing's rope has come unclipped.

"That's strange," she mutters, shaking her head. "I could swear I just saw you sitting in the reception area." She hobbles away, befuddled. I have a sharp sense of déjà vu. I see my mother, who would walk away exactly like Miss Pershing just did, when I used to pretend to be Angie. All of a sudden, it clicks. I jump out of my chair and fly out the door.

"Mary?" says Judy, after me.

"Be right back, pardner!"

And I'm gone, leaping up the stairs, two by two, until I reach the reception area. I see her, sitting by herself on a white sofa that has no support. She looks just like me, except that she has a pixie haircut. And a suitcase.

She rises to her feet when she sees me. "Hello, beautiful," she says.

ACKNOWLEDGMENTS

I think it was Chekhov or Tolstoy, one or the other, who said something about someone being the most extraordinary ordinary person he'd ever met. Such people exist, I know, because I'm friends with them, and I met many others in researching and writing this novel. In fact, I know so many of them by now that I'm quite sure they constitute the world's sum total, and I worry that you are fresh out of luck.

The first such person is my agent, Linda Hayes of Columbia Literary Associates. It was Kermit the Frog—I'm on firmer ground here—who said something about the wonderful things that can happen when one whole person believes in you.

Linda was the first one whole person (not related to me by blood or affection) to believe in me. She nurtured me, and this book, as if she had given birth to both of us. Linda is truly extraordinary. I am forever in her debt.

And she's a great judge of character. She introduced me to Carolyn Marino, another extraordinary ordinary person, who became my editor at HarperCollins. Carolyn believed too, and I thank her for that. Also, while she appreciated what worked in the novel, she knew how to improve it. That she managed to tell me so, and for me still to find the editorial process so much fun, is a tribute to her grace, intelligence and sensitivity.

Thanks, too, to Chassie West, for her enormously valuable (and fun-to-read) suggestions.

I also met a number of extraordinary ordinary people in researching the book. There were good Catholics, mountain climbers, a priest, women's health care providers, officers of my local police department and the Philadelphia Police Department, an ex-nun, an order of cloistered nuns, and Eileen at the Dusty Rhoads Gun Shop, who knows more about revolvers than anyone should. These people answered every question I had, carefully and without once checking their watches, and all I was to them was some lady with a legal pad. Thank you.

Finally, all my love and thanks to my family, the first whole people who believed, and to my daughter. To my very supportive friends—extraordinary ordinary people all—Rachel Kull, Judith Hill, Susan White, Laura Henrich, Franca Palumbo, and Jerry Hoffman. Special thanks to

Fayne Landes and Sandy Steingard for the psychiatric consults (not mine, my character's), to Liz Savitt, whose enormous energy and bravery got me writing in the first place, and to Marsha Klein, who helped me find a smidgen of bravery in myself.

SARAH LACEY

FILE UNDER: DECEASED

It really wasn't Leah Hunter's lucky day.

True, the handsome stranger in her arms was a bit of a Tom Cruise look-alike. But he was also dead.

Leah, a lively twenty-five year old tax inspector, can't resist a challenge. And when she finds that the dead man's tax records are suspect she delves deeper into what begins to look like a murder case; despite warnings, from the dishy detective sergeant, to stop meddling.

Before long it becomes uncomfortably clear that some-one thinks she knows more than she should. And her Yorkshire town begins to seem an extremely dangerous place to live.

Sarah has found a real winner in Leah Hunter
Liza Cody

A sparky debut; if only the Inland Revenue's one-liners were half as amusing!
The Observer

HODDER AND STOUGHTON PAPERBACKS

CAROL BRENNAN

IN THE DARK

Just as the lights dimmed, I heard it. Its androgynous hoarseness was burned into my memory, into my dreams, where I'd hear it, and I'd kill it. Or it would kill me.

Behind her in the cinema is the voice that has haunted Emily Silver's dreams for twenty years. Everyone around her silenced the protests of a small child and told her that her parents weren't murdered, that they killed themselves. But Emily knows better.

Shocked and terrified, Emily reluctantly lets her lover try to discover more about the voice. But when Mike dies suddenly she is propelled on a hunt for the killer. A hunt which takes Emily first to strangers but then back into her past and dangerously close to home . . .

HODDER AND STOUGHTON PAPERBACKS

THOMAS DRESDEN

TALKING TO A STRANGER

All of a sudden, Claire Garrison's world is falling apart. Her husband is having an affair. It looks like her closest friend is the woman involved. And trouble is brewing with her work as a researcher for her charismatic but volatile Russian father.

But Claire's problems have only just begun. When the bloodstained clothing of her young sister-in-law is found on the banks of the Thames, a chain of horrifying revelations comes to the surface.

And, as everyone around her seems to have become a stranger, Claire puts her trust in a man she has only just met. Although somehow she senses she's known him all her life.

A chilling woman-hunt by a man with a nightmarish mind . . . a book you'll find difficult to put down
Anthony Barwick, author of *Shadow of the Wolf*

HODDER AND STOUGHTON PAPERBACKS